THE DEVIL'S MARK

A DI GRAVES THRILLER #BOOK THREE

WD JACKSON-SMART

BLOODHOUND
— BOOKS —

First published in 2022 by Bloodhound Books.

www.bloodhoundbooks.com

Print ISBN: 978-1-5040-8008-8

ALSO BY WD JACKSON-SMART

THE DI GRAVES SERIES

CHAPTER ONE

The thudding of her trainers hitting the concrete was extremely satisfying as she let the beat from her headphones flood over her. The morning was sunny, but cold: winter hadn't yet broken but it was edging closer towards spring – finally. It was perfect for a run. Fresh, bracing.

A combination of guilt about Christmas over-indulgence and the thought of Natalie Adams – a ferociously athletic woman in her yoga class – looking smug had spurred Nicola Clement into starting running again. She had bought new Nikes in the January sale, treated herself to some new purple and blue running leggings and a better sports bra, and had already clocked up five decent runs since Christmas. She was even using an app to track her routes, times and calories.

As she took a corner, Calvin Harris spurring her on, Nicola felt smug herself. Hyde Park was beautifully quiet, with barely another soul out and about, yet here she was keeping up her New Year's resolution of improving her health and fitness while others were getting ready for work or still in bed. She couldn't help smiling. Maybe next time she went to yoga she'd even fish for a compliment from Natalie or the painfully attractive cardio-pump instructor Tony.

Nicola unzipped her jacket, instantly feeling refreshed as the cold air chilled her sweat. She had been going for twenty minutes and had started to heat up.

After a speedy walk to the park, her run had started at the entrance to Queensway Tube – the one closest to her flat. She had run past Kensington Palace, across the park to the art gallery and Princess Diana memorial fountain, over the Serpentine, and now looping back up towards Lancaster Gate when she realised she needed the toilet.

Slowing down a little, Nicola considered her options. She wasn't close enough to any of the public toilets, and the Sackler Gallery wasn't yet open. She stopped, took a deep breath and surveyed her surroundings while she jogged on the spot. There was no one in sight.

'Perfect,' she said to herself. After another quick double-check to make sure she was alone, Nicola stepped off the path and into the trees and hedges to her left. Even though it was winter, there were still a lot of leaves to contend with. Nicola pushed her way through them, trying to find the ideal spot. She needed somewhere far enough from the path not to be visible in case anyone passed by. Ahead of her was a small clearing in the undergrowth. As quickly as she could, Nicola pulled down her leggings and peed, immediately feeling embarrassed. She hated doing it and felt thoroughly self-conscious but it was over in seconds and she hadn't been spotted. She would be able to emerge from the trees and continue her run, no one any the wiser.

Nicola was about to head back in the direction of the path when a waft of wind washed such a horrid stench towards her that she coughed and slapped a hand over her mouth and nose. The smell was disgusting but not too unfamiliar – kind of like the roast chicken carcass she had left in her kitchen bin for too long the other week.

Her mind ran through a few scenarios. It could be a dead animal. Maybe a dead person. Neither was something she wanted to see, especially the latter. It could also be a homeless person. Homeless people apparently slept out in parks. She'd read about it in the paper. The smell still threatening to make her gag, Nicola made a decision. She knew it would bug her if she didn't find out what was causing it. Moving in the opposite direction to where she had come off the path, she made her way past a few more trees. The smell grew stronger.

'Oh God, Nicola, what the fuck are you doing?' she muttered, worried that the organic cereal bar she had eaten before leaving the house would make a reappearance.

In the thick line of hedging in front of her was a gap – one that didn't look entirely natural. It looked like someone had cut away a load of branches quite deliberately. More curious despite the smell, she reached the gap. After a second's pause she pushed her way through into the clearing. After just a few seconds, what she saw made her turn away and vomit. She spat out bile and oat chunks onto the ground.

Taking slow, deep breaths, Nicola turned back to what had caused her to be sick.

The clearing was small, perhaps six metres square. In the centre was a wooden post, taller than her, pointing to the sky. Projecting out from either side of it were more pieces of wood, four either side, like ribs. And from each wooden rib hung a human body part – an arm, a leg, a partial ribcage, strings of organs that she didn't attempt to identify. Nearly every inch of the wooden structure had been covered in what she assumed was blood, dark where it had soaked in and pretty much dry.

Nicola couldn't believe her eyes. She'd heard about joggers stumbling upon bodies before, even seen it happen on some crime show or other, but this was something else – next-level fucked up. She didn't even have the words for it. Her skin crawled; she was repulsed and fascinated in equal measure.

Pulling her phone from her arm strap, trying not to be sick again, Nicola filmed the structure in front of her, getting as close as she dared, capturing it from a number of angles and zooming in to some of its more gory features. Next she called the police, giving them her approximate location, based on the GPS on her phone. Last, as she made her way back to the path to find air that didn't reek of death, she googled the *Daily Mail*'s news tip hotline and placed a call. She informed the man who answered that she had one hell of an exclusive that he would most certainly want to pay for.

CHAPTER TWO

'This is different,' Detective Inspector Daniel Graves said, standing as far back as he could from the remains, pulling his coat collar up over his nose and mouth to act as a barrier between him and the smell. He could feel the hedge touching his back. He had rubbed Vicks under his nose, a trick he had been taught by a morgue attendee. But it was only partially working, because he could still smell the rotting flesh only metres from him.

'Reckon the Blair Witch did it?' DI Charlie Palmer said, a smirk on his face.

Daniel hadn't seen any of the films but did know they had something to do with twigs fashioned into strange shapes and people dying in the woods.

'You know I don't like horror movies. Too much horror in the real world,' Daniel answered, gesturing at the effigy. 'Case in point.'

'You should – horror films are fun. And there's evidence that people actually watch them specifically *because* the real world is such a nightmare. They act as a kind of release.'

'If you say so. Not so fun when it's real, though.'

'Well, no, it's pretty fucking grim. What are we thinking? Some sort of weird ritual murder?' Charlie asked, getting closer to the strange wooden structure while attempting to stay out of the way of the crime scene photographer.

'That's my guess at the moment,' Daniel said, although in truth he had no idea what to think. The ribcage-shaped structure with pieces of a person strung up on it like baubles on a Christmas tree was like nothing he'd ever seen before. He was a little surprised he hadn't been sick. Perhaps he was finally getting more resilient, though he wasn't convinced that was entirely a good thing.

'It doesn't seem like it was left here to be found,' Daniel continued, looking around at the location. 'This little clearing, the wall of hedges – it's surprisingly well hidden, given that we're standing in the middle of London in a busy, popular park. It was dumb luck that the runner found it – if you can call discovering something like this lucky.'

'Nicola Clement. Claims she needed to urinate while out jogging, so was looking for some privacy among the trees. She noticed the smell and curiosity got the better of her.'

'How could she not notice it? It's putrid,' Daniel said, pulling a face. Again he pulled his collar closer to his face, although he knew it wouldn't really help. If eucalyptus rub wasn't helping, a bit of fabric in front of his nose definitely wouldn't cut it.

'So someone brought the victim here, did their ritual and then – what? Just left? Job done, off they go?'

'I guess so. Although I don't think they brought the victim here necessarily, unless they took parts of the body away with them. There are no massive splashes of blood in the surrounding vicinity, and it looks like we're missing a few pieces.'

Though the remains had not yet been touched by any of the investigation team, it was obvious that there were not enough parts to comprise a full human. The head was noticeably absent, for starters.

'So you think they brought the pieces with them? Just hauled over some body parts in a bag or a collection of Tupperware?' Charlie asked. 'We need to find out where this person was killed.'

'That's just one of a million things we need to find out. I want to know who the victim is,' Daniel said. 'The parts might not even be all from one victim.'

He had yet to spot anyone from the coroner's office who might be able to shed some light on identity, but he knew someone would be nearby. The space in the clearing was limited and there were a lot of other people outside the circle of trees, including officers trying to keep the area off-limits to anyone passing by in the park. A perimeter had been set up, but Daniel was glad the killer had decided to be so private. It made his life easier. It also prevented news teams from getting any pictures, though it wouldn't have surprised him if a drone was hovering somewhere overhead.

'And hopefully that might tell us who did it. I can't even begin to fathom a motive right now,' Charlie stated.

'Me either. Not a sane one, at least,' Daniel admitted.

'Excuse me, Detectives?' came a polite voice with a mild Scottish accent. They turned away from the body parts tree to see who had entered the wooded circle of death. The woman in front of them was small and petite, Japanese, and dressed very formally in a black trouser suit with a light pink shirt and a knee-length grey winter coat. Daniel thought she looked quite young to be at a crime scene: she had a 'fresh out of university' quality about her.

'Hi, can we help?' he said.

'You're the detectives on this case, right? I'm sure you can help if so,' the woman said with a confident smile. 'I'm Emi

Kobayashi. I just started working under Stephanie Mitchum.'
She thrust out a hand in greeting, and Daniel and Charlie shook
it in turn.

'Lucky you. How's that going?' Charlie asked, raising one
eyebrow.

'It's good. Challenging,' Emi said thoughtfully.

'Very diplomatic answer.'

'Nice to meet you, Emi. I'm DI Daniel Graves, and this is
DI Charlie Palmer. You must be new. I take it you're here on
behalf of the coroner's office?'

'Yes. Miss Mitchum is busy and I am new, yes, but I promise
I'm more qualified than I may appear. I'm heading up this one
from our side.'

Daniel heard Charlie mutter something under his breath,
but ignored him. Daniel felt some relief too, though. Kobayashi
seemed to have a friendlier disposition than her boss, which
would make a refreshing change.

'Perfect – we look forward to working with you. I believe the
CSI team has yet to do a thorough analysis?'

Emi nodded.

'In which case, can you let us know as soon as everything
has been catalogued? And let us know if you are able to ID our
victim. Or victims, if it turns out to be remains from multiple
sources,' Daniel said.

'Plus tell us anything else you find out about the remains.
Cause of death, stray particles, that sort of thing,' Charlie added.

'Don't worry, Detectives,' Emi answered. 'Like I said, I
know what I'm doing. You'll get a full and detailed report as
soon as it's ready.'

'Great stuff,' Charlie said with a smile. 'Shall we, Graves?
I'm not sure what else we can do here while we wait for Miss
Kobayashi's report.'

Daniel nodded his agreement. They had next steps to take,

of course. They needed to speak to the park management company, for a start, and get CCTV footage from the area. He also thought it might prove useful to ask a small team to look into similar cases – murders that involved anything relating to ritualistic behaviours or iconography.

There wasn't anything else they could do at the crime scene. The remains had been well hidden and he knew they wouldn't find any witnesses. Whatever had happened in the closed-off circle of hedges had probably occurred overnight.

Daniel led the way out of the enclosed area, nodding a hello to an officer who had offered a 'Morning, Detectives' to them.

'Think there's any point talking to Nicola Clement any more?' Charlie asked once they were outside the cordoned-off area.

'Probably not, at the moment. She found the body, but that's it. Not sure what else she could tell us. She told the officer who got her statement that she's already contacted the *Daily Mail*. Clearly she's happy to get some cash as a sort of messed-up finder's fee, but I highly doubt she knows anything. I think we should go and talk to the park management people. There was at least one person from the park team here earlier, but I didn't catch a name and I can't remember for the life of me what they looked like.'

'She's already contacted the press? What an opportunist. That'll cause us a few headaches. And you know, I think you were right that time you joked you had partial face-blindness. Good job we don't rely on you to point out suspects in line-ups, huh?' Charlie laughed, jamming his hands into the pockets of his pea coat.

'Told you.'

After some googling, Daniel found the Royal Parks website and a contact number. It turned out they were close to the Old Police House, which served as the park lodge. A woman named

Helen answered and told Daniel she had been expecting them, that they could head over right away.

'Dammit,' Charlie said. 'I was hoping to get a bite to eat first. I skipped breakfast.'

'Seriously – you're hungry after seeing that?' Daniel gestured in the direction of the crime scene.

'Yup.'

'You're a very strange man, Charlie Palmer.' Daniel turned and headed towards the park lodge, following the map on his phone.

'So, afterwards, then?' Charlie asked.

'Sure. Now come on, would you?' Daniel smiled over his shoulder as Charlie jogged to catch up with him.

The Old Police House was a period building, full of character, and its orange brickwork was pristine in the morning light. Google had told Daniel that the building dated back to 1902, and he thought its features were a beautiful fit for the surroundings of the park. Apart from the tarmac roads, there was still a very 'ye olde London' feel to the place. Even the old gas street lamps were still present, although they had been updated with electric fixtures. It occurred to him that at night it might feel like Jack the Ripper was waiting among the shadows, ready to strike, but despite the macabre thought there was no denying the beauty of the architecture.

'Shame our offices don't look like this,' he said as he and Charlie headed up to the front entrance and stepped into the welcoming warmth inside.

The park management team had its own police force, which was part of the London Metropolitan force, but neither he nor Charlie had ever worked with them before. Daniel hoped they were co-operative.

'Can I help you, gentlemen?' the woman behind the desk in the entrance hall asked. 'I presume you're the detectives who just called?' She tucked a strand of red hair behind one ear as she stood to shake their hands. The rich colour of her shoulder-length hair was stark against her white shirt.

'Hi, yes. DI Graves and DI Palmer. We spoke to Helen on the phone a minute ago?'

'Yes, that's right. Officer Mader. I'll call for her. Take a seat if you like.' The woman pointed towards the armchairs across from her. Daniel had not even taken his coat off when Mader appeared, a thin smile on her face.

'Officer Helen Mader. Nice to meet you in person, circumstances aside obviously. Do you want to follow me?' Mader led them down a corridor – lined with sepia photos of London and decorative sculpted motifs edging the ceiling – into a much more basic meeting room, a typical white-walled box with simple, clean furnishings.

'Now it's more like our offices,' Charlie whispered with a smile as they took a seat.

'Horrible business, isn't it? This sort of thing just doesn't happen inside the park,' Mader started as she took a seat across the fake wooden table. 'Assaults, muggings and that sort of thing are alarmingly common, and there's always the possibility of knife crime, certainly at the moment, but it's rare that we have human remains on our hands. Especially like the crime scene discovered this morning. We're ready to help in any way we can.'

Helen Mader was a tall woman, slim in build but not lacking in any authority. Her face was friendly, framed by curly brown hair that was neat but not overly styled, and she had a real sense of business about her. Her words and her manner so far suggested that Daniel's fears over collaborative difficulties were unfounded. She seemed genuinely interested in helping them out – something that, surprisingly, wasn't always the case when working with other police forces or departments.

'This is our first time dealing with your department, so that's reassuring to know, thank you,' he answered. Charlie nodded his agreement.

'What we really need to know, to start with, is if there is any surveillance in place around the park. As you already know, the crime scene is well hidden and was only found by luck, to be honest. Even so, we suspect whatever happened there, ritual or otherwise, occurred at night. The park is locked up at night, correct?'

Mader nodded. 'Yes, of course. We have staff who lock up the entrances at midnight all year round, and constant security patrols. And we do have CCTV around the park, dotted along paths and of course focused on key locations such as the entrances, the cafés and the galleries.'

'Would you be able to share footage with us? All the entrances and, I guess, anything from cameras in the radius of the remains.'

'Of course. I need to put in the request with our security company so it might take a little while, but I'll do what I can to expedite the process.'

'Amazing, thank you,' Daniel said. 'I'm not sure what else you might be able to help with at the moment, but perhaps you could give us the names of the guards who patrol the park at night? We could speak to them.'

'And it would be good if your team could hold off from making any statements,' Charlie added. 'We'd like to control that aspect. If that's okay?'

'No problem to both. In terms of park guards, I'll check who was on duty last night and send you their details,' Helen answered, writing a note in a pad she had retrieved from the shelf behind her. The detectives handed her their cards and stood up from the table.

'Officer Mader, thank you once again for your help.' Daniel smiled as he pulled on his coat.

'Of course. Like I said, our team want to help as much as possible. The thought of someone being butchered like that and left in the park...' Mader shuddered. 'I want you to catch whoever did this and lock them away. The thought of them doing something like this again...' Her voice trailed off.

'Agreed. We'll be in touch.' The men shook hands with Mader again and headed back to the entrance.

'So, breakfast then?' Charlie said the second they were outside. Daniel couldn't help laughing, despite himself, almost forgetting the horror they had seen just half an hour ago. Almost.

CHAPTER THREE

Notification after notification pinged onto the home screen of Sarah Boyd's phone. She put her latte down and picked up the device, curious about what could have set it off.

'Don't you hate it when that happens? One person trawling through your Instagram and liking a shitload of posts?'

'Woe is you,' Angelica Okeke said, rubbing her forefingers together in mocking tiny-violin style. 'It must be so hard to be popular.' She burst into laughter when Sarah flicked a sugar cube across the dated Formica table at her. The old man sitting adjacent to them glared at them, which only made them laugh more. He scowled and Angelica mouthed 'sorry' at him. The woman behind the counter in the café smirked.

'Nah, it's weird,' Sarah said. She felt a pang of misery that it had been a stranger, not her ex Mike Turner, who had liked all of her posts. He hadn't liked anything she had posted since he had ghosted her, not even the vintage horror poster she'd snapped the week before to get his attention.

'You need to stop that now,' Angelica said, her face suddenly serious. She pushed a few stray strands of her afro hair off her forehead.

'That obvious?'

Her friend nodded. 'I know you liked him, loved him maybe, but he acted like a total dick.' And here it was, right on cue, the fiery side of Angelica that Sarah knew oh so well. 'He led you on, made you think he was into you, then he fucked off to God knows where and left you in the lurch. He's a twat, Sarah. You need to block him. Number, Instagram, everything.'

Sarah gave a thin smile of agreement. She knew Ange was right, but she still wasn't ready to face the reality of it. She still had feelings for Mike, even though she knew he hadn't treated her well – at least, not at the end.

But they were very different people. Angelica was the loud, fierce, strong friend and Sarah was the meek one who acted like a doormat and let people trample all over her. Angelica would yell at her for even thinking that was true, of course, and she would nod and agree – ironically only cementing it further.

'Yeah, maybe,' she admitted.

Meek, her inner voice whispered to her.

'No maybes about it. If he was a decent guy, he wouldn't have done that. You know I'm right. He would have given you an explanation. God, a fucking text or something.' Angelica picked up her green tea and took a sip, her eyebrows raised at Sarah as if expecting agreement.

'You swear too much,' Sarah said. 'Still hurts, though. Am I that bad? Really?' She instantly cringed at her clear attempt to fish for a compliment, and smiled when Angelica threw back a knowing glare.

'No, dickhead, you're not that bad.'

Sarah flicked another cube of sugar at her. 'Yeah, all right, fine. He's a twat. I'm amazing and he's a twat and should know better.'

'Too right! That's better, much more what I like to hear.'

For a moment they sat in silence, sipping their drinks. Sarah felt calmer, glad she had called Ange for a chat. She felt less calm when Angelica threw an idea into the ring, breaking the momentary serenity of the quiet café.

'What about we go to a party on Friday? My mate from work is having a moving-in kinda thing. Cocktails, hopefully some fit men. We can get dressed up.' Angelica had a glint in her eye.

'I mean... I'm thirty-four. I'm too old for some random house party.'

'Fuck off, you're not an old maid. Come on. My colleague is single and I bet he's got single friends who will be there too. It'll be fun. And if there are no hotties, it'll still be fun. Say yes. We haven't partied together in ages.'

Sarah rolled her eyes. 'We went out in Shoreditch less than a month ago.'

'Exactly! Almost a month ago! Almost as long as cockface Mike has ghosted you for.'

The old man pulled another face at Angelica and put his coat on, then left the café with a huff.

'Ugh, fine. Text me details.' On the table, Sarah's phone buzzed again. Another Instagram notification, only this time it was a comment, from the same account that had liked so many of her photos.

Looks like you're a creative woman – you should come to our group. A safe space for all women, inspiring and welcoming.

Sarah held up the phone to Angelica so she could read it.

'What exactly does that mean?' Angelica asked with a dismissive frown.

'Dunno – weird, huh? Sales crap probably.' Sarah dropped

her phone into her handbag, not wanting to face the fact that the message had bothered her, had somehow got under her skin.

The studio was a mess. Sarah groaned as she dumped her jacket and bag on her desk and surveyed the space, hands on her hips. She had only been renting the studio for six months, but already her start-up business was outgrowing it. She used to work in a design studio for a small fashion brand based in Notting Hill. She loved the work but hated the woman who owned the business, so Sarah had decided to branch out on her own. She had quickly settled on accessories, and before long had designed a small range of silk scarves and some beautiful leather purses and handbags, embellished with neon colours and gold and silver clasps. She was selling online and out of two London boutiques and couldn't be happier with how things were going.

But the space was too small.

After checking her post, which she had brought in with her, and finding none of it interesting, Sarah sat down and pulled her MacBook from her bag. She processed two orders that had come through, checked her emails, then started a quick search for bigger studio spaces to rent. Google brought up a veritable feast of options, ranging in price quite dramatically.

Clicking on one in Clerkenwell, which Sarah knew to be a hub for art and design companies, excitement tingled through her. Could she really grow the business further? She was just about managing with the production of her goods, a combination of handmade work and some pre-crafted elements she sourced and imported from Portugal, but she knew she could do more. Her mind raced. She'd need someone to help, her first actual employee. She'd probably need to get better accounting software and a business manager that wasn't just an online service. It felt terrifying but exciting.

Plucking a neon green handbag from the shelf behind her, Sarah artfully arranged a set-up on the desk. A corner of a notebook, a dry flower, a sleek metal pen and the bag. She took a shot and posted it to her company Instagram account with a caption about women in business and exciting things to come. Before she could put her phone down it buzzed – notifications coming through.

She recognised one of the accounts. It was the same one that had liked all her photos while she had been with Angelica.

'Stalker much?' she muttered, clicking on the account. It had the username EnchantedWomenLDN and seemed to be about female empowerment, as far as she could tell from its images of inspiring women and motivational quotes. That made sense, correlated with the message the account had sent to her. There was a link in the bio, and she clicked on it. Her phone redirected her to a basic but attractive website offering mentoring, networking, creative workshops and more for women in London.

It struck Sarah that this could be something she'd actually find useful. Perhaps they ran sessions about business and taking charge, leading the way, that sort of thing. Sarah filled out the on-site contact form, enquiring about an introductory session. She also followed the account.

CHAPTER FOUR

'God, I hate this place,' Daniel Graves said to the world in general. The world needed to know his discomfort.

'I don't think anyone really likes morgues, Dan,' Charlie said, his voice flat, as though Daniel had been stating the obvious.

'I bet *he* does.' Daniel nodded in the direction of Samson Lepard, an experienced mortuary technician with an always present grin, a wiry frame and slim black-rimmed glasses. Samson had worked on a number of their cases and Daniel liked the man, but he had never got used to his constant exuberance. How Lepard could be so alive and full of positivity when spending over forty hours a week in rooms filled with dead people was beyond Daniel entirely.

'Exception to the rule,' Charlie said as they watched him from across the cold, sterile room. Lepard read through something on a clipboard before scrawling his name on the bottom.

'Oh good, you're here,' came a Scottish voice behind them for the second time that day. They turned to say hello to Emi Kobayashi.

She pulled a face. 'Are you okay, Detective? You look a little... peaky.'

Daniel could tell she had selected the word carefully, her tone implying as diplomatically as possible that he looked like shit. He suspected that she was probably correct. Charlie leant around him to inform Emi that Daniel was not a fan of morgues.

'Who is?' Emi responded. 'Although, given your surname—'

'I know, ironic isn't it, blah blah,' Daniel said before she could finish. No new person he met could ever resist saying something about his name and his career choice. There wasn't a joke about it that he hadn't already heard.

'Anyway,' Emi continued, unabashed, 'thanks for meeting me. As I said on the phone, Mr Lepard informs me that he has found something that could prove useful for your investigation. I thought it was best that you came to see for yourself. Always nice to do things in person, I think.'

Daniel felt it was unlikely that she or Lepard couldn't have informed them of their discoveries over the phone. Stephanie Mitchum normally did that. It was efficient and saved him time. He resisted mentioning that, keen on fostering a good working relationship with the new Coroner Administration Assistant.

'Let's get on with it, then,' he said. 'Samson, are you ready for us?'

Lepard adjusted his glasses as he beamed at them, at least fifty per cent perkier than Daniel felt he had a right to be.

'I'd say so, Detective. Let's get this body parts show on the road!'

Lepard led them across to the opposite side of the morgue to a metal table covered with a semi-translucent plastic sheet. Daniel could clearly see the body parts beneath and held back a gag. With a flourish that reminded Daniel of a party magician, Lepard pulled the sheet away to reveal the remains, neatly laid out to form a rough human shape.

'As I'm sure you already knew, and can definitely see now, we're missing a few pieces of this chap,' Lepard started.

'Chap?' Daniel clarified.

Lepard nodded. 'Indeed it is. One man. I know you thought perhaps there was a mixture of victims here, but all the pieces belong to the same unlucky fellow.'

'Okay, that's a good start,' Charlie said. 'You have more for us, though, right?'

Lepard put his hands on his hips and pouted, his head tilted to one side. 'Detective Palmer, do I ever disappoint you?' Not waiting for a response, he leant forward and pointed at the severed ends of a piece of forearm and shin. 'See how ragged these cuts are? The flesh has not been neatly sliced, and there are multiple striations on the visible bone of both of these segments. In layman's terms, they're messy – not the work of a pro, if you get my drift.'

'So our killer just hacked this guy to pieces?' Daniel asked, shuddering at the mental image. 'That would make one hell of a mess, right?'

'Oh yes, most certainly,' Lepard agreed. 'Wherever this man was killed would probably feature a significant pool of blood.'

Daniel thought about what that meant for the killer. They would need a decent-sized space and would probably have covered it in plastic first. But given the amateur skill at work, would they have thought it through well enough, been that prepared? Surely at least some trace evidence would have been left behind. The killer wasn't Dexter. It was something to keep in mind – once they had a suspect.

'Okay, does that mean we're looking for someone who probably hasn't killed before? And someone who has a space big enough to chop up a body.'

Charlie didn't look impressed. Daniel knew what his

partner was thinking. It wasn't enough to go on. Not yet. Evidently Lepard had understood the expression too.

'Fear not, for I have more. Your killer may be a brunette woman. I found a long strand of hair. I mean, it could be from a man, it's impossible to tell for sure. You can't tell sex from a hair sample without the root. Given the length and its condition, though, I'd say female in origin with fair confidence.'

That took Daniel by surprise. A woman might have done this? Hacked up a man and strung him up in the middle of Hyde Park?

'Told you it was worth coming down in person,' Emi said, her arms crossed and a knowing smile touching her lips. Daniel had to admit that Lenard had found out more than he had expected.

'Wow, okay. That's good to know. She's probably not a serial killer. There's less than a handful of active serial killers in the country right now, and none are thought to be women. It seems she hasn't got her methods down yet, so... a crime of passion, an accident, maybe? She panics and wants to get rid of the body. But that doesn't explain the whole ritual thing,' he said, his brow wrinkling.

'Yeah, that's certainly a problem. Do you know who the victim is yet?' Charlie asked.

'No,' Emi answered. 'We have some partial prints, which we're running through the criminal record database. No teeth for dental records, which is a shame.'

'We can cross-reference with missing persons as well,' Daniel noted. 'Okay, anything else?'

Lepard shook his head.

'Okay, thanks both. Great start.'

Daniel and Charlie bid farewell to Emi and Lepard and left the morgue, heading upstairs and outside into the darkening evening. Daniel found the fresh air welcome, as always after visiting the morgue.

'Right, I'm knackered. See you tomorrow,' Charlie said as he headed across the car park. 'I reckon it's going to be a busy one,' he said over his shoulder as he went.

'See you,' Daniel said before heading towards his own car. It had been one hell of a day. The weird ritualistic crime scene was entirely new to Daniel and offered up a myriad of questions. Add that to the amateur technique the killer had shown, and the fact that their killer may be a woman, and it made for a highly unusual picture. Plus, it was all over the evening news. Charlie was right. Tomorrow would be a very busy day indeed.

It still felt unusual for Daniel to drive home to his new flat, a two-bedroom place in Stoke Newington on a quiet street not far from Finsbury Park. It didn't feel like his home yet, more like somewhere he was simply visiting. As he checked for post in the communal hallway shared with the downstairs flat he tried to slough away some of his discomfort and admit the truth: that he'd had no choice but to move, and this was his new normal.

The problem was that things were so complicated and unresolved. Daniel had been thrown for a loop. Finding out that his sister's ex-boyfriend had known Jenny Cartwright – a woman who had been killed to get at him, in apparent revenge – was a lot to process.

Daniel had met Jenny Cartwright when she had become involved in a case of his a year ago, not long after he'd moved to London. There had been an instant mutual attraction. She had ended up providing Daniel and Charlie with valuable information on a prime suspect in a homicide, a woman named

Cassandra Salinas. As a result Jenny had been attacked twice by Salinas, a ruthless woman who had killed numerous other people. Jenny had survived, and Daniel and Charlie had closed the case after Salinas had been shot dead by a special firearms officer. And that should have been that. After the case was over, Daniel had the opportunity to date Jenny – a vibrant, exciting woman he had come to know and like. As it turned out, someone had other plans. Jenny had been killed. Worse, her killer had left her heart in a box on Daniel's doorstep for him to find. Jenny's death was revenge for Salinas's death – or so a note written in blood informed him. Since that horrific gesture, Daniel had been constantly uneasy, on guard, wondering what would happen next.

The next thing to happen had been a note to Daniel, left as a comment on Jenny Cartwright's Facebook memorial page. It told him that Salinas's death had not been forgotten. It was short and to the point, and sent Daniel reeling. Shortly afterwards Daniel had found out that his own laptop had been used to leave the message, and that someone had broken into his flat to do so. Whoever wanted to get to him was dangerously close. It didn't end there. An unknown driver behind the wheel of a Range Rover with blacked-out windows had then tried to drive him off the road. Daniel hadn't been sure if the intention had been to hurt him or simply scare him, but he was definitely scared.

Amanda Graves, Daniel's sister, had unwittingly provided a connection between everything that had happened. Daniel's sister had been dating a man who knew Jenny Cartwright and who had repeatedly made trips to London from up north at around the same time someone was messing with Daniel. This man was called Greg Armstrong.

And then everything had gone quiet again – unnervingly so. Three months had passed without further incident. Greg

Armstrong had simply disappeared. His phone had been disconnected, the property he had been living in had been abandoned. It seemed that he had vanished entirely. Whoever he really was, he had become a ghost – presumably after finding out that Amanda had visited Daniel in London and had told him everything.

Superintendent Peter Hobbs, Daniel's superior, had initially allowed police resources to be used to try and find Greg Armstrong. After they had found nothing within a fortnight, however, Hobbs had been forced to pull the resources back for other cases. Daniel had been left in a sort of limbo. He still looked over his shoulder each day, waiting for Armstrong to emerge and terrorise him once more, but he no longer had much power to do anything about it. And all because he had just done his job and stopped Salinas.

It was a lot to deal with. The easiest thing to do in the short term had been to move, so that was what he had done, but he was not yet used to his new place. It was slightly bigger than his last flat, the upstairs of a converted house rather than a new build. It was nice, lovely in fact, even given Daniel's lack of furniture and belongings beyond the essentials. It just didn't feel like home yet.

Daniel stood in the kitchen, which was open plan, just like his old flat, wondering what might make it feel more homely, more his. He wasn't sure, and decided he'd wait until inspiration struck organically. After rustling up some pasta and putting on some low music, he felt more at ease, if not fully relaxed.

Before he went to bed he checked his front door again, double-locking it and pulling the chain across. He tapped in the code to set the alarm. He suspected he would dream of blood-drenched effigies as it was; he didn't need to add the subconscious worry of someone breaking in as well.

CHAPTER FIVE

A fter a night broken by odd, uncomfortably intense dreams, Daniel Graves was surprised to find that he wasn't totally exhausted the next day as he looked for a parking space just off Mile End Road. He hadn't needed a huge coffee or an energy drink to keep him alert either – a change from the norm. He wondered if the strangeness of the new case was enough of a stimulant, although strange cases were starting to feel like his speciality.

He and Charlie had scheduled a mid-morning appointment with a professor of humanities and social sciences at Queen Mary University of London. It was a fact-finding mission. They needed to know more about rituals and effigies to figure out the significance of the crime scene from the day before.

It was not as sunny as the past few days, back to normal early spring temperatures. As Daniel clambered out of his car, dragging his satchel out after him, he felt a low wind sneaking whispering tendrils over his skin. He looked over at the Queens' Building across the road, shaking off a feeling of foreboding that had arisen with the breeze. The looming clouds and heavy sky seemed an all too fitting backdrop to the impressive period building that was the focal point of the campus.

A car horn beeped, and he turned to see Charlie's shiny new Renault SUV pulling in just down the road from him. It was a good-looking car. Daniel was kind of jealous. After his previous car had been written off a few months ago, he'd got a cheap second-hand Kia to replace it. The Kia was decent but not in amazing condition, and it was by no means his dream car. It made him laugh that Charlie had bought such a big vehicle just to drive around gridlocked London.

'Just in from your manor in the countryside, are we?' he joked. Charlie headed his way, buttoning up a thin black jacket he evidently hoped would keep out some of the chill in the air.

'Just in from the scrapyard?' Charlie fired back with a grin. Daniel laughed and together they crossed the road to the university campus, stopping in front of a board showing a map. They located the library, where they had agreed to meet the professor, and dodged their way through groups of students chatting or smoking – and, in one couple's case, putting on a very public display of affection.

Professor Molly Goodings was waiting for them at the main reception desk in the library entrance. She was dressed in jeans, boots and a soft grey jumper, with her long wavy brown hair falling around her shoulders. There was little trace of make-up on her naturally attractive face, and her warm smile lit up her features as she headed over to them. She didn't look like Daniel had expected a university professor to look. She was younger and less academic than he had imagined. Clearly the world of teaching had moved on since he was in higher education.

'Detectives, lovely to meet you. I'm Molly Goodings. So, you're here to talk about rituals and murder, correct? Fun stuff!' Without pausing she spun and, beckoning to them, led them past the circular reception desk and into the library proper. As they followed her the vibrant smell of books filled the air – a scent that brought Daniel back to the days of his studies. A mixture of old and new, the building was a tranquil oasis, with the only sounds the quiet whispers of students, pencils scribbling on notepads, and the soft whoosh of book pages turning. It was remarkably relaxing.

Professor Goodings led them to the back of the building, up a flight of stairs and into a private study room.

'As you can see, I did some planning ahead based on the quick conversation I had with DI Palmer this morning.' She tapped the stack of books on the table as she sat down. The detectives sat too, staring at the spines of the books. Words such as 'witchcraft', 'demonology', 'rituals' and 'sacrifice' stood out, and Daniel shuddered, particularly at the word 'demonology'. He'd had more than his fill of that with his first homicide case in London. He hoped that wasn't where they were heading with this new case too.

'That's quite a collection,' he said, frowning.

Molly smiled. 'Well, I figured I'd try and cover all the bases. I didn't have much to go on from the phone call.'

'Fair enough,' Daniel admitted. 'Before we go any further, can I ask you to sign a non-disclosure agreement? Even though the woman who found the crime scene sold her video of it to the press, there are obviously details that aren't public, so this will cover us.' Daniel opened his satchel and pulled out the requisite paperwork, which the professor signed without even reading it.

'Okay, then,' he said and pulled out another file. 'I've only got a few photos to show you. Be warned: they aren't pleasant.'

Molly nodded as Daniel passed them to her, and he and Charlie waited to see her reaction. She grimaced but otherwise seemed remarkably unfazed. She pulled a photo out from the stack, then held it up. 'This one, where we can clearly see the shape of the effigy used, could be quite useful if we can find some comparisons for it. I don't recognise this form, but if it references something I'm sure we'll find out what it is with some digging.'

Molly scanned the spines of the books and pulled one out of the pile before handing it to Daniel. She then chose another different title, which she offered to Charlie.

'The practice of rituals, particularly ritual murder like this, is very rare – at least, in modern times. Satanic ritual abuse has been connected to physical and sexual abuse in various cases around the world, most prominently in the 1980s and 1990s, but is not often heard of now.'

'Do you think it could really be something like that?' Charlie asked as he flicked through the book she had given him. 'Satan worshippers or something?'

'I suppose so, though satanism as a modern religion is more about collections of people who are interested in the subject matter and who class themselves as "other" in regard to religion. It's not really about holding demon-summoning rituals and sacrificing goats. A common misconception. I don't know of any public groups in the UK that are affiliated with the Church of Satan or similar – they're mostly based in America, but I think we'd be foolish to rule it out as an avenue of investigation.'

'Even though you said that satanists aren't about sacrifice?' Daniel asked.

Molly nodded. 'The person who committed this crime could still be involved with satanism somehow. In terms of similar, I'm sure you're aware of modern cases that have ties with ritualistic killings, such as the torso of the young boy found in the Thames in 2001. That's one of the few high-profile, vaguely recent cases I know of in the UK. Historical links to ritual murder are more common – often associated with anti-Semitism as late as 1939, actually. And of course rituals in general are regularly linked to witchcraft and the occult across the world. Punishment effigies were used as part of law enforcement in the 1700s, though these were wooden or straw sculptures that were normally burned to send a message to the criminal. The criminals themselves were not sacrificed in this way. Frankly, I've seen nothing like this.' She looked back down at the photos splayed out on the table.

Daniel tapped the image of the blood-soaked effigy that Molly had initially singled out. 'So it could be a number of things, but what can we learn from this specifically? This structure? And the use of a structure of any description?'

The three studied the photo for a quiet moment before Molly continued. 'Typically, effigies are meant to represent a person or an entity. Modern versions are often politically charged, again nothing like this. This definitely speaks to something occult in origin. Sometimes effigies are deliberately damaged or destroyed as a way to cast something out or cause harm. This one looks intact, though.'

The detectives nodded. Apart from the addition of the body parts and blood, the wooden effigy had appeared basically untouched after assembly.

'Could it be related to voodoo?' Daniel asked.

'Technically, yes, I suppose so. I'll need to do some proper research to see if I can find anything resembling this specific structure, but voodoo dolls are a form of effigy too. This structure certainly has a bodily form to it, namely the ribcage shape, but it could also be meant to symbolise a demonic or god-like entity.'

'Could it just be a display of brutality? Someone showing off?' Charlie suggested.

'You tell me – you probably know serial killer psychology better than I do. But yes, I wouldn't rule it out, although you mentioned that the crime scene was quite private, correct? That suggests actions with a different intent.'

Daniel thought about everything that Molly had told them so far. He already knew about the use of effigies in relation to politics, and figures such as Guy Fawkes, but he was struggling to get into the mindset of whoever had created the monstrosity in Hyde Park. He'd had dealings with the occult before, had even at moments been tempted to believe elements of the supernatural to be true, but this was new. Had the killer sacrificed someone to appease a supposed entity? Had they done it as punishment for something? Was it merely a show of some sort, not related to the occult but a mere display of power?

He looked down at the books in front of them, knowing some heavy reading was in his future. 'Can we borrow these?'

Molly nodded. 'Of course. And I have more books that could offer some useful insights or avenues to look into. I will also do some research myself, see what I can find out.'

Knowing that they didn't have time to waste, Daniel stood, pulling his satchel over his shoulder. He needed to get in touch with their criminal profiler, Martia Franklin. She would have a field day with this one.

They also didn't have a suspect yet. Of that he was painfully aware.

'Thank you for your time, Professor Goodings – it was really helpful. And I hope you don't mind if we keep in touch? Perhaps continue to use you in a consultant capacity?' Daniel offered her his card.

'Contact me any time – I'll help whenever I can. You have my number. And now I have yours,' Molly said with a charming smile that promised something more. She reached out to shake Daniel's hand and he felt himself flush. He hadn't expected his attraction to her to be seemingly reciprocated. Awkwardly returning the handshake, he said he would, taking a last glance at Molly.

'Thank you. We'll show ourselves out,' Charlie said, and they left.

Outside, Charlie nudged Daniel. 'I think you need to call her, mate,' he said with a sly smile as they headed for their cars.

'I will,' Daniel answered. 'I'm sure we'll need more help on this case.'

Charlie stopped walking and glared at Daniel. 'Don't be dense. I mean, you need to call her for a drink. She was clearly into you – I saw that little moment as we left.'

'Whatever,' Daniel said. They reached their cars and split up. As Charlie got into his SUV he held a thumb and little finger up to his cheek, the universal signal for a phone call. In return Daniel gave him two fingers and a smile. He couldn't help agreeing, though. There had been a spark of something there, totally out of the blue. He shook himself. 'Focus, Daniel. You have a murder to solve first,' he said to himself.

He'd just eaten a tuna and cucumber sandwich, a bag of Popchips, an apple and a can of sugar-free Relentless. Daniel frowned at his phone. Emi Kobayashi was calling. He didn't want to bring up his lunch at some horrifying piece of news she might share with him.

'Hi, Detective. I have some good news for you about the victim from the park.'

'Okay, hit me with it,' he said, hoping that he wouldn't need to go back to the morgue.

'We have an ID for the poor guy. His name was Anthony Gallagher. He was reported missing three days ago by a friend. Apparently Anthony missed two football sessions and when his friend couldn't get hold of him, he called it in. Samson found an old sports injury on the left tibia that matched with Gallagher. He's our guy.'

'Amazing – that is good news. I don't need to come down to the morgue again, do I?' Daniel asked.

'No need. The remains couldn't tell us anything else. I'll email over what we have on him.'

Daniel thanked Emi before hanging up. Just two minutes later, the files came through to his inbox and he printed them out. 'Time to find out all we can about you, Mr Gallagher,' he said to the picture on the man's driving licence. 'What happened to you?'

Heading back to his desk from the printer, he scanned the open-plan office to see who was around to assist with the research. Ideally he wanted to bring in Sergeant Amelia Harding again. She had supported him on two of the high-profile cases Daniel had led in the last year and both times had proved invaluable. She wasn't at her desk, however.

Daniel spotted another face he recognised, and called the man over. 'Junior Sergeant Hayes, can you come here for a sec?'

Ross Hayes crossed the office, a mug of coffee in hand. 'Hi sir, yes sir, what can I do for you?' he asked, his youthful face lighting up with curiosity.

'Do you know where Sergeant Harding is?' Daniel enquired, still scanning the office as though mentioning her name would make her suddenly appear. When he looked back at Hayes, he saw the man's disappointment.

'Oh right, yes, she's assisting DI Bellows, I think. We got a call about a guy in Camberwell, seen with a machete in the street.' Ross sounded dejected, and immediately Daniel felt guilty.

'Okay. Well in that case you can help me instead,' he said. He didn't know the junior sergeant well, but was aware that Ross had helped Amelia to carry out research on his home invasion serial killer case a few months back, and Amelia had fed back with positive remarks on his performance.

'Of course, happy to.' Ross put his coffee down on the nearest desk and rubbed his hands together.

'Perfect. Can you do some research for me? Man's name is Anthony Gallagher. He was killed some time in the past two to three days, and his remains were found yesterday. I need to know why someone wanted him dead. Did he have debts? Was he into drugs? Did he piss off the wrong person? All that sort of thing. Anything you can find out would be great. By the end of the day, if possible.'

Daniel handed Ross the printouts, and the junior sergeant took them with an enthusiastic nod. 'Of course, sir. On it!' Ross grabbed his coffee and shot off across the office, a bounce in his step.

Daniel smiled to himself, then pulled out his phone. His call rang out, unanswered, so he left a message. 'Hi, Martia. It's Detective Inspector Graves. We've got an interesting new case and I could do with building up a picture of our possible killer. You in?'

CHAPTER SIX

The day before had been a whirlwind of new orders. As the morning rolled on Sarah Boyd decided it was time for a break from the manufacturing side of her business. She had fulfilled her urgent orders and decided that the others could wait for another day.

Since she'd signed up to receive more information on EnchantedWomenLDN and the services it could provide, her mind had been full of exciting thoughts about her business and where the women's centre could take her.

She'd received a welcome email that morning, explaining what the centre was about in more detail and listing some of the benefits of joining, such as creative workshops, networking and social events. Sarah wasn't that fussed by the idea of social events, but women around her age and older were her target market. She was convinced she could, if nothing else, sell some pieces to new people she met, perhaps build up good word of mouth for her products.

The email also invited new applicants to come and visit the centre, to give them a better idea of how everything worked and to see if it was for them. An induction of sorts. And that's what Sarah had decided to do with her day.

Making sure she'd responded to any urgent emails, Sarah set off across the city on her business adventure, her stride confident, her mind ready to absorb new information that would grow her business. When she finally made it to the address provided by the website, her positivity was overflowing. As she stood outside the building, however, she felt it all drain away, as though she had stepped on something sharp and it was leaking away through the hole that had been made.

The building was ugly. It looked like a warehouse, on a plot of gravel and weeds stranded between Deptford and the Thames. Nothing about it was inviting. As Sarah studied the warehouse, she decided she'd made a mistake. Either she had it wrong and had somehow googled the wrong place or EnchantedWomenLDN was a load of crap and not worth her time. She couldn't even see a sign on the warehouse front, just a set of double doors in plain grey metal. Her disappointment was palpable.

'It's what's on the inside that counts,' came a voice behind her.

Sarah screamed, almost dropping her handbag as she jumped and spun at the same time.

Behind her was a concerned-looking Asian woman in her fifties who had clearly not meant to scare the living hell out of her. 'I'm so sorry. I didn't mean to make you jump!' the woman exclaimed, taking a tentative step forward and offering a smile.

Sarah sucked in a few deep breaths and tried to calm her pounding heart before returning the smile as best she could. 'It's okay. No harm done. I scare easily.' She laughed before putting a hand on her heart, settling herself.

'Not the best introduction, was it? I'm Mira. Are you coming in?' Mira gestured to the warehouse.

'To be honest, I was going to, but then...' Sarah wasn't sure how to finish the sentence without sounding horribly rude. For all she knew, this woman had founded the place. Who was she to judge, at least to Mira's face?

'Trust me, I know. It looks like a dump from outside. And the name is a bit misleading too. But I think what's inside will change your mind. What are you here for?'

'I... Well, I run my own business and I thought... maybe networking. Or focus groups perhaps – for my products, I mean. Some start-up business mentoring.'

'Then you're in the right place.' Mira smiled. Sarah frowned as she turned back to look at the warehouse.

'What do you have to lose?' Mira asked.

'Nothing,' Sarah admitted.

Again Mira gestured to the front doors, and this time Sarah did as instructed. Dubious, but figuring if she hated the place then she could just leave, she pushed one of the metal doors open. The colourful cacophony inside was such a jolt to her system that it almost took her breath away.

'Told you.' Mira giggled as Sarah stepped into the reception area of EnchantedWomenLDN, awestruck.

The interior was everything Sarah had imagined a creative space to be. Huge skylights allowed warm light to stream down on a large open central space with rooms coming off all around it. A small but inviting café sat in the middle, and the delicious scents of coffee, cinnamon and fresh pastries wafted over to Sarah. Small vases of flowers were on almost every available surface. Art adorned most of the wall space. About twelve women of different ages and ethnicities milled around, some with drinks, some holding art supplies, others in deep discussion. It looked like heaven.

'Good morning, how can I help?' asked the young woman sitting behind the reception desk, her smile wide and as charming as the curly black hair piled on top of her head and kept in place with a rainbow ribbon.

'I shall leave you to it, enjoy!' Mira said, waving hello to the receptionist and heading towards the back of the building.

'Thanks,' Sarah called after her before turning to the receptionist. 'Hi, my name's Sarah Boyd. I emailed about joining? I thought I'd pop by and see what's on offer, how it works, that sort of thing.'

'Lovely to meet you, Sarah. I'm Abby.'

The next forty minutes went by in an excited haze. To start with, Abby explained all the types of workshops, creative sessions, mentoring, and even therapy on offer and that, apart from paying a low monthly membership fee, Sarah could just pay as she went, tailoring her use of the space to suit her own needs and interests.

After this, Abby's colleague Hailey showed Sarah around the two art studios, the quiet spaces, the bookable meeting rooms, the small but well-designed lecture theatre, ending up back at reception, where she offered Sarah a leaflet that covered events for the next three months.

It was incredible. Before leaving to head home, Sarah took a photo of the café. It looked so nice, no filter was needed. She posted it to her business Instagram account, promising exciting things ahead for her start-up and tagging EnchantedWomenLDN. Before she had made it up the road, her phone had buzzed with seven notifications liking the post.

Sarah felt invigorated. It felt like a good move. This place, this community, full of women who shared a passion for development, for creativity and learning, would surely bring good things her way.

How could it not?

CHAPTER SEVEN

E ven though he had looked around to make sure Daniel wasn't present to overhear, Charlie still didn't feel safe to take the call where he was. He ducked into the nearest stairwell, hoping that his signal wouldn't drop out.

'Hey, Kel, what's up? I'm at work.'

Kelly sighed with frustration, a sound he was getting all too familiar with. 'Would you just tell him already? He's a big boy, he'll cope. It's not like it'll be a total surprise,' she complained.

Charlie was not, in fact, entirely certain that Daniel would cope with the news that he was back with Kelly Malone. He expected a less than positive response, not an understanding smile and congratulatory high five. To be fair, though, that was Kelly's own fault.

Charlie and Kelly had first dated over two years ago. It had all started well enough. Loved-up trips to nice restaurants, pop-up bars and the like. A number of weekends spent in bed. Kelly had even met Charlie's dad, albeit briefly. And then she had written a story for her paper leaking information about a case that had not been made public, that she shouldn't have known. That Charlie shouldn't have told her. It was the first time

Charlie had been in genuine trouble in his career. He was pulled off the case, given a written warning. One more slip-up like that, he'd be out of the force. It had devastated him, that Kelly, the woman he was falling in love with, would do that to him, would jeopardise his career to get a leg up in her own. He'd immediately ended their relationship, breaking his own heart in the process.

Since then they had run into each other on occasion when Charlie worked a case and Kelly approached him for a scoop, but he'd never said more than a curt hello to her and he had otherwise successfully avoided her.

But when he and Daniel had begun working on a high-profile serial killer case, he and Kelly had crossed paths again properly. The brutal home invasion murders just a few months ago. Somehow Kelly had been tipped off about the first victims and had been the only journalist at the initial crime scene. She hadn't heard a word from him or Daniel but still managed to break the story. As the case became more infamous, so did Kelly, resulting in her furiously trying to keep her position as the go-to news source for the murders.

Kelly had always been pushy, Charlie's experience of her proved that, but her uncompromising dedication to her job meant that she had ended up putting herself in danger to stay ahead of the competition. She had managed to track down one of the suspects related to the case, then had broken into their base of operations, looking for anything she could use for an explosive story. She had almost been killed as a result. Charlie and a member of the armed forces unit that had taken down the two killers had saved her, seconds from death. It had triggered something in Charlie, the thought of losing her despite everything. He realised he still had feelings for her, and they were mutual.

Daniel Graves knew what Kelly had done to Charlie in the

past, and had immediately taken his friend's side. He made no attempt to hide the fact that he hated what Kelly had put Charlie through, and he was very reluctant to accept she had changed. He had little time for her. When he had seen her and Charlie coming out of the abandoned building that night in Lewisham, Daniel had been concerned for Charlie. Luckily for Charlie, Daniel had other more pressing issues to deal with at that moment, and he hadn't mentioned Kelly since.

Which brought Charlie back to now, a few months later, standing in a stairwell to take a call from his girlfriend because their rekindled romance was still a secret. No one knew about it apart from one of Kelly's closest friends. Charlie didn't think anyone else would understand why he was willing to give her a second chance, including Daniel.

'I told you, I need to wait for the right time. And if you really want to build your relationship with the department and get back on the invite list to our press conferences, then Daniel has to be okay with you. The superintendent too. Hobbs needs to trust you – and me. And Daniel's support will go a long way.'

Kelly knew about the new ritual murder case, though she only knew the details that had been covered in the video that had been in the news on day one. Charlie had not told her anything else. No way was he going to let slip confidential information for a third time. She had immediately asked for an exclusive but he had shot her down. He still wondered if she was with him again to try to get stories. He didn't think so, not after spending the last few months together, when he'd seen a new side to her, but the worry was always there in the back of his mind. It wasn't that simple, anyway. After the shit she had pulled to write stories on the home invasion case, her name had been blacklisted. The *City Post*, where she worked, had been tarnished too. She had been suspended for two months, and was still only working there on the proviso that she was limited to entertainment and lifestyle content, nothing to do with breaking news stories. He felt bad for her, knew that she had struggled since, but it was her own fault. He felt that she had made her bed and she needed to lie in it. She was lucky to still have a job. He thought she should be grateful that things hadn't turned out worse for her.

'Oh, fine, I'll be patient. But please don't take too long. I miss working on stories about cases like your new one.'

'Thank God I know you love me, otherwise I'd swear you were using me again,' Charlie answered. As he said it, he ignored the small part of his mind that warned him she could love him *and* use him. She really did seem different. Nearly being killed had clearly changed her – for the better. She was still driven, but he now knew how sweet and funny and caring she could be when she spent less time chasing headlines. He had to hope his faith in her was well placed, and he had to have faith in *himself* that he wouldn't fall for it yet again.

'Stop it, you know I love you. Since I almost died, I'm a new woman, and I'm going to keep proving that to you. Even if I never get to cover another murder. Anyway, I suppose I should get back to work. I still need to be employed!'

'That you do. Are we still on for dinner tomorrow?' Charlie asked, feeling himself relax a little.

'Yep, I'll text you some options later.'

They hung up and Charlie sighed, releasing some residual tension, before emerging onto his office floor. He walked straight into Sergeant Amelia Harding.

'Wow, careful, sir!' she exclaimed, turning to him. 'You look a little flustered – is everything okay?'

Amelia was smiling. Charlie could feel his cheeks reddening, even though she couldn't possibly know that he had been hiding on the stairs.

'Er, yes, sorry, family stuff,' he lied, figuring she wouldn't press for further details. He quickly changed the subject. 'You helping us on the new murder case?'

'Oh, the sacrifice in the park? I wanted to, but just my luck – I was out on another case when DI Graves wanted some research done. Ross is helping him.'

Charlie could see the disappointment on her face. He knew that Amelia was a hard worker. She'd helped him and Daniel out numerous times before and had proved very valuable. He also knew she was after a promotion.

'I'm sure you can assist Ross. I believe he's been looking into our victim. If you have capacity, I reckon it'd be good for you to go over with him what he's found. We're trying to put together a profile of our killer so we'll need to cross-reference with anyone in our vic's life soon.'

'Perfect! Thanks, sir.'

Charlie watched Amelia head off in search of Junior Sergeant Ross Hayes. He was glad of the extra assistance on the case. An extra brain could help speed things up, especially one as bright as Amelia's. They still didn't have much to go on, suspect-wise, and Amelia had a track record of finding useful information. He hoped she would again.

It was early afternoon by the time CCTV footage came in from Officer Helen Mader, who Daniel and Charlie had spoken to after visiting the Hyde Park crime scene two days before. It had taken longer than Daniel wanted, for which Officer Mader had apologised profusely but, as it turned out, she and her team had done some of the work for them already.

'It'll take us a while to run through facial recognition, but they isolated all people caught on camera around the times we needed. That will save us some work,' Patrick Marsden had told Daniel.

Daniel had watched a small section of the footage while with the tech team, concerned that the footage was too dark in places and that it didn't cover enough angles into and out of the park, but Patrick had assured him they could enhance it fairly easily. The head of the Digital Forensics department, Patrick knew what he was talking about, and Daniel trusted him. Would the CCTV have captured anything useful? Would anyone in the footage come up on their database? Daniel wondered. He wasn't holding out for a clear suspect just yet. According to Sampson Lepard, the autopsy had shown that whoever had killed Anthony Gallagher had shown no signs of expertise in the art of dismemberment. It might also be a woman who had killed him. Daniel doubted that there would be footage of a woman entering the park at night, dragging a body bag in one hand and wielding a saw in the other.

Patrick had told him not to expect anything for the rest of the day. As the dull, late winter afternoon outside started to darken Daniel's office, he took advantage of the moment of calm. Taking a seat at his desk and pulling out his phone, he started to compose a message. He shook his head and deleted it, not sure of the right approach. He felt nervous, like a bloody teenager. The thought made him laugh.

'Don't be such a loser,' he muttered to himself, writing the message again.

Hey Molly, this is Daniel Graves. I'm just checking in to see if you've found out anything else about our Hyde Park effigy. Also, if you're free tonight, do you fancy going for a drink?

He pressed 'send', his skin tingling with anticipation. He'd been out of the dating loop for a while and wasn't sure how to play it, so he decided that honesty was probably the best approach. He really hoped that he and Charlie had read that moment at the university correctly, because Molly had been on his mind regularly since then. Sure, he could brush it off if he had been mistaken, but it would be embarrassing. But he was excited to feel this way again, to genuinely want to go on a date with someone. Since Jenny, he hadn't allowed himself to think about the possibility of meeting someone. Her death had been such a blow to him, even though they never had the chance to date. Now, with his whole body hoping that Molly would text back a 'yes', he knew he was ready.

His phone buzzed and he flinched. He opened the message.

Nothing on the effigy yet. Seems to be a rare one! Will let you know when I find something. M.

'Is that it?' he said, disappointed. He had started to text back a casual thanks when his phone vibrated again.

Also drinks would be great but I can't do tonight. How about Friday?

Daniel's heart soared. Again he laughed at himself and his swinging emotions. He texted back immediately, asking where Molly fancied meeting.

London Bridge? Lots of nice places around there. I know a really good pub. Shall we meet at the station at 7?

Daniel confirmed, already excited about the date. It was Wednesday, so he only had to wait two days. He wondered if he could keep it a secret from Charlie for that long; he didn't want Charlie to add pressure on top.

CHAPTER EIGHT

S arah Boyd had already been to two workshops at
EnchantedWomenLDN. She didn't want to waste any
time. The first workshop had been a simple networking session
where she met a few other women who had started up small
businesses. Led by a woman who was a successful entrepreneur
three times over, the participants had discussed the challenges
they were facing, great discoveries that had helped them, and
had asked questions of the group. Sarah had loved every minute
of it, and had already looked into one of the investment
companies a woman called Kerry had mentioned. With a bump
in capital, she could expand her business...

The second had been totally different – a still-life drawing
class. Sarah had paid £7 for the materials for the class, but that
was all. In one of the bright, airy studios built in an extension at
the back of the warehouse, she had spent an hour and a half
listening to beautiful classical music and trying her hand at
drawing a variety of objects. She wasn't bad, either; her
experience of sketching designs for bags and clothing had come
in handy. She had left the class with a warm sense of
achievement, the teacher's compliments still circling her mind.

She had enjoyed it so much that she returned for a second class, this one on a Thursday morning, and she had not come alone.

'I'm not very creative, you know,' Angelica said as they waited for the class to start. 'I can't draw for shit.' She tapped her pencil on the intimidating blank white expanse of paper in front of her. The surface seemed to be waiting with bated breath for that first permanent mark that would forever taint its crisp, fresh expanse.

Sarah rolled her eyes. 'Does it matter? We're here to enjoy, not judge. Just soak it in, have fun. And anyway, everyone is creative in some way. I don't buy that excuse.'

'Okay, well, prepare yourself for my squiggles. I can't believe I'm doing this on my day off.'

'Shush. You'll love it. And if not – well, we can go for lunch and a wine afterwards and I know you'll love that!' Sarah laughed at Angelica's enthusiastic thumbs-up.

A moment later the teacher, a short, stout woman in her sixties with big purple earrings and an equally purple headscarf, swished with the remnants of a dancer's grace into the room, beaming as though she literally lived for running drawing workshops. The woman pressed 'play' on the battered CD player that sat on the windowsill, and Sarah felt soothed when violins started to play.

Her stillness was broken by a giggling gasp from Angelica.

'You didn't say it was a life drawing class!' Angelica whispered, her grin stretched as wide as her face, her eyes lit up with amusement.

'I didn't know,' Sarah admitted. 'Now, enjoy the session and get drawing that dick,' she said with as straight a face as possible when the man in the centre of the room dropped his robe to the floor and struck his first pose for them.

Angelica had been staring at her drawings for a good few minutes after the class had ended. The music had been switched off and the students were efficiently tidying up after themselves.

Sarah stood behind her friend to take in the drawing. It wasn't amazing but Angelica had captured something, at least, a sense of life and motion.

'Not bad. See, I said you were creative.'

'Yeah, I'm quite impressed with myself, to be honest. Just you wait, I'll have work hanging in the Tate before the year is out.' She laughed, gathering up the pencils she had been using, then putting them back in the large ceramic pot the teacher was taking around the room to collect them in.

'I'll be there at the private viewing with canapés and wine in hand, singing your praises,' Sarah joked, smiling at the teacher. 'Do we keep these drawings?'

'Oh, of course, dear, if you wish to. Feel free to recycle them if you're not desperate to take them home.' She waved a hand towards the large plastic bin that contained some scrunched-up paper balls already. Clearly not everyone had been enamoured by their artwork.

Sarah rolled up her drawings and watched Angelica do the same.

'Lunch and wine, then?' Angelica asked. 'I feel like you kind of promised. Is there anywhere around here?'

'We can walk to Greenwich – it's only down the road,' Sarah answered, thinking of the many pubs that were dotted around Greenwich near the *Cutty Sark*, which overlooked the Thames. She wondered if she should go back to her office to work later, but knew what she and Angelica were like. They'd write off the afternoon in a sea of Sauvignon Blanc.

'Sounds perfect.'

Sarah heard her phone ping from the depths of her handbag and knelt to dig it out.

'You've got to be kidding...' she hissed, still crouched as she read the message.

'What is it?' Angelica asked.

Sarah turned her phone and aimed it up at her friend.

'And out of the woodwork he comes to ruin your day. Just delete it.'

Sarah considered what Angelica said, knowing that the sensible option would be to ignore Mike Turner and get on with her life. After a few seconds, she dropped her phone back into her bag and tried to forget that Mike had asked her to meet up for a drink.

'Yep.' She nodded and stood up, mentally brushing away her feelings for the man. Angelica muttered something about finding a loo, and Sarah found herself alone as she pulled on her leather jacket and swung her bag over her shoulder, ready to leave. She realised she was looking at her bag, as though attempting to see through the fabric to the text message, when someone spoke to her unexpectedly.

'Man trouble, is it?' the voice asked. Sarah's instinct was to tell whoever it was to sod off and mind their own business, but for some reason she didn't. Instead she locked eyes with the woman, who was standing just a metre from her. She had appeared there so suddenly that it was as if she had materialised out of thin air.

The woman was tall and slim, all angles, with piercing green eyes and the shiniest red hair Sarah had ever seen. It draped around one side of her face and fell over her shoulder. She was dressed in black trousers and a silk shirt that matched her eyes almost exactly. While she wasn't exactly dressed for the red carpet, something about the woman made Sarah feel out of place, like a ruddy-cheeked maid who had accidentally found herself in the private quarters of the castle in the presence of a queen she was not supposed to lay eyes on.

'You know, I find that men are very rarely worth it,' the woman continued.

'What? Oh, right. Yes. My ex,' Sarah answered, wondering how the woman had known what she and Angelica had so briefly talked about.

'I take it we don't like him much,' the redhead said. Sarah noticed the use of the word 'we', thinking it rather strange.

'No, not really. I mean, I did, but...' Sarah trailed off, feeling horribly awkward. She couldn't believe the effect this woman was having on her. Sarah couldn't remember the last time she had been near someone with such a dominating character.

'You know, you should come to one of the sessions I run. Female empowerment. No woman should feel less than at the hands of a mere man. Especially a beautiful woman like you.' The woman smiled, her stare slicing through Sarah, who had never really thought of herself as more than fairly pretty. Maybe she could be considered a beauty, Sarah thought. One that Mike did not deserve.

'Saturday mornings, nine sharp. You can register at reception.' The woman gave another tight but exceptional smile. 'I'm Beatrice, by the way. Lovely to meet you, Sarah.' Then she moved past Sarah to leave the classroom and she was gone, the mysterious, magnetic woman who had seemingly owned Sarah for the last few minutes and somehow knew her name. Sarah shook off the daze that had fallen over her, letting out a nervous laugh.

'I just saw the most stunning woman,' Angelica said as she rejoined Sarah.

'That would be Beatrice.'

'Do you know her?'

'Not even vaguely.'

As they left the warehouse Sarah paused to sign up for Beatrice's class, excited by the chance to learn from such an incredible woman – and, in fact, any others that EnchantedWomenLDN threw her way.

The haze of the afternoon's wine still lingering over her in the late evening, Sarah did what she swore to Angelica that she wouldn't do.

She texted Mike back.

Over drinks and fish and chips at the Gypsy Moth in Greenwich, Angelica had preached at length about how Sarah should always go forwards when it came to relationships, not backwards. When a boyfriend didn't work out it was for a reason, one that should be respected. Sarah had nodded along, but she didn't really agree. At least, not entirely. She had kept quiet, though.

Angelica had then brought up Richie, a guy she had been dating but had not yet introduced to Sarah. They had been seeing each other for two months, and it wasn't working out. Angelica was trying to come up with a nice way to break up with him. But Richie was extremely determined. Nothing she had said to him to hint that things weren't working had sunk in, and she was wondering if a blunt approach would be best after all.

'Maybe you should come with me to the empowerment workshop, Ange,' Sarah had suggested. Angelica had vaguely acknowledged the notion before moving the conversation on.

Sarah hadn't told Angelica her own plan. She was going to see Mike and find out what he had to say for himself. Once she knew all the facts, she would be able to decide a logical course of action and perhaps use what she would learn at the empowerment workshop to get rid of him for good. If that was what she decided to do...

She texted him back. He replied straight away.

Friday sounds perfect. Cocktails? Meet me at Sushi Samba at eight?

It was just like Mike to suggest such an expensive and stylish place, but she would happily let him pay as he tried to explain why he had ghosted her. And then she would either take him back or wash her hands of him.

CHAPTER NINE

Daniel Graves felt a tingle under his skin as he and Charlie pulled up outside the house on a quiet suburban road just round the corner from Earl's Court Tube station. The properties were tall, sleek affairs, classic London buildings with columns on either side of their front doors, all painted white and all three storeys high, plus a basement. While a few needed some love and a lick of paint, the one in question was immaculate.

Daniel had always wanted to live in such a property, but when he had arrived in London he had quickly come to understand just how expensive they were, even the ones split into flats. They were out of the question unless he won the lottery.

As they climbed the steps to the dark-blue door, the paint glossy and reflective despite the grey of the cloudy day, Daniel realised that this house was still one unit.

'So she's loaded,' he said as he reached for the doorbell, Charlie standing beside him.

'Rich people have just as many vendettas as poor people,' Charlie answered. They both knew this was true.

They waited for a few seconds, then Daniel rang the doorbell again.

'Hang on a bloody second, I'm coming!' came a flustered voice from inside. After another few seconds, the door opened wide to reveal the owner of the flustered voice. Wearing a blue skirt that flared slightly, a cream wool jumper with rolled-up sleeves, and an apron dotted with small baby-blue blossoms, the flour-covered woman looked like a 1950s housewife. Her cheeks were flushed, her blonde hair pulled away from her face by a soft pink ribbon.

'Can I help you?' she asked with no real sincerity. She looked genuinely irritated. Clearly whatever she was baking was more important than some random at her front door.

'Celia Gallagher?' Daniel asked.

She nodded but quickly corrected him. 'Celia Hartley now, but yes.'

'Is that your maiden name?'

Celia raised her eyebrows at them, silently asking why they were standing on her doorstep enquiring about her name.

'Look, I'm clearly busy,' she said, indicating the flour dusting her clothes. 'Can you get to the point?'

It was Daniel's turn to raise his eyebrows. He turned to look at Charlie, who gave a resigned shrug, indicating that Daniel should be honest with the woman.

'As you wish. We're here with bad news, I'm afraid. We have identified recently discovered remains as those of your ex-husband, and we have strong reason to believe that he was murdered. I'm very sorry to have to break this news to you. Can we come in, ask you some questions?'

The expression on Celia's face changed as Daniel's words sank in. Slowly she stepped back, allowing the detectives to enter the house.

'I'm Detective Inspector Graves and this is my partner, Detective Inspector Palmer.'

'Right. Shit. You'd best follow me. Tea?' Celia asked as she led them past a staircase on their left and closed doors on their right into the kitchen, a bright open space with a partial glass ceiling extended from the main building. Tall windows overlooked the perfectly landscaped garden beyond. The kitchen was a mess, with bowls and spoons everywhere, but nonetheless Daniel was impressed by the house interior. It was beautifully done and had no doubt cost a fortune.

Rich indeed, he thought.

Celia flipped the switch on the chrome kettle and started to tidy up, dropping her apron on the central island and wiping her hands. She retrieved three mugs, even though neither Daniel or Charlie had confirmed that they'd like tea, and plated a selection of cookies from Fortnum & Mason. Daniel heard the rattle of the mugs, an indication of Celia's upset, or perhaps nerves.

'Please, have a seat,' she said. They all sat down at the white wooden dining table, just as the kettle boiled.

'So, Tony is dead. What happened?' she asked, her face wrinkling with what looked like a mixture of discomfort and sadness. It seemed she didn't really want to know. Daniel didn't really want to tell her either – not all the details, anyway. He wanted to gauge her reaction to the conversation as genuinely as possible, so chose his words carefully.

'Anthony's remains were found three days ago. He had been left in Hyde Park, and–'

'Oh God.' Celia's face blanched. She held a hand up to her mouth. After she'd taken a few shallow breaths, she dared to ask them something. 'Was he... the video of that structure, with the body parts...'

Evidently she had seen the news that week. Daniel was sure that almost everyone in London had heard about it. The video the runner had sold to the papers had hit hundreds of thousands of views within an hour of going live. He knew now it was past a few million.

'We're afraid so,' Charlie said. 'We identified him from an old sports injury.'

'Football, yes.' Celia nodded, lifting a finger to one eye to dab away a tear. Despite this, Daniel thought she seemed remarkably calm, not as shaken by the news as he would have expected.

'We looked into Anthony's history and nothing major came up. Except you, that is,' he said, throwing the statement out there with deliberate intent. Celia's eyes narrowed and she suddenly seemed less amiable. She reached for a biscuit and took a bite, standing to make the tea.

'Right,' she said, clearly unamused.

Deliberately, Daniel waited until Celia had made three teas and returned to the table before he carried on, letting her soak in the tense minutes of silence. He didn't want her feeling too comfortable; he found that the truth often came out more easily when the person being questioned was on edge.

'Our records show that you called in a number of domestic incidents over the last three years. The most recent one was reported last July.'

'Yes, our divorce was finalised then.'

Daniel expected more, some comment on the reports at least, but Celia was clearly not in the mood to be forthcoming.

'Right. And these incidents,' Daniel continued. 'You called in quite a few, but no charges were ever pressed. Can you tell us why that is?'

Charlie and Daniel watched Celia Hartley closely as she

took a controlled breath and adjusted her position on her chair, her posture much less relaxed. 'Detective, I can see what you're getting at, so I'll be open. My marriage to Tony was one of heat, of passion and fire. But with that came... rather extreme moments of anger too. Passion runs both ways, of course. Sometimes Tony was physically aggressive. But I must admit, so was I. I reported him out of anger mostly, to annoy him and get under his skin. Like a power play, perhaps. But I was just as responsible, so I never pressed charges. We'd have an explosive fight, then go back to normal. In the end, we divorced because it just wasn't sustainable. We were exhausted. I bear no ill will towards the man. I have no reason to murder him, before you ask. I know you want to.' Celia took another slow breath, then leant forward to sip her tea, eying the detectives over the rim of the cup, as though she too was attempting to gauge their reactions.

Daniel believed the comment about the power plays. Celia Hartley was clearly intelligent, poised and controlled when she wanted to be. She had waited to discern the direction of the conversation, then seized the opportunity to take control of it as soon as she had the chance. Her pre-emptive answer seemed genuine enough, but he thought they should take it with a grain of salt. Had she practised it? Thought over her personal position and narrative? If she had killed her ex-husband, or had anything to do with it, she would have known that the police would pay her a visit at some point. She seemed to be prepared for most eventualities.

'Yes, we were going to ask that,' Charlie said. 'What about your divorce? How amicable was it? Was there a lot of money at stake?'

Celia rolled her eyes at the mention of money. 'Again, I can see where you are going. Not to be crass, Detective Palmer, but

Tony and I both came from money – me more so than him, perhaps, but he was plenty well off. We split things fairly and appropriately. If I'm honest, we had a minor argument about our property in Los Angeles, one we had bought together, but that was it.'

'And why did you argue?' Daniel pressed.

Celia sat still for a moment. Daniel couldn't tell if she was actually thinking or just pretending. She was remarkably difficult to read.

'He wanted to sell it; I wanted to buy it off him. It's a lovely property and I thought I'd like to keep it. What I was willing to pay for his half was not enough for him. I remember him being convinced we would get more for it if we sold it properly rather than me buying him out. That caused a few rows. In the end we did sell it and he was right, we made a fortune on it. But why he was so adamant he wanted the extra money, I'm not sure. Perhaps he needed a quick lump sum; he was rather pushy about it. But I never asked him.'

'Interesting. So you think perhaps he was in trouble? Financially?' Charlie suggested.

'I don't know. Honestly.'

Daniel looked closely at Celia's face for any trace that she was lying, but she seemed genuine. She took another sip of her tea, then reached for a second biscuit, which she nibbled the edge of with no real enthusiasm.

'And can you think of anyone else who may have had something against Tony?'

'I really can't. Even when we were married, Tony could be quite the closed book. He may well have been up to no good, but I know nothing about any such issues.'

Again Daniel thought she was telling the truth. 'Okay, I think that's probably all we need from you for now, Ms Hartley, but please take our cards. If you think of anything at all that could be useful, please do call either of us. We won't take up any more of your time today.'

Daniel gave her a sympathetic smile and both detectives passed over their business cards, which Celia took, running a finger over their edges before placing them on the table. Daniel suspected she would not call, but it was better for her to have the option at least.

'No problem, Detectives. I'm sorry I couldn't be more helpful.'

Celia returned Daniel's smile but hers was thin, with no real warmth in it. She showed Daniel and Charlie to the front door, where they thanked her again, then she was gone, shut away behind the glossy blue barrier.

Out on the street, Daniel waited until they were at Charlie's car before asking for his thoughts.

'She was tough to read,' Charlie answered.

Daniel was glad to hear this.

'I mean, I feel like she was telling the truth, she came off as fairly authentic, but I wouldn't be surprised if she had kept something back from us.'

'I agree. I was hoping for something more helpful from her, especially when she mentioned them arguing. I suppose it's possible she might know more about his death. All that fighting, she could have reached her breaking point. If she was going to kill him, though, I doubt she'd do it herself, and she would do it without the ritualistic theatrics.'

The pair clambered into the car and Charlie started the engine. 'The money issue and the brutal way he was killed, that could be something. Some sort of gang killing, perhaps? If he pissed off the wrong people? The whole ritual angle is weird.'

As they drove away from Celia Hartley's luxury home, Daniel gave that some thought. Even if it was nothing to do with his ex-wife, had Anthony Gallagher had serious money issues?

Did he owe someone a lot of cash? And if that was the motive behind his death, why would his killer go to such lengths to display his remains?

It all seemed possible, but something just wasn't adding up for Daniel.

CHAPTER TEN

Sarah Boyd was sitting in the central café of EnchantedWomenLDN, a cooling latte in hand, when Angelica Okeke came bustling through the big metal doors, smiling as she walked over to greet Sarah, whipping off her black leather jacket with a flourish.

'Sorry I'm late. It's such a pain to get here, I can't believe I agreed to come again.' Her face told Sarah she was half joking. Angelica was a north Londoner at heart and Sarah was the only reason she was ever willing to go south of the river.

Sarah looked at her watch, then back at her friend. 'We have one minute.'

Together they hurried over to the studio, where they were taking a fabric-printing class. Sarah knew about the process already, but despite designing the patterns for her range it had been a long time since she had done the printing herself, and she felt like it would be a nice way to refresh her memory. Angelica was just there for fun, although it quickly became evident that she wasn't enjoying herself.

Throughout the session Angelica barely spoke, occasionally

muttering that she wasn't keen on what she had created or that she just wasn't feeling it. By the time the lesson came to a close, Sarah was irritated. She hadn't forced Angelica to come, and would have been just as happy to have been alone. Angelica had agreed it sounded fun – in fact, had become more sold on the women-focused community centre as a whole. It was time to call her out.

'Okay, Ange, can you stop complaining for a minute and tell me what's the matter?' Sarah asked as she took a few photos of the designs she herself had made, wanting to post them on her social channels later.

Angelica huffed, dropped her own fabric prints on the table and leant back against the counter behind her, fussing at a fern that brushed her shoulder with its leaves.

'Leave the fern alone. What's going on?'

Angelica frowned. Sarah's question had been loud. A couple of the other women tidying their stations were watching them, perhaps hoping for gossip.

'Richie, that's what's up.'

'And we just failed the Bechdel test. Did you finally break up with him, then?' Sarah asked, moving closer to Angelica, lowering her voice.

'Yes, I did. Except he hasn't paid any attention. He hasn't stopped calling or texting, then this morning he came to my bloody flat, started getting arsey at me when I told him to piss off.'

'Sounds a bit weird. I'm sure he's just upset. He'll soon back off.' Sarah wasn't sure what else to say. She had never even met Richie, which was odd now that she thought about it. Usually Angelica was quite open about her dating escapades. Sarah couldn't help wondering what was odd about Richie, other than his apparent neediness, that would have stopped her friend from introducing him to her.

'You don't get it. He was really...'

'What?' Sarah didn't like the look on Angelica's face, and felt concern starting to bubble in her.

'He was aggressive, I suppose. That's the best way to put it.'

'Physically?'

'No – I mean, not to me. He didn't touch me. But he was shouting, he swore at me, and he kicked the door open when I tried to close it on him.'

Sarah suddenly felt sick. 'Ange, fuck, why didn't you tell me? That sounds horrible! No wonder you feel like crap.'

Angelica nodded silently, wiping her eyes gently in a bid to stave off tears. 'Yeah, I didn't expect it, to be honest. He just... he was a bit scary.'

'Of course. God, come here.' Sarah wrapped her arms around Angelica and hugged her hard. 'Want me to kick his ass?' she said over Angelica's shoulder.

'Yeah, maybe. If he decides to come back.'

Sarah pulled herself out of the hug but kept hold of Angelica's shoulders. 'You don't think he will, do you? Do we need to call the police?'

'I don't know. Maybe. Probably not.'

They stood still for a moment, their gazes locked.

Sarah flinched when a woman appeared behind Angelica.

'There is something else you could do,' the woman said. Sarah and Angelica turned to look at her.

The woman was tiny. Sarah thought she looked a bit like Kylie Minogue, if Kylie dyed her hair almost jet black and wore heavy mascara and eyeliner. She wore a black wool jumper with a turtleneck and a dark grey and green striped skirt. The tips of leather boots poked out from under the hem.

'Sorry?' Angelica asked, clearly wondering why this woman had interrupted them. Sarah was confused too, and angry that, whoever this woman was, she thought it was okay to stick her nose into a private conversation, especially a clearly emotional one.

'Other than the police, I mean. If you don't want to go the official route.'

'Who are you?' Sarah asked bluntly, wanting rid of the woman.

'Call me Cally. And I can help you send some negative karma this guy's way,' the woman said to Angelica, as though she was trying to shut Sarah out. 'A little bit of... you know. The craft.'

Sarah caught the twinkle in Cally's eye and felt a shiver travel down her spine. Was the woman mad? Eccentric? Sarah had no problem with other people's beliefs but some random woman chiming in to tell Angelica to tap into what she assumed was witchcraft was just weird.

'The craft?' She smirked. 'Like the schoolgirls in that film? Don't be so ridiculous.' Sarah could hear the venom in her tone but made no real effort to dampen it. 'Can you leave us alone, please? And take your witchcraft crap with you?'

'Sarah!' Angelica snapped, surprising Sarah and making her step backwards. 'Don't be so rude!'

'I... sorry, but... I mean, come on, Ange.' Sarah raised an eyebrow at Angelica, questioning why her friend was even giving Cally the wannabe witch the time of day.

'I'm sorry,' Angelica said to Cally. Sarah felt her cheeks go red as her friend apologised for her, feeling a potent mixture of anger, irritation and shame.

'Oh, don't you worry, my dear. Not everyone is so enlightened about the beliefs of others.'

Sarah felt guilt knife through her. She suddenly felt like a complete bitch for the sharp judgement and narrow-minded outburst she had just displayed. She watched in silence as Cally handed Angelica a business card. Sarah was desperate to say something to her friend, but bit her tongue.

'Call me if you want to try a session,' Cally said, and with that she waltzed out of the classroom, seemingly unfazed by Sarah's scathing dismissal.

Angelica put the card in her jeans pocket. 'Well, that was rude.'

Sarah went to agree before she realised Angelica meant her. 'Yeah. Sorry,' she muttered. 'It's just... she interrupted. And with something so stupid too. I mean, witchcraft? Really?'

Angelica brushed a few dark curls away from her eyes. 'You don't have to believe in what she does, but you didn't need to be so dismissive. Would you have done that if she had mentioned a religion you don't believe in, too?'

Sarah was silent. It was now becoming apparent just how rude she had been to Cally. She had genuinely thought she was more tolerant of others than she had just proved.

'Thought not. Anyway, let's go. I'm tired. I want to go home.' Angelica left the classroom. Sarah was about to follow, when someone else spoke to her.

'She's harmless, you know. I wouldn't worry.'

Sarah turned to face the woman who had spoken. It was Beatrice, who she had met the other day. Sarah had not been to one of Beatrice's Saturday empowerment classes yet, though she intended to. Perhaps she should go to a tolerance class if they ran one, she thought, still feeling the hint of shame on her cheeks.

'I'm not a believer either, but if Cally wants to employ the so-called healing power of herbs and crystals and incantations as a solution to her problems, who are we to judge?' Beatrice gave Sarah a knowing and painfully wise smile and wink before leaving her to it. Sarah felt her cheeks flush again, and was glad to be temporarily alone. She took a few seconds to herself, then followed Angelica out, cross with herself for her behaviour.

CHAPTER ELEVEN

It was early, the air was bitingly cold, and Andy Davis really did not want to take the dog out for his morning walk. Andy had stayed in bed as long as he could, feeling the effects of the wine he'd consumed on his date last night still floating through him. Bosley had other ideas. The black-and-white French bulldog had been huffing and whining outside Andy's bedroom door for almost an hour. He was a living alarm clock, seemingly set to go off before dawn each day.

Bosley really did love his walks. He bounced happily down the steps of the apartment building, restrained by his lead. Andy made him wait at the bottom so he could zip up his hoodie; the wind coming off the river was snapping at him. Bosley threw Andy some impatient side-eye, keen to go and smell trees and cock his leg against things.

Andy lived in one of the fairly new apartment buildings that lined the Thames just past Greenwich, and the usual route he took Bosley followed the water towards the Greenwich Peninsula. On a sunny day it was a popular route, dotted with cyclists, joggers and those out for a casual stroll, but on cold and gloomy early mornings like this one, barely anyone was around.

He'd only seen one woman, bundled in a huge coat, presumably going to start an early shift, and one Lycra-clad man out on a run. He and Bosley had the route to themselves.

Andy could feel the hangover in the back of his throat as he and Bosley headed past the apartments on their right to the narrower path that meandered along by the river. He rubbed sleep out of his eyes, feeling sorry for himself. Why Bosley couldn't sleep in longer, he'd never know.

Andy registered the painted sign for Morden Wharf not too much further ahead. That was where they normally walked to before turning back. At least the walk was half done and he could feed Bosley and be back in bed in less than thirty minutes.

An unused pier jutted out into the Thames, and he let Bosley lead him down it rather than continuing along the normal path. Often he saw people standing at the end of the ugly concrete slab of pier, taking selfies with the river and the O2 Arena in the background, but, just like the rest of the route, no one was around this early.

As they neared the end of the pier, Andy saw something lying on the ground, along with some paint, like graffiti. It was new, whatever it was. People occasionally tagged patches of wall that lined the walk with scrawls of graffiti, but he'd never seen anything on the pier before.

'What's this then, Bos? Shall we go look?'

The dog turned to look at him, his tongue hanging out in what looked like a grin, then trotted on, leading Andy towards the pier's end. At first Andy's bleary eyes couldn't make out what he could see. Rubbing his eyes again, he stepped closer. Bosley also went in for a sniff. At the sight of the severed arm, its hand outstretched, balanced on top of a viscera-covered ribcage, placed in the centre of demonic symbols that had been painted in what looked like – and smelled like – blood, Andy lurched to the railing and vomited into the river.

'Okay, I'm going to ask the obvious question,' DI Charlie Palmer said. 'Where is the rest of the body?'

He and Daniel Graves were standing side by side on the pier in Greenwich, the pleasant, gentle breeze carrying the scent of the Thames making a horrid juxtaposition with the second ritualistic crime scene they had experienced in a week.

The pier was a hive of activity. It had been cordoned off at its entrance and was guarded by an officer doing her best to prevent people from trying to get a closer look. The nature of the pier meant that no one could physically get near the scene, but at the same time it was a very open area, with nothing to hide it from view. Passers-by regularly stopped to gawk and take photos, some of whom could surely zoom in and snag a few good shots. Graves and Palmer knew it wouldn't be long before the gory details were online.

'In the river, maybe?' Daniel suggested, staring down at the pallid arm and ribcage at the centre of the painted symbols. The blood had darkened considerably, soaking into the concrete, but it was still clear enough for them to make out the lines and curves in the iconography on which the body parts had been posed. A variety of football-sized symbols had been painted in a circular layout around one much larger symbol, which looked like a circle with two half-moons on either side of it, each facing outwards. That central circle contained the body parts.

Charlie turned and leant over the railing. 'Yeah, it would be easy to chuck someone in there. The body could go miles downriver before anyone found it – if it was found at all.'

'Are they that strong? The currents?' Daniel asked, glancing out over the water. The thrum of a river boat and the waves that followed it carried over to him. It would be a nice spot, if it wasn't for the pieces of human on the ground.

'Maybe we should monitor any areas where detritus from the river washes up. It would help us to identify the victim if we had more remains. One arm and some ribs is not much to go on.'

A crime scene worker who had introduced himself as Chris had been taking photos of the limb, bones and the markings, and he stood to speak with them again.

'I'd say the arm was severed a day ago, tops. And there's not much blood, so it wasn't cut off here. It's hard to say if the ribs belong to the same person. I would bet against other pieces being dumped in the water, personally. I think these parts were likely chosen and brought here specifically.'

'Thanks, Chris. That actually matches up pretty closely with the remains in Hyde Park. It has to be the same person, right?' Daniel asked, though it was a rhetorical question. Someone was using body parts for devil-summoning sessions or whatever the hell they were doing, and leaving them in specific displays. It wasn't about sacrificing someone there and then, Daniel was fairly sure of that, otherwise there would be bodies left behind, not just small pieces.

'The limb was cut off hastily as well. It's very messy, like the other remains,' Chris added. 'Same MO, I'd say, from a quick look anyway. If we're lucky, we might be able to find a few bone striations and match them to a tool that would link the two directly as well. As you can see, the arm was cut just below the shoulder. Clearly it belongs to a white male in his late twenties, I'd hazard. The arm has pronounced musculature, so a man in good shape, a regular gym-goer or fitness addict. Certainly someone who worked out more than average. I would guess that the ribcage belonged to a man, too, given the size, but I can't be sure. The coroner's office will be able to confirm after an examination.'

Charlie leant in to get a closer look at the arm, which was

pale from blood loss. Daniel resisted a closer look. He could see it all too well from where he stood.

It was the blood-painted symbols beneath the arm and ribs that actually held more intrigue for him. 'This is different to the shape of the effigy left in Hyde Park. Again it has a structural quality but the actual presentation isn't consistent, and it's smaller. But it's clearly ritualistic, designed to mean something. The ribs could be a reference to the wooden effigy that was itself shaped like ribs, perhaps. I'm very curious to find out what the hell it means.'

'A good excuse to get in touch with the hot uni professor,' Charlie said, not attempting to hide his grin.

'I already have, if you must know,' Daniel said casually, not looking directly at Charlie, immediately regretting letting the words slip out.

'What?' his partner exclaimed, jabbing at Daniel's arm. 'Why didn't you tell me? This is very exciting news!'

Chris gave Charlie a look of distaste at his sudden joviality, and moved away to speak to another crime scene investigator.

'Because I didn't want you to react like this,' Daniel hissed. 'Calm down. It's a first date, no point getting too excited. Focus on your own love life,' he said, trying to shut Charlie up. It worked, and he thought he saw a flash of something in Charlie's changing expression, though he couldn't decide what exactly.

'Well, obviously, you know me, a dating machine.' Charlie laughed awkwardly. 'But still, this is great. I'm excited for you.'

Daniel gave him a smile, but he was done with the subject for now. Sure, he thought that Molly Goodings had seemed genuinely interested in him, but who knew how their date would go? If it was a disaster, he didn't want to have built it up too much in advance. The disappointment would only be that much greater.

'Anyway, yes, we should ask Molly about these symbols, see

if they're connected to the first effigy,' Daniel said, shifting his brain back to the matter at hand. 'Chris, do you know if Emi Kobayashi will be here soon?'

Chris turned from his conversation to nod. 'She'll be here in about a half hour, I think,' he said before turning away again.

'Let's chat with her then, see if her team can definitely connect this to the first murder.'

'Do you think it's money-related? Or a woman scorned, perhaps?' Charlie asked. They still hadn't got a clear motive.

'God knows. Let's see if we can find out who that arm belonged to, try to connect the dots.' Daniel looked out over the water again. London was already bustling and the day was brightening a little, the city's residents unaware that the ritual in Hyde Park was evidently just the start and that more victims were no doubt in the killers' sights.

Daniel sat patiently in the newly set-up taskforce room back at the department, waiting for Junior Sergeant Ross Hayes to fill him in. Hayes had found an interesting piece of information on Anthony Gallagher. As was always the case, photographs had been pinned to the wall detailing both crime scenes. Although he was never keen to examine gore up close, Daniel had looked over the images side by side, trying to discern any visual commonalities. The obvious connections were the ritualistic set-ups and the severed limbs, but the actual symbolism was quite different between the two scenes. Daniel had not yet called Molly Goodings about the second case, but he hoped she would be able to identify the symbols at the pier. The concept of chopping someone up was, despite being horrible, easy to grasp at some level, but the weirdly ceremonial elements and possible associations with demons or witchcraft was much harder to get his head around, even with his recent experience of demonology.

'Sorry to keep you, sir,' Ross said as he came into the task force room, laptop in hand and Sergeant Amelia Harding close behind.

'No problem. I hope you have some good stuff for me. Amelia, what are you doing here? I didn't think you were on this case,' Daniel said with genuine surprise. He got on very well with Amelia. He knew she was a hard worker and a valuable asset, but he had not been told she was helping. Daniel liked processes and disliked pissing off his superintendent, who would surely have something to say about sergeants hopping onto cases without permission. There was, after all, a system in place to monitor cases and workloads.

'Did DI Palmer not tell you? He said I could assist on this one. You know me – I love a good murder case,' Amelia answered quickly, sounding awkward. 'He said he thought I'd be useful.' There was a flutter in her voice, subtle but noticeable nonetheless.

Daniel got the impression it was the other way round. He knew how determined Amelia was, and suspected she had asked Charlie if she could join the case. He didn't like being the last to know, but in the end he supposed it didn't matter as long as Hobbs signed off on it. They now had two victims. Presuming that both murders had been committed by the same person, they could well be dealing with a serial killer. If they didn't find who was responsible soon, then he expected another body to turn up. Then the case would explode even more than it already had, and he'd get Amelia as a resource anyway. He knew that the evening news would feature the Greenwich murder scene. Twitter had been flooded with blurry pictures and poorly shot videos from phones as soon as the police had turned up at the pier, and a few breaking news tweets had gone viral not long after. Violence in the capital was prime content, and comments on the tweets already mentioned gang warfare and terrorism to full-on conspiracies trying to explain the murders.

'Okay, as long as DI Palmer said it was okay, you know I don't mind having the extra brainpower. Ross, do you want to go through everything?'

Ross had sat down and opened his laptop. He angled the screen towards Daniel while Amelia hovered behind them, looking over their shoulders.

'Sure. I looked into everything I could about him, but what has stood out most so far is his finances. It didn't take long to find something a bit unusual.' Ross opened up a chart that showed the victim's bank account, his incomings and outgoings. 'If you look here, Mr Gallagher had a large amount of money come in six months ago, then just two days later a huge chunk of it went out again. Then a few weeks later, he wired more money to the same account. He had a separate account that he seemed to almost exclusively use for storing lump sums, moving them back and forth. Kind of like he would hide money in the second account, then transfer it to his first account before paying it out. Overall he sent more than a million pounds.'

'Palmer and I spoke to Gallagher's ex-wife this morning. She said that they sold a shared property last year, so that would likely be the large amount coming in. The timeline fits. Who did he send the money to?' Daniel asked.

Ross went to answer but Amelia cut him off.

'That's the weird thing. You'd think he'd buy something expensive like a new house or flashy car, but the money went to a private account based out of the country. We couldn't get any other info on who owned the account or what it was set up for.'

Ross nodded. He also frowned at Amelia, then his eyes widened when he realised Daniel had spotted his frown.

'Er yes, like Amelia said, that much money going to

something so private seems a bit odd,' Ross said. 'But that's not all we found out.'

'That's right,' Amelia chimed in again, although Ross's mouth was still open to speak. 'It seems our victim might have been involved with some shady people, according to some of his neighbours – possibly people he owed money to.'

Although Amelia was highly animated, Daniel saw that Ross seemed rather downtrodden. Amelia was stealing the junior sergeant's thunder, and the poor guy was not happy about it.

'Good work, both. Really helpful, thank you,' Daniel said, ensuring that he made eye contact with Ross. He wasn't about to shame Amelia publicly for overshadowing her junior, who had clearly done most of the research, but he wanted Ross to see his appreciation. Ross clearly read his intent and gave him a pleased smile in return, looking more cheerful.

'Do we know who the second victim is?' Amelia asked, clearly keen to get ahead.

'Not yet. Hopefully the coroner's office can give me a name soon. You guys can actually help out on that. Ross, how about you stay on victim one and dig a bit more? I'd like to know more about these so-called shady people he had associations with. Speak further with his neighbours, friends and such. Maybe we can find a motive, identify some suspects. Amelia, we know that victim number two was a white male likely in his late twenties who worked out a lot – weightlifting, bodybuilding, something similar. Why don't you tackle that? Check in with missing persons to see if you can find anyone who fits that description?'

Both nodded, and Ross closed the laptop and got up.

'Amelia, can I have a quick word?' Daniel asked.

She smiled and waited until Ross had left the room, pulling the door shut behind him.

'What's up, Graves?' she said jovially, immediately more friendly and less formal now it was just them.

'You want to progress, right? In your career?' Daniel asked, keeping his tone calm, knowing he was about to pull the rug out from under her feet.

'Of course – always!' she answered keenly, her eyes lighting up.

'Good to know. But here's the thing. Please don't take offence, but... you need to practise letting others have their moment. Don't take credit or talk over them, okay? In people management and leadership, it's important to know when to allow others to shine, and when to step back, offer up space and simply listen. It'll help you to learn that skill now rather than later. Good leadership is vital if you want to move further up. I've been there myself, wanting to show up, to really prove myself, and stepped on toes in the process. It didn't go well for me but maybe you can learn from my mistakes.'

Amelia's smile vanished and all of a sudden she looked embarrassed, like a schoolgirl brought before the head teacher for swearing in class. 'Oh God, I'm sorry. I wasn't trying to – I mean, I just got caught up in it and... shit.' Her whole body deflated.

'Amelia, you know I like you, that I value you as a friend and colleague, and that I'm impressed by your tenacity and work ethic. But I'm also your senior and I know that someone with determination like yours can occasionally step on others' toes. I want everyone to contribute and work together, not jostle for credit. Okay?'

Amelia offered a weak smile and shook herself, clearly trying to regain her composure. 'Yes, all good. I understand. Sorry again.' Her words came out in a babble, and Daniel couldn't help feeling bad. He'd been in her position before, being told off by a senior colleague. It felt horrible.

'Great, that's all I wanted to say. But maybe say sorry to Junior Sergeant Hayes.'

Amelia nodded and left the room, her head hanging lower than when she had entered. Daniel turned back to the photos on the wall and took his phone out of his pocket.

'Hi, Molly? It's Graves. Daniel,' he said when Molly Goodings answered. He was trying to strike a tone somewhere between professional detective and friendly. He had no idea if he had nailed it or not.

'Hello, Daniel. You're not calling to cancel tomorrow, are you?' Molly asked.

'Oh no, of course not.'

'Good,' she said simply. One word, but it was enough to send a tingle of electricity through Daniel. He realised he was grinning, despite the photos of body parts in front of him.

'No, this is a professional call, I'm afraid. We have another crime scene. Another ritual of some sort. Could I send you some images to look over? See if you can tell me anything about them?'

'Of course,' she answered. 'I have some time this evening. That'll give us something fun to talk about over drinks as well, huh?'

'You know we need to keep all murder talk private, right? I'd be sacked if I was overheard chatting about a case in the pub.'

'I won't tell if you won't.' She laughed.

Again Daniel's body tingled in anticipation of their date.

CHAPTER TWELVE

I t was almost seven in the evening when, while he was considering packing it in for the day and going for a workout to de-stress, Charlie got a call from Kelly Malone. He didn't get a chance to say more than hello before she launched into a rant.

'A second ritual death, and I found out on bloody Twitter? Jennifer Khan, my delightful colleague, just tagged me in a snide tweet asking why I'm not covering the case, even though she knows full well why not. It's fucking mortifying, Charlie! I really need this work punishment period to be over. It's really getting to me.'

His gym bag slung over his shoulder, Charlie looked around the office to make sure Daniel wasn't around. 'I know, it's shit, but we've already talked about this. Your track record has made you very hard to trust. What do you want me to do about it?'

'Well, you could start by telling the smug young man sitting at your reception to let me up and see you.'

The wind was knocked out of Charlie as effectively as if she had punched him in the stomach, and he felt himself panicking. 'Excuse me? Are you actually downstairs?'

'Yes!' Kelly snapped. 'I want to talk to the superintendent

and see if I can work something out with him, but this jobsworth won't let me in.'

'Of course he won't let you in, Kel, are you kidding?' Even as Charlie ran for the lifts he could hear Kelly arguing with the poor guy manning reception, who was getting it in the neck for just doing his job.

'Just wait there, okay? I'm coming down.'

The lift doors pinged open and Charlie hopped in, stabbing the ground floor button so hard that he hurt his finger and hissed in irritation.

As the lift hummed down, Charlie started to question everything. What was wrong with Kelly? Did she want to get him fired? Was she worth it? Their hidden relationship, that she was constantly threatening to make public? Kelly was beautiful, intelligent, driven, and he loved her for all of that, but she had so many issues. It was stressing him out that no one knew about them, especially Daniel. And he had already got in trouble at work before for letting slip case details to her. That was on his record. He had thought that would have been enough to stop her relentless ambition.

And yet here she was, going rogue again, ignoring the impact she could have on his career. What would his colleagues think of him, still dating the woman who caused chaos everywhere she went because of her ruthless journalistic pursuit of stories and success? Was she really just a liability? The notion that she could ruin him seemed all too real. Was the fact that he loved her enough of a reason to keep things going when she posed such a threat to his livelihood?

His heart was pounding as the lift doors opened on the ground floor and he made his way down the corridor to reception. He could hear Kelly before he could see her. She was still bickering with the receptionist.

'See?' she exclaimed as he rounded the corner and passed

through the security barriers to where she waited. 'DI Charlie Palmer, down here because of me.'

Her hair was in a ponytail and she wore a leather jacket over a blouse, skinny jeans and heels. She would have looked stunning if it hadn't been for the anger on her face, making her distinctly less attractive.

'Hey, Kel,' Charlie said, casting a quick, apologetic smile towards the receptionist, David, who didn't look willing to accept it.

'Just because DI Palmer knows you, Miss Malone, does not mean I can let you through. I've already told you that's not how it works. We have very strict security measures. Especially with journalists. Especially with you, for that matter.'

David glared at Kelly as he made the cutting remark, and Charlie moved quickly to step in between them. Kelly looked like she was about to hit something. Or someone. He blocked her view of David.

'Calm down, okay? He's doing his job. Let's go outside.'

Kelly huffed, but seemed willing to comply, and Charlie gave a quick sigh of relief. Together they headed out of the entrance and off to the side of the main doors.

'What are you doing? Do you want me to lose my job?' Charlie hissed.

'Come off it, Charlie–' Kelly started.

'No! You need to listen to me. You cannot just turn up here and start kicking off. I've already got in trouble because of you. Twice, in fact.'

'I apologised about that.'

'Yeah, you did, and I appreciate that, plus I know full well that I was to blame too, but it hasn't stopped you doing this, has it? You promised me you were a changed woman. How do you think it would look to my superiors if they saw you causing trouble here, distracting me from my case in the process? The same person who almost got herself killed by a serial killer because she doesn't know when to quit?'

Kelly's anger dropped off her face and was replaced by embarrassment and guilt. All the fury that had animated her minutes before seemed to blow away and she shrank into herself. 'Oh shit. Shit! You're right. I'm so sorry, babe. I'm doing it again, aren't I? God, I... I don't think I really realised until right now just how much everything has been affecting me. I didn't mean to cause you trouble; I didn't think. I'm just...'

'Frustrated?'

Kelly nodded. 'Understatement.'

'Look, I know not covering this case is getting to you, especially because of what Jennifer's like. But you royally fucked up when you tricked the officer at the hospital to get access to a key witness, and then broke into the building in Lewisham to try and keep your serial killer story going. It didn't reflect well on me, but more importantly, you could have been killed. Is it all worth it?'

'I know, I know. When you put it like that, it makes me sound batshit crazy. But honestly, sometimes I think that it *is* worth it. I'm not sure what else I have, Charlie, if I'm honest. I've got fuck-all friends, my mum lives in Chicago so I never see her... this job, it's so important to me. And I'm good at it, I'm really bloody good at it. I can't... I'm scared to lose it. If I do, then what will I have left?'

'You have me, you know,' Charlie said, insulted.

She caught his frown and called him out. 'Come off it. I don't have you until we're officially together and people apart from us know, so that's not fair. When you commit to us, then that argument will hold weight but right now, you could disappear like everything else.' She hitched her handbag onto her shoulder and put her hands on her hips, trying to be defiant but looking more miserable and worn down than anything else.

Charlie didn't know a huge amount about her upbringing, but he knew it hadn't been easy, knew she had created this harsh external barrier for a reason, more often than not to keep people away and allow her to ignore her feelings and focus on other things, namely her work. He felt her misery.

'You do. And I'll tell the guys, I'll tell Daniel. I love you, I'm not going anywhere. But this? It needs to stop. You have to be patient about the work stuff, okay? Enough of the ruthless, manipulative behaviour. Rebuild some of the bridges you burned – and you can't do that by shouting at our receptionist.'

Kelly huffed but gave him a weak smile of defeat. Defiant she might be, but he also knew she was pretty self-aware. She was a smart woman. It was one of the reasons he'd fallen for her.

'Come here,' he said, pulling her close to him. Her eyes shone with tears that she fought back. Charlie welcomed her warmth against him and they kissed, slowly, enjoying the moment. Then the doors next to them swung open, and instinctively they broke apart. Charlie's stomach sank when he saw who was standing just metres from him and Kelly.

'Oh. Hi, Daniel,' Kelly said awkwardly, wiping her eyes.

'Daniel! I... er... I thought you'd left already,' Charlie muttered, not sure what to say. He registered disappointment in his friend's eyes.

'Oh, Charlie,' Daniel responded, ignoring Kelly. He sighed, then started towards his car.

'Dan, come on,' Charlie said after him, fumbling for words.

'I don't have time for this, not now,' Daniel said over his shoulder without stopping. Moments later, he had disappeared into the night.

Charlie turned back to Kelly. 'Fuck.' He crossed his arms, feeling sick. It was the worst way for Daniel to have found out.

'Well, at least now he knows,' Kelly said. 'Come on, let's go for a drink. You look like you need one.'

'I was going to go to the gym,' he said weakly.

'You're buff enough, babe. One night off won't kill you. Come on.' She held out a hand and he took it, then walked with her across the car park to the gates, hoping that he'd soon start to feel some sort of relief that his secret was now out there.

Daniel felt bad for ignoring Charlie after the night before, but he just wasn't in the right frame of mind to deal with his partner. He was still surprised by his reaction to seeing Charlie and Kelly together. Daniel knew she had sunk her claws deep into his partner from the get-go, even before the night in Lewisham last year when Charlie had saved her life.

But Kelly was trouble, pure and simple. She would do anything to get what she wanted, no matter who she took down in the process, and she had already hurt Charlie twice. Even put his career at risk. Who was to say she wouldn't do it again if the opportunity arose? He was furious at her for using his friend and didn't see how that would change any time soon, even if she really did have feelings for him.

He was also pissed off at Charlie. How could he be stupid enough to go back to her?

After catching them kissing, Daniel had driven home and immediately phoned Rachel, his best friend from up north and his go-to person when he needed a rant. She'd helped him see things from Charlie's point of view, which was annoying, but fairly effective at defusing his irritation. Rachel had admitted that Kelly seemed toxic, though. She hadn't met Kelly Malone, but this wasn't the first time that Daniel had ranted about her.

Now, back at work the next day, Daniel wasn't sure how to

act. He'd said a brief hello to Charlie earlier in the day and had sensed that Charlie wanted to talk to him, but he had made an excuse and avoided him. He did need to focus on their case, not let their private lives get in the way.

He felt like a hypocrite when just before lunch Molly called. His mind went into overdrive in anticipation of their date.

'Hey, Daniel, how's it going? Thought I'd call you to save us chatting too much about body parts over drinks. Are you free to talk?' Molly began.

Daniel was relieved that she hadn't been calling to cancel. 'Hi, Molly – yeah, I'm good. And that makes sense. About the body parts talk, I mean. Do you have something then?'

As Molly began to speak about the effigies found at the crime scenes, Daniel's hopes began to rise. He believed the symbolism behind both scenes to be the key that would help him unlock the puzzle of who was doing these killings, and why.

'Kind of. It's a mixed bag. First thing is the ribcage motif, which I think we can agree is there at both scenes, even if one is an actual ribcage.'

'Yeah, I'd say that connection is deliberate.'

'The symbolism behind ribs can vary, but there are a few key meanings. In the Christian religion there's the obvious connection to Adam and Eve – God removed one of Adam's ribs to create Eve, therefore women in general. Both victims are men, so that could be relevant.'

'Especially as we have some evidence to suggest our killer could be a woman.'

'Exactly. And, assuming it's a woman for a second, she is clearly severely pissed off. Nothing like a woman scorned, huh?' Molly said with a laugh.

'Is that a warning?' Daniel joked back. Molly laughed again.

He smiled at how easy it was to talk to her. It gave him high hopes for their drinks after work.

'Nah, I'm not too fierce, don't worry.'

'Good to know.'

'Anyway, the ribcage is also associated with the protection of emotions – literally protecting the heart.'

Daniel thought about that for a moment. If they were dealing with a woman who was revenge killing, was she taking out men who had wronged her? It was quite the move. But surely it wasn't as simple as that, and that didn't explain the ritual angle. You could kill someone to try to right a wrong without displaying their corpse for all to see.

'Okay, that could make some sort of sense. It's very extreme and oddly public, but if we're dealing with a female killer and her malicious intent is specifically aimed at men, that's a narrative that fits. What about the other symbols? The ones in blood at the second crime scene?' Daniel asked, feeling like they were getting somewhere.

He heard Molly utter a sigh of what sounded like frustration.

'Not got anywhere with those, then?'

'Well, that's why I said this was a mixed bag. The thing is, only one of the symbols, the one in the centre, is easily identifiable. It's the symbol for goddesses – different ones depending on the culture, but effectively representing the divine feminine, intended to invoke the blessings of goddess energy. It points us towards a female killer again, don't you think? None of the smaller symbols are as easy to define, and certainly none relate to religion in a way that's easy to clarify. Are you in front of your computer?'

Daniel cleared the screensaver on his monitor and opened up the photos taken at the crime scene on the pier, as Molly instructed.

'Do you see the symbol that looks a bit like antlers? Left of the hand?'

Daniel scanned the image, looking at the symbols, which were drawn in a rough circle around the severed arm and ribcage. He spotted the antlers. 'Yep, got them. Weird that they have lines over them.'

'Exactly. Antlers tend to represent masculinity, and are often seen in records to do with male witchcraft. That doesn't fit with this being a female killer. But then there are those lines, which almost make it look like it has been crossed out. It could be a reference to killing a man, erasing masculinity, maybe, but I can't say for certain.'

'Fits, though,' Daniel said.

'Then there are some symbols that look like they originate in alchemical practices, but again none of them are clear. If I had to guess, I'd say our killer is kind of doing a symbol pick and mix.'

'Is that normal?'

'Not really, no. Normally practices would be fairly specific to one faith or area of focus. All of this added together speaks of witchcraft, but the strange mixing of elements is something I've not come across in my research.'

'Okay, that's weird. Thanks, Molly. This is still really helpful, even just as a theory. Let's end the creepy talk of witches and body parts for now, but let me know if you find out anything else, okay? Otherwise I'll see you this evening.'

'Wouldn't miss it. See you later!'

Molly hung up and Daniel sat back in his chair, basking in the glow that washed over him. Even without knowing all the details of what the ritualistic symbols meant, what Molly had found out so far seemed to back up his and Charlie's theory that they were dealing with a woman out for revenge.

And then there was Molly herself. Even given what they had been talking about, he felt certain that there was something between them. He enjoyed talking to her, felt they sparked off each other. His chest hummed with excitement for the day to end and his evening with her to begin.

CHAPTER THIRTEEN

She'd only been waiting fifteen or so minutes, but Sarah Boyd was starting to wonder if Mike had stood her up. She was waiting outside the entrance to Sushi Samba, as agreed, feeling awkward every time someone walked past and looked at her as if they knew her date wasn't coming. Although she wanted to be wrong, it certainly fit with Mike's patterns. He had done it to her twice before when they had been dating.

She was a jumble of emotions. She felt sexy, having made a huge effort to impress Mike, even though she knew she didn't need to. She just wanted to make sure he knew what he had been missing out on. Her silver shimmery top, black leather skirt and patent black Louboutin's, combined with the best make-up she felt she had done in years, made her feel shit-hot, even with her jacket hiding the full effect. And she felt excited about seeing Mike, knowing how much she fancied him, how much she liked him. She also felt stupid that she was setting herself up for yet more disappointment, and there were hints of embarrassment swimming around the edges too. Was she just being totally gullible?

She still hadn't told Angelica that she was meeting Mike.

That said it all, really. She knew her friend would be pissed off at her and for her – whereas if Mike was a decent guy and Sarah had faith in him, wouldn't she have chatted about it with her best friend?

'You look fucking gorgeous,' Mike said, suddenly right in front of her. She smiled widely, took him in. Six foot, a toned body shown off nicely by his tailored white shirt and chinos, a navy trench coat protecting him from the chill of the night. He ran a hand through his wavy blond hair and grinned at her. In an instant she felt like putty in his hands, although she could still hear a little voice in the back of her mind telling her to be cautious.

'Thanks, you look great too.'

'You haven't been waiting long, have you?' he asked and she shook her head.

'Shall we, then?' Mike put an arm around her shoulders, a move that made her feel at home, and they took the lift up to the restaurant. Sarah couldn't help feeling that things were going to go well.

Despite his best efforts, Daniel had lost the argument over whose round it was, and Molly had gone to the bar. He sat watching her, smiling unabashedly as she ordered their drinks. The date was going well – better than he'd dared to hope.

He thought he'd fluffed it when they went to Aqua in the Shard first, for cocktails. It was a nice bar and the drinks were great, but it was very busy and Molly had politely informed him that she was more of a pub woman. He'd felt stupid for not having checked first, until he realised that she wasn't complaining, simply telling him her preference. They finished their drinks, took in the city skyline for another few minutes, then left, finding a pub around the corner on ground level instead.

'Now this is more me.' Molly had grinned as they entered and were surrounded by wooden furniture and pictures of London past. It was wildly different to the sleek glass of the Shard, but just as busy.

'I love a classic pub – you can't beat them.'

They'd found a table as a group of London Bridge office workers had left. Two more pints later, the date was still going strong.

Molly presented Daniel with a Peroni and sat down. Pulling a face she stood again, moved her stool closer to him and sat again, their legs touching. 'That's better.'

Before Daniel could take a sip, Molly leant in and kissed him, a long, lingering kiss exploding with sparks. Then she pulled back, flashed him a smile and took a swig of her beer. Daniel didn't know what to say, and she laughed at him.

'That good, huh?'

'Er, yeah. That good.' He smiled, took a breath and let himself calm down. 'Cheers.'

They clinked glasses.

Standing in the hallway, with her front door just a metre away, Angelica Okeke debated the pros and cons of opening it. Part of her wanted to ignore the incessant knocking and pretend that she wasn't home. The other part of her was well aware that Richie knew she was in. Maybe if she opened the door and was firm with him, he would give up and leave. He had last time, after all.

There was more banging on the door. Angelica took a slow breath, trying to stay calm and collected.

'Come on, Angie! This is crazy! Just let me in so we can talk.'

Taking a step closer to the door, her hand outstretched, Angelica assessed the situation one more time. She had her phone in her other hand, ready to call the police at the first sign of real trouble. Surely that was security enough. Her fingers trembled as she twisted the bolt to unlock it. After another calming breath, she opened the door.

'Richie, please. Just go, will you? There's nothing to talk about,' she said quickly, the door open just wide enough that she and Richie could see each other, but not too wide that she couldn't slam it shut.

'I knew you were in. Come on, Ange, are we really doing this?'

Angelica saw the flowers in Richie's hand, and almost laughed at his assumption that something so basic would work.

'You need to leave. My neighbours will complain,' Angelica said firmly.

If you looked at Richie, you'd never guess that he could be aggressive or threatening. A well-dressed, handsome Chinese guy who had an athletic, but not imposing, build, was well spoken and was always smiling did not scream danger. On the surface, he was exactly the type of guy her mother would like her to be with. She couldn't forget the way he had made her feel when he had last turned up on her doorstep, though. There had been something underneath his charming facade that she had been concerned by, and she didn't want to find out how false his facade might really be.

She realised he had taken a step closer to her, thought she could smell alcohol on his breath.

'Just let me in, Ange. You opened the door – you must have wanted to see me.'

'I opened the door to tell you this needs to stop, and I want you to leave me alone. That's it. We're over. Move on. Goodbye, Richie.'

For a moment there was a stand-off as they locked eyes. It took mere seconds, however, for Angelica to sense that her words weren't going to be enough when she saw the upset expression on Richie's face change to anger. His lips curled, making her skin crawl. She went to shut the door.

'Don't you fucking dare!' Richie snapped, thrusting a foot out to stop the front door from closing. It bounced back and almost hit Angelica. She staggered in surprise and before she knew what was happening he had pushed his way into the house. The click of the door closing behind him made her heart stop.

Sipping her gin and elderflower cocktail, Sarah listened to Mike chat about his job, about his friend Dave, who had just bought a boat, about how his dad was off to the Riviera again, and she tried to get a handle on how she was feeling. Since they had arrived, the date had gone smoothly and she was genuinely enjoying herself. Still, her brain kept telling her she had a few facts to face. She waited for a pause in Mike's chatter to make her move.

'So, are you having a good time tonight?' Sarah asked, deliberately looking Mike in the eyes.

He smiled back and nodded. 'Yeah, of course. I'm glad we arranged it. I missed you.'

'So why did you ghost me? I thought we were together and you... well, you clearly didn't. So I'm wondering why we're out now, having drinks?'

Mike took a sip of his whisky but kept quiet. Perhaps he hadn't expected her to put him on the spot.

'Let's cut the crap,' she said, surprised at how blunt she was being. Perhaps it was the gin spurring her on. 'Are you actually interested in me? In going out with me? Or are you just after a fuck?'

Mike's eyes widened as she swore, and he put his drink down, leant forward and put a hand on hers. 'Look, Sarah, I'm sorry. I really am. I've been thinking about you constantly and... I don't know why I stopped messaging you back, stopped calling. I think maybe I got scared.'

Now it was Sarah's turn to be surprised. 'What on earth could scare someone like you?'

'Truthfully? I know what people think of me – that I'm some rich dude that throws cash at what he wants and that I'm shallow, only after fun and a life of excess. I caught myself acting that way with you, maybe to impress you, and I think it got me doubting myself, you know? But that's not me. And I know you know that too. I guess I got scared that the real me wouldn't be what you want – not good enough or something.'

He took his hand off hers and slumped back in his seat, looking downcast, vulnerable even, something Sarah had never expected.

'Is that true? Genuinely? You know I liked the man I saw behind the wallet, not the wallet itself. The funny, caring, sometimes geeky guy. Before the ghosting, obviously.' She felt as if she was seeing a new person in front of her, a new man that she could actually be with, and one to whom she was even more attracted.

Mike looked up at her, nodded, bit his lip as though fighting to hold back tears.

She leant forward to take his hand and they kissed over the table. Mike smiled, wiping a finger under one eye. He seemed embarrassed, but to Sarah he seemed more genuine than she had ever known him to be.

'Well, now I feel like a total twat.' He laughed awkwardly. 'Messing you about all this time when I could have just been honest and...'

'Come on, let's get out of here. I think I've had enough fancy cocktails, and I reckon my bed is calling,' Sarah said, catching Mike's eye with a wink.

'Really?'

'Yep, really.'

They stood and, hand in hand, left the bar. Sarah felt her heart soaring; she was happier than she had felt in weeks.

'Oh my God, I can't tell you how much I needed these.' Molly grinned as she stuffed chips into her mouth. Daniel took a handful and did the same. After so many pints, the stodgy chips and cheese tasted amazing.

'Me too. Although we must look like drunken messes, with our faces full of food.'

Molly shrugged and pulled Daniel close to her, kissing him quickly before popping a few more chips in her mouth. The man behind the counter in the kebab shop laughed.

'See? He gets it,' Molly said, laughing herself.

They headed out, the cool night breeze refreshing on Daniel's face, and together they finished off the chips sitting on a bench by a bus stop.

'Is this where we part ways?' Molly asked.

'I guess so, for now.' Daniel had wanted to ask her back to his place, but each time he had prepared himself his internal dialogue made him back down, saying it was too soon, that a clumsy, drunken one-night stand after their first date might ruin things.

'Well, I had a lovely time, thank you. But I'm not getting the bus!' Molly pulled her phone out and booked an Uber. Daniel did the same, not fancying the thought of the night bus either.

They waited in silence for a minute or two before Daniel took Molly's hand and turned sideways to look at her. 'Tonight was amazing. I'm so glad you agreed to go out with me. I don't do this often, what with work being crazy all the time and... and yeah. Then you came along and blew me away. You're gorgeous, confident. But if I'm honest – and I probably shouldn't say this – I expected you to notice Charlie, not me.'

'Why would I have only looked at Charlie?' Molly asked, one eyebrow raised.

'Because he's stupidly good-looking, charming, the whole lot. He walks into a room and everyone looks at him.'

'And you're not?' she asked.

Daniel didn't answer, just pulled a face.

'Then you clearly don't see what I see, cos I think you're extremely handsome, Detective Inspector Graves. In fact, I think you're so handsome, maybe you should cancel your Uber.' She grinned and the glint in her eyes was unmistakable.

'Are you sure?' Daniel asked, surprised at how the evening had gone: it had been too perfect for words.

'You bet your sexy drunk ass I am! Come on, get your phone out and cancel that car.'

Daniel did as he was told and then they were kissing passionately, still on the bench, hands in each other's hair, wanting to explore further already.

'Hey, are you Molly?' a man called from a car that had pulled up right next to them.

'Shit, I forgot about him!' Molly laughed and they fell into the back of the taxi, all over each other like teenagers.

'This is not okay, Richie. You need to leave. Now!' Angelica yelled as she backed into her kitchen.

Richie filled the doorway, trapping her. 'I told you I just wanted to talk. See if we can work things out. I love you, Ange!'

'Are you fucking kidding? Do you scare the shit out of everyone you love?' she spat, edging back to the counter, aware that the knife drawer was behind her.

'What?' Richie said, suddenly deflated. 'You're... scared of me?' he mumbled, apparently shocked.

'Of course I am! The way you banged on the door, then charged in here... Please, Richie, this is over. You know it is. Just leave, okay? I don't love you. That's why I ended things.'

Richie looked like he had just seen someone shoot a kitten. Tears welled in his eyes as he dropped to the floor, sobbing.

Angelica couldn't help feeling bad, but she was still scared. She didn't know what to do. Her mobile phone still in her hand, she considered dialling the police. Even with the situation defused, she wanted her ex gone, and she wasn't sure he would go easily. Tentatively she tapped the phone screen. She was about to press 'dial' when Richie spoke again.

'What are you doing?' he asked, looking up at her.

'You need help, Richie. I'm just calling someone to come and help you, okay?'

'You'd better not have called the police, Ange,' he said. The hurt in his voice was gone and anger was back in a flash, so quickly Angelica couldn't believe it.

'You need help – it's the only way.'

'Don't you dare,' he warned again.

Feeling shaky, fear flooding back through her veins, she pressed the button to connect the call. She had no time to raise the phone to her ear before Richie charged at her. Within seconds he had a hand round her throat. Angelica felt the phone drop to the floor, heard a crack, then she began to choke, struggling against Richie's weight as he pinned her to the counter. His breath was hot in her face and he was seething, his eyes crazed. The smell of stale alcohol wafted over her.

'You stupid bitch!' he snapped, spittle spraying across her cheeks and lips. She balled a fist and hit him as hard as she could in the ribs. He let go of her throat and she shoved him back.

'Get away from me!' she screamed.

As Richie paused, his face full of fury, Angelica yanked open the drawer next to her and pulled out a kitchen knife. 'Get the fuck out of my house!' She waved the knife in front of her.

'Fuck you,' Richie muttered before turning and stalking out of the kitchen. The front door slammed behind him. Angelica dropped to the floor, letting the tears come hard and fast until she felt drained. She was barely able to believe that she was safe again. Even with the sudden quiet in her house, she didn't feel safe – not really.

CHAPTER FOURTEEN

Checking for the third time that she had the correct address, Angelica Okeke knocked on the dark-brown front door, staring at the silver metal numbers fixed to it. Sixty-six. She wouldn't have been surprised if there had been a third number six. She shivered at the thought, wondering what on earth she was doing. But deep down, she knew why she was there.

The police had been kind and understanding when she had called the night before, and an officer had come to her house to check out the situation. As it turned out, though, they were powerless, at least for the time being. There was no evidence that Richie had done anything, that he had threatened her, other than her word and slight bruising to the left side of her neck, which was helpful but not enough by itself. There were no witnesses, no neighbours to back up her claims. The officer had taken down a full report, photographed the bruise, promised he would take any further information very seriously and would send someone to visit Richie and have a word with him, but there was nothing else he could do unless things escalated. He had tried to assure her that, after a caution,

Richie would back off, that men like him normally did. She had smiled and nodded and tried to convince herself that she felt better. She didn't, though. She felt horribly vulnerable and in need of another option – one that didn't rely on Richie coming back again, and perhaps acting more violently than he had before.

That was why she was standing in front of the small unassuming house in Clapham Old Town first thing on a Saturday morning, ready to see a self-professed witch and reclaim some semblance of control.

Although nothing about the house screamed 'weird' or 'supernatural', as the front door opened it creaked like something out of a cheesy horror movie. Angelica jumped. She couldn't believe how on edge she felt.

The appearance of Cally Buchanan's smiling face was a relief, defusing some of the tension that rippled under Angelica's skin.

'Hello, my love. Nice to see you again. Please come in,' Cally said warmly, gesturing for Angelica to follow her. The house was dark but smelled nice, of incense of some sort, and Angelica moved down the small hall to a sitting room at the rear of the property.

'Oh my...' she muttered, not able to stop the words as she stepped into the room after Cally.

The sitting room was swamped in flickering shadows, with the curtains pulled tightly shut. They seemed to be fitted to block all light from coming in, for not a wisp of daylight broke through. Candles were everywhere, with waxes of differing shades, their flames dancing. Numerous incense sticks burned, giving the air a smoky, cloying feel. On the floor in the centre of the room was a velvet throw on which sat two large cushions and, right in the middle, surrounded by crystals, what looked like the skull of a sheep or a goat. It was exactly what Angelica had feared when she had first considered resorting to the 'craft', and now she wasn't sure what to make of it all.

'This… this all looks…' she started, flinching when Cally took her hand and led her to the cushions.

'Please, sit, and we'll talk over everything. It's not as scary as it all looks. The scents in the air will calm you in no time. And do ignore Edgar here – he just works so nicely for visual representation, I feel,' Cally said with a gesture at the skull. 'I'll get some chamomile tea – back in a moment.' The dainty woman strode out of the dark room, leaving Angelica alone with her thoughts, which were spinning.

Reluctantly, Angelica took a seat on one of the cushions. She had always had some faith in things outside what she supposed would be classed as normal scientific and quantifiable reality, some belief that there was a higher power of some kind, even though she had never decided what it might be. She was certainly not religious. She wanted to feel like she had some control over her life again. If sitting and chanting over some crystals and an old animal skull gave her something even remotely approaching calm, then perhaps it was worth it. And who knew? Maybe whatever she and Cally were about to do would actually help. Maybe the cosmos would shine down on her and help her to remove Richie from her life.

Cally returned with two mugs of tea and put one down on the throw in front of Angelica, then took her place opposite her. 'On the phone you said you were looking to try something different. To help you feel like you have some balance again and to rid yourself of a negative person and their damaging energy. Tell me about that,' Cally said before taking a sip of her drink.

Reluctant to go into too much detail, Angelica sipped her tea too, then explained briefly that her ex had been bothering her and she wanted him gone for good, that frankly she wanted some negative karma to be sent his way. She left out the choking and the fact that she had got the police involved.

'A classic, to be sure, the old "revenge on an ex" tale. Tell me, do you actually believe in this sort of thing?' Cally gestured to the room.

'Honestly? I don't know. I've always felt that there had to be some truth to magic, to the supernatural. There are just too many stories around the world for it to all be totally false. And my mum always said there were other things at play in our world, other sets of eyes watching over and manipulating things. Sometimes she just seemed paranoid, but at other times I believed she was on to something. To what extent I believe it, I don't know. But I'm willing to try it. If nothing else, I think it might give me some short-term peace of mind, you know? That I took some action myself, even in a small way.'

'Well, that's good. It helps to be open. Makes everything much more likely to stick,' Cally said with gusto, instantly more animated. 'Now I'm going to try a few things with you, and I will explain as I go. You just tell me what you're up for. The cost is the same – a session is a session. But I must ask you to respect this space and this process. You must not tell anyone what we do here today. We need to keep the energy of what we do clear, and others can bring in unwanted negativity, which can cause all manner of problems. Trust me on that!'

Something in the woman's tone made Angelica shiver again. She wasn't sure what she had expected, but the seriousness with which Cally spoke seemed surprisingly genuine. She simply nodded, nervous but also curious.

'We'll start with some healing, a bit of light reiki and crystal work to help balance you out. Does that sound good?'

Angelica nodded again.

'And then we'll move on to the task at hand. You brought a

picture of this person, like I asked, this negative presence? And something that belongs to him?'

Angelica handed Cally the photo-booth print of Richie, taken at a club in Shoreditch two months earlier. She had deliberately picked the one of the four photos that she was not in. On the back she had written his name, as instructed over the phone. She also handed over a T-shirt. Richie had left it at her house on one of the last times he had stayed over. It was black and had a tattoo-style female pin-up on it, naked, the woman's modesty only partially covered. She hated it, thought it was tacky to have sexualised images of women on clothing. What made it worse was that Richie had a similar tattoo on his leg, of a naked woman squeezing her tits together. How she hadn't realised earlier that he wasn't the man for her, she didn't know.

'Perfect – these will do nicely. Remember, this must all stay between us, okay? Let's get started.'

Angelica swallowed the lump in her throat as she looked down at the photo of her ex-boyfriend, placed in front of the skull before her. Candlelight flickered over it, almost making Richie look alive on that small piece of glossy paper.

CHAPTER FIFTEEN

After having Saturday off and enjoying every minute of the morning he spent with Molly after their date the night before, going back to work on Sunday was a shock to Daniel's system. Not only did he miss having full weekends off, but he also wanted to spend more time with Molly. She had suggested a trip to South Kensington and a wander around one of the museums as an activity for Sunday and he'd been upset to have to turn down her offer. He was giddy – it was a fantastic feeling that he was fully embracing. He was passionate about his work, though, and murder cases didn't wait. Plus, there had been a development.

'So we know who our second victim is!' he said enthusiastically as he entered the task force room, scanning to see who was present. Charlie, of course, plus Ross Hayes and Amelia Harding.

'We do indeed!' Amelia answered with matching energy. 'Ross? Care to do the honours?'

As was usual with weekend meetings, someone had brought snacks. Daniel reached for one of the original glazed Krispy Kremes in the box in the middle of the table, then took a huge bite. 'God these are good!' he said, smiling as he chewed. Charlie threw him a look, one eyebrow raised.

'What? They are!' Daniel laughed as he devoured the rest of the doughnut. The raised eyebrow didn't disappear but Charlie moved on.

'Go on, Ross,' he said, nodding at the junior sergeant.

'Right, well as it turns out, it was quite easy to find the identity of the victim just from looking at the musculature of the arm left at the crime scene, the age of the victim, and the fact that Miss Kobayashi spotted that the skin showed traces of an oil used by competitive bodybuilders. Combined with the time frame, we only had one option from missing persons, and the coroner's office has confirmed it's a match.'

A laptop was open on the desk. Ross tapped it. The television behind him came to life, the screen filled with photos of a man who was clearly a bodybuilder. In most of the pictures his skin shone with dark-brown tanning oil, used to make muscles stand out more on stage. He was clearly white, despite the fake tan, and not that old.

'This poor chap is Alistair Watts, amateur bodybuilder. Twenty-seven years old, originally from Manchester but living in London. Records show he was renting a place on the Isle of Dogs.'

'That's not far from the crime scene,' Daniel noted. He reached for another doughnut and took a big bite. Again Charlie stared at him, his expression one of curiosity. Daniel wondered if he was waiting to ask him about his date after the meeting.

'Yeah, we thought that,' Amelia said, tucking a strand of brown hair behind her ear. 'But we couldn't figure out if it was relevant or not.'

Ross bobbed his head in agreement.

Daniel could tell that Amelia was being careful. She was still her enthusiastic self, he could see the familiar glint in her eye, but she was definitely more reserved than normal. He wondered if it was due to his dressing-down the other day. He was pleased to see that she was saying 'we' instead of 'I', and that she was allowing Ross some time to shine. He wanted his team to be at ease working together, to be collaborative rather than jostling for praise.

'He was reported missing by his trainer a week ago. As soon as we got photos, we sent them over to the morgue for comparison. They said they couldn't be one hundred per cent sure without the rest of the body or doing a DNA test, but everything lines up. They said that they could fairly closely match the arm from the scene with some photos of him. Apparently they rehydrated the limb and could compare veins, muscle growth and such, to get a surprisingly accurate result.'

Ross pulled a face at that, his nose wrinkling, and Daniel had to admit it sounded revolting.

'Assuming, then, that this is our victim, which is highly likely given what you've just said, why was he killed? That's what we need to know. Did he piss off the wrong person – a woman, maybe? Although let's not forget we don't know if we're correct about the female vendetta angle. Sex aside, who had it in for him? Do we have anything on that?'

'I've looked into that already,' Amelia piped up before awkwardly looking at Ross, then at Daniel.

He had been right; she was trying her best not to overstep. She clearly had something, so he had no intention of shutting her down just to prove a point.

'Go ahead, Amelia.'

She bent down to retrieve her bag and pulled out her own laptop, quickly switching the HDMI cable from Ross's computer to hers. After a few taps, the TV screen changed. Now there were images of a different bodybuilder – and his Facebook account.

'This guy is Jared Afolabi, twenty-eight, from Croydon. Also a bodybuilder. Turns out he and Watts had a beef.'

She clicked through a few of Afolabi's posts, then showed them some of his comments on Alistair Watts's Facebook profile.

'That's pretty blunt language,' Charlie said. 'And look, there he says he'll kill Alistair. He may or may not have meant it literally, but I'd say it gives us enough reason to question him. Anything about an ex-girlfriend on Alistair's account?'

'Not that I could find. Watts didn't actually post much. I managed to find his Instagram account but it's solely about bodybuilding, workouts and pictures of food. No photos outside of that. Nothing about an ex of any description. Also, as far as we can tell, there's no connection to the first victim.'

'I guess we're going to Croydon today then,' Charlie responded, looking at Daniel. 'We can have a chat in the car.'

Daniel knew that his friend and partner was ready to grill him about Molly. He was extremely pleased that he had good things to say.

'Do we have an address for Afolabi?' Daniel asked.

Amelia nodded. 'Just emailed it to you.'

Daniel checked his phone. 'Got it. Let's go. Great work, both of you,' he said as he got up. Charlie followed. As soon as they were out of the room he spoke, clearly unable to contain himself.

'So your date clearly went pretty fucking well then. Details on the drive to Croydon, please.'

Daniel laughed as they headed for the lift, thinking about Molly and how sexy she had looked in bed just hours earlier.

'I'm impressed!' Charlie exclaimed when Daniel told him that Molly had stopped at his place after the date.

'Try not to look so surprised.' Daniel frowned. He signalled and pulled past a Sainsbury's van that had parked awkwardly to deliver food.

'Come on, you know I think you're great. I just didn't peg you for a sex-on-the-first-date kind of guy.'

'It was her idea,' Daniel answered quickly, trying to pay attention to the road.

'Good on her. I'm a fan of a woman who knows what she wants. You're a catch and obviously she knows it. I'm chuffed for you, mate.'

'Thanks. She is pretty great. Intelligent, funny. Beautiful.' He felt his cheeks go red but was surprised to find he didn't care.

Charlie continued to grill Daniel about the date, trying to get more juicy details on what Molly was like, but as they drove past Clapham North, heading for Crystal Palace, their conversation shifted into dicier territory.

'Are we going to talk about Kelly then?' Charlie asked, looking at Daniel, who kept his eyes on the road.

'We can if you want. I'm not sure what to say, though.' It was true. Daniel was still at a loss for words. Charlie didn't respond, and Daniel glanced at him. His partner was fiddling with his fingernails, looking awkward and downcast.

'Look, you know how I feel about Kelly. I don't think she's good for you, I think she's a user.'

The car was painfully quiet, the hum of the engine and traffic around them barely breaking the silence.

Daniel had briefly asked for Molly's opinion on the matter, and had decided to try her advice and make it less about him and more about Charlie.

'I can't say I know her, not really – obviously not like you do. Look, you're the one dating her. I know you love her...'

'I do,' Charlie muttered.

'Just... okay, please promise me something. Don't let her break you again. You don't deserve that. And for fuck's sake, don't tell her anything about this case. I'm sure she's chomping at the bit to cover it.'

'She is, and I won't, I promise. On both counts. And you're right – you don't know her, not the real her. She's funny and passionate and... maybe you should meet her properly, unrelated to work. Over drinks or something. You could bring Molly!' Charlie said with a sudden rush of enthusiasm.

Daniel thought about it. He didn't really want to get to know Kelly Malone, but Charlie was a good friend and Daniel wanted him to be happy. Perhaps he should try to compromise, be less stubborn. Maybe if Molly did come, he'd be able to keep his opinion of Kelly under wraps. Maybe.

'Okay, sure. I can do that.'

'Awesome, I'll set it up,' Charlie said, smiling again, but with an edge of nerves showing through still.

Daniel quickly changed the subject. 'Do you think this other bodybuilder did it?' he asked, hearing the doubt in his own voice.

'Nope. I mean, I could see him maybe murdering Watts to get rid of the competition, assuming that's why they have issues with each other, but then setting up the whole bloody ritual scene on the pier? It doesn't make any sense. It doesn't fit.'

Charlie had vocalised what Daniel had been thinking since Ross and Amelia had shown them the profiles of the bodybuilders. He could believe that high levels of stress from competitions could lead to murder, but if that was what had happened then what did the severed arm and ribcage surrounded by symbols of witchcraft mean?

'What I'm hoping, to be honest, is that Afolabi will be able to tell us more about Watts in general. Maybe lead us to something else, maybe another suspect. Someone who's more inclined towards the dark arts.'

'Fingers well and truly crossed,' Daniel answered.

Jared Afolabi wasn't in. Daniel checked the man's Facebook account and quickly discovered the local gym he worked out at. 'Amazing what you can find out about someone on social media, isn't it?'

'I'm amazed more people haven't cottoned on to the fact we check social channels to help with cases,' Charlie answered. 'If people paid attention to how much we get off their profiles, I bet they'd be far more private. The ones who commit crimes, anyway.'

When they entered the gym, they were met with a cacophony of smells and noises. The air con was blasting and so was the music, Drake rapping over the sound of people working out. The converted warehouse smelled like sweat and cleaning products. It was well lit and kitted out with equipment that Daniel didn't recognise.

Daniel had gone to a gym on a few occasions, but had always struggled to put on bulk, so had resigned himself to being lean. He was more interested in running and swimming, anyway – not that he'd had time for either in the past month. It occurred to him that if he wanted to keep Molly interested, then maybe he needed to find the time. Guilt washed over him at the thought. Molly didn't seem shallow in the least.

He shrugged it off, knowing that his own insecurities had made the thought pop up. He looked at Charlie – over six foot, in great shape, able to hold his own against some of the bigger men working out in front of them – and couldn't help feeling small. He just couldn't compete.

But I'm faster, and fit enough. And Molly likes me – that's what counts. He made a mental note to go for a run as soon as he was free – for himself, not for Molly – then forced his brain back to the matter at hand.

'There he is. Got your badge ready?' he said to Charlie. He had spotted Afolabi, who was bench-pressing an obscene amount of weight. They headed over to him and waited patiently while he finished his set. When he registered their presence, he looked confused.

'Jared Afolabi – correct?'

The bodybuilder nodded, sitting up on the bench and wiping his forehead with the back of his hand.

'I'm DI Graves and this is DI Palmer. We'd like to talk to you about Alistair Watts.'

At the mention of the name, Jared rolled his eyes and bent down to get his water bottle from the floor. He took a swig. 'Why? What's he done? Bitched about me or somethin'?'

'Not exactly. Is there somewhere we can go that's more private to chat?' Daniel asked, glaring at a personal trainer who was lingering near them on the other side of the bench.

'Fuck's sake...' Jared muttered but he nodded, then led them across the gym to a small room that was seemingly used for consultations. As they sat down, Daniel informed Jared that Watts had been murdered, and that they wanted to find out some more about Jared.

'Do I need a lawyer?' Jared asked without pause, an eyebrow raised, his face sharper. The large muscles in his shoulders and arms had tensed.

'Not at this stage. We just have some questions, so we'll get to the point. Someone killed Watts and we're investigating why. What can you tell us about him?'

'Not much. He was all right as a bodybuilder. I'm better. We weren't friends or nothing, just used to see each other at competitions. He was always trying to beat me. Never did.'

Daniel saw Jared flex his muscles, and wondered if he actually thought that would impress them.

'We know you had some pretty heated competitions with him, and you frequently expressed your feelings online.'

'Seriously? He's just a competitor. Was... I mean, I don't – didn't – like the guy, everyone knows that. But kill him? Nah, not my style. It was always just banter between us. Macho shit, you know?'

Charlie pulled out his phone, opened a photo and held it out to Jared. 'This screenshot of one of your comments on his Facebook page paints a more extreme picture. Care to explain?'

Jared huffed. 'Come on, man, that's just chatting shit online. It don't mean nothing. Just ribbin' him, you know? Smack talk.'

'Let's hope so, for your sake. What can you tell us about Watts as a person?'

'He was okay – bit of a twat but not that bad. Decent bodybuilder, to be fair. If I'm bein' honest, he could have gone far. Pretty chatty, although he was a cocky fuck whenever he had an audience. Liked showing off, you know? Especially round girls.'

Daniel nodded, taking some brief notes on his phone. 'Was he seeing anyone, do you know?'

'Dunno. There was one girl a bit back but he dumped her.'

'How far back?' Daniel asked, leaning closer to Jared. If this woman had sought revenge for being dumped, that would fit their theory. It was probably a leap, he knew that, but sometimes leaps paid off.

'Like... maybe a month, two.'

That seemed too far out to Daniel. His shoulders sagged. Still, he couldn't rule this woman out as a suspect.

'What can you tell us about her?'

'Nothing.'

'What, at all?' Charlie asked, clearly not convinced.

'Never saw her. Just heard about her. So nothing.' Jared folded his arms across his broad chest, looking bored, as though he knew he wasn't in trouble so didn't care anymore.

Daniel tried a different avenue. 'Okay, so do you know about the rest of his life? Had he pissed anyone off? Did he have money troubles? Anything like that?'

Jared rolled his eyes again but made some effort to think before answering. 'He wasn't flush with money, but I don't think he struggled. He always seemed to have decent training kit and I know he didn't have a sponsor. As for anyone being pissed at him, like I said, he was a cocky prick so maybe, but he was harmless. Just a lot of swagger.'

Daniel took notes – not that there was much to add to what he had already written.

There was a moment of silence, which Jared seized. 'That it? I've gotta get back to training.'

'For now, yes. Thank you.' Charlie handed Jared a card, telling him to call if he thought of anything.

Jared got up and headed back across the gym, immediately chatting with his trainer.

Daniel and Charlie asked around about the woman Alistair Watts had been seeing, but no one seemed to know anything about her. A few people agreed that he had been rude and arrogant but, just as Jared Afolabi had said, no one could think of a reason someone would want Watts dead.

'Bollocks,' Charlie said as they left the gym, as though reading Daniel's mind. 'What next?'

CHAPTER SIXTEEN

The evening was unseasonably warm. Sarah Boyd sat on the bar's roof terrace, looking out across the new buildings of King's Cross. The area was full of shoppers, diners and travellers. She was surprised by how quiet it was up there, away from the road, even with the constant stream of people coming and going. The breeze even seemed refreshing.

'There you go,' Maisy Peters said as she placed the fishbowl gin and tonic in front of Sarah. A slice of cucumber bobbed in the drink. Maisy looked as cool as always, her bright-red hair in plaits contrasting with her faded black Aerosmith T-shirt. Angelica Okeke was close behind her, holding her own drink and a bowl of pistachios. She looked good – certainly better than the last time Sarah had seen her. She looked more lively, as though she had been restored somehow.

'Cheers, ladies,' Sarah said once they had settled. They clinked glasses. All took a sip, a trio of smiles.

'Maisy, is that a new tattoo?' Sarah said, spotting the skeletal mermaid figure on Maisy's right forearm.

'Yep, had it maybe four weeks? Wow, have I not seen you in that long? I love it now it's finally healed. Cool, huh?' She held her arm out so Sarah could see the tattoo more clearly. It was beautifully done, the delicate black line-work showing real care and detail.

'Do you get them done for free?' Angelica asked, nodding at the mermaid.

Maisy worked in a sleek little tattoo parlour that had opened a year back in Shoreditch to rave reviews. Sarah knew that Angelica wanted ink of some sort. She kind of did herself, though she wasn't sure she'd cope with the pain.

'Fishing for a discount, Ange?' Sarah grinned as she sipped her gin.

'Hell, yeah!'

Maisy laughed and cracked open a pistachio shell. 'Afraid not. Not free. Matt did this one and gave me a good rate, but not free. I can probably get you a discount if you really want one. But you're so indecisive!'

'True. But good to know. I saw some girl with these really pretty flowers on her shoulder the other week. I'd have loved that, but I think my skin is too dark for it.'

'Well, let me know when you've decided. I'll ask Caleb if I can give you mate's rates. I bet he'll say yes. He's a pushover, bless him. Then you can do a consultation with him.'

Sarah thought she felt her phone buzz in her handbag, which hung over the back of her chair. She assumed it was Mike, since he'd said he would call, but she chose to ignore it, not wanting to get into a discussion about him with Angelica – not yet, anyway. Neither friend noticed her distraction, and she let out a small sigh of relief, then began to tell Maisy all about EnchantedWomenLDN.

'It'd be right up your street. They do loads of creative workshops and stuff. Might give you some cool ideas for tattoo designs.'

Maisy took out her own phone and looked them up on

Instagram. 'Oh, you're right. They do a wicked-looking line drawing class. Where is it?'

Sarah saw her click 'follow'.

'Deptford.'

'Middle of nowhere.' Angelica laughed. 'To be fair, she's dragged me to a few classes and it's a nice place.'

'Pained you to say that, didn't it?' Sarah joked.

'Deptford... that's pretty easy to get to for me. DLR straight there. I might book something.' Maisy smiled, scrolling further on her phone and double-tapping a few images.

'Amazing – let me know when you go. Just be prepared for some typical artsy weirdos. And claims of witchcraft.'

Angelica huffed, and said something under her breath that Sarah didn't catch.

She turned to her friend. 'Oh, what? I know I was rude to that woman but come off it, she was weird. All that babble about crystals and stuff. You really buy into that?'

Angelica glared at her.

'I mean, whatever,' Maisy said. 'I'm a weirdo artsy type too so I'm sure I'll cope. Witchcraft, I can probably avoid. It's not some coven, is it? I wouldn't be signing my life away if I went?'

Angelica coughed as she took a sip of her wine, and Sarah and Maisy stared at her.

'What? Like I'm going to suddenly start wafting crystals in the air,' Angelica said with a frown, wiping her chin.

All three of them laughed, any tension that had been hovering gone.

Sarah felt her phone buzz again but ignored it, as she was happy chatting and gossiping with the girls. Mike could wait. After all, he'd made her wait plenty of times. It was only fair.

It was past eleven when Angelica made it back home, slightly tipsier than she had planned. She hesitated at her front door, thinking about the other day, when Richie had barged his way in. She shivered, then turned her key in the lock.

Flicking on every light as she passed to banish the shadows from her house, she headed into the kitchen and grabbed a glass from the cupboard next to the sink. A pint of water normally warded off the worst of her hangovers unless she had truly overindulged.

As she leant against the counter she couldn't help recalling fending Richie off with a knife, her tearful phone call to the police, then her tears when they said they couldn't do anything at this stage.

Sarah and Maisy had laughed off witchcraft and magic, of course they had, but was it really so strange that she had tried a ritual with a supposed witch in an effort to make herself feel better? And she hadn't heard from Richie since. Not even a text.

That seemed a bit weird. After the first time they had argued, when he'd scared her a little, he'd begged for forgiveness, called her numerous times, before again showing up at her door. This time? Nothing.

Angelica moved to pick up her handbag from where she'd dumped it at the end of the counter, and retrieved her phone. Her heart skipped as she saw she had a WhatsApp notification. She clicked on it, and saw it was from Maisy, saying it was great to see her and Sarah and they needed to meet up more often. She texted back a quick message of agreement. Then she clicked on her chat history. At the top of the screen it showed what time Richie had last been online.

Last seen yesterday at 02.37

That meant he'd not been online since the small hours of

that morning. That seemed strange too. Even if he hadn't messaged her, surely he'd have been on WhatsApp at some point during the day? When they'd been dating, he was constantly on his phone.

She supposed he could have deleted the app, but a knot of fear started to grow in Angelica's stomach and she felt a little queasy. On Saturday morning she had gone to see a witch and together they had performed a ritual to get rid of Richie from her life, with Richie's picture and an item of his clothing. Had it worked? What had happened?

'It can't have...' she muttered.

She felt dizzy, not sure what to think. The ideas buzzing through her mind were ridiculous. Magic was fake, she knew that. The ritual had just been to make her feel better. It hadn't actually done anything to Richie. It couldn't have.

Yet he hadn't tried to contact her, and he hadn't been on WhatsApp in more than twenty hours.

'Nope. He lost his phone,' she said loudly, as though trying to convince the world, not just herself.

That had to be it. Witchcraft was fiction. No matter what Cally Buchanan thought.

Feeling a little better, brushing off her paranoia and crazy thoughts, Angelica drank the rest of her water and headed upstairs to bed. Despite her worry, she was asleep in a few minutes.

Bright light streamed through the open curtains, and Angelica winced. It took her a second to realise she was in bed, and her head thumped as she reached for her phone from her bedside table. It was almost midday.

Dragging herself out from under her duvet, Angelica

assessed her hangover. She was pleased to discover it was actually quite mild. She would cope. *Thank you, water!*

Phone in hand she headed downstairs, glad that she had the day off. She rarely went to work after drinking the night before. Any day with a hangover always dragged.

She made a coffee, grabbed a granola bar from the cupboard and moved into the living room, where she slumped onto her worn but still very comfortable sofa, which absorbed her as though she had sat on a big marshmallow.

Turning on the television, she flicked through a few channels before something made her pause. A breaking news report. On the screen a female journalist was standing in a kids' playground. The ticker tape at the bottom of the screen revealed that someone had been murdered.

'... not many details have been provided yet, but what we do know is that the crime scene seems to echo two other recent crime scenes in London. Bloody symbols were painted on the wall behind what we can only describe as an effigy, like those found in Hyde Park and Greenwich.'

The woman on-screen looked uncomfortable. Angelica shuffled forward to get a closer look at the television. She had read about the two murders on the *Daily Mail Online*. And the *Metro*. In fact, every news outlet had published something on them. She'd seen coverage all over the internet.

'... not able to share images or specifics of the crime scene at this time, but police at the scene have confirmed that the remains are of a man in his early thirties. While no articles that would identify the man have been found at the scene, we are able to share the following image of a tattoo on the victim. Police are urging anyone who may recognise the tattoo to contact them immediately. We will now show the image. Viewers may find the image distressing and viewers of a sensitive disposition may wish to look away.'

An image appeared on the screen, cropped into a square. There was no blood on the pale skin. Just the tattoo. A black-and-white image of a woman, part of the image pixelled out to hide nudity.

The mug fell from Angelica's hand. It bounced off the rug and coffee sprayed across the floor. She didn't notice. Didn't move or react in any way. She couldn't. She was frozen, her gaze locked on the image of the tattoo, which she recognised all too well.

'Oh God...' she managed. She grabbed her phone, hand shaking so much she could barely unlock it. 'Sarah, oh thank God, Sarah... something has happened. Oh shit, something bad. Can you come over? Now?'

CHAPTER SEVENTEEN

The day had been chaotic, and Daniel Graves was starting to really feel the pressure. A third victim left with another bloody effigy in an even more public place, and still he and Charlie had no suspects, just theories. And the press were going wild.

'Kelly will be furious she's missing this,' Daniel had said to Charlie on their arrival at the latest crime scene.

'She's already messaged me. She's upset, worried that her name is no longer synonymous with big murder cases to people in the industry,' Charlie had said.

Daniel felt bad for Kelly, in a way. If he'd been taken off cases like this, it would have hit him hard. He knew the passion Kelly had for her job and he respected it. He didn't like Kelly or her methods, but he wondered if maybe they had some common ground there at least. Something he could chat to her about when they went out for drinks.

Emi Kobayashi had once again been at the scene. Her boss Stephanie Mitchum had also turned up. Emi had been tasked with leading the case for the coroner's office, and Daniel wondered why Stephanie was here today. He had thought Emi was doing a good job, but perhaps not? As it turned out, curiosity had simply got the better of Stephanie.

'I wanted to see the scene for myself,' she had said when Daniel expressed his surprise at seeing her. 'These are not the type of remains we normally analyse.'

Daniel suspected she also wanted to monitor how Emi was doing, but this remained undiscussed. After half an hour at the scene Stephanie departed, leaving Emi in command again.

'Still going okay?' Daniel asked her as they watched Stephanie leave the playground. 'Stephanie seemed confident about leaving you to it.'

Emi pushed some strands of black hair out of her eyes. 'Yes. I mean, don't get me wrong, she's tough. But she's a good teacher, knows her stuff.'

'You don't find her a bit too... cold and robotic?'

Emi laughed, her face full of emotion. She was very different to Stephanie Mitchum. 'Well, yes, sometimes. But I know where I stand with her, and I like that she's straight to the point.'

'Yes, she is ruthlessly efficient,' Daniel said.

'She sure is. Came to the same conclusion as I did on this one, but she took half the time. I don't think I'm quite as willing to commit to an analysis as she is; I'm nervous of making a mistake. I'm glad we think the same, though. Quite vindicating!'

Daniel could see the relief in Emi's eyes. 'And what is your analysis, then?'

They headed back towards the area of the playground where the remains had been discovered.

'To be honest, very similar to the last two murders. No precision has been used; the remains were hastily chopped up. The victim was not killed here either, although there is a bit more blood spatter here, which suggests there was less of a time gap between the murder and setting up this display.'

'Sounds fairly consistent.'

'There is one thing that may take you by surprise,' Emi said, turning to face Daniel. 'And Stephanie agrees with me.'

'What's that, then?' Something about the way Emi was looking at him put him on edge. Her tone, the way she was biting her lip, unsettled him.

'I don't think you're going to like this, but there are a few things about this scene that made me think... this is not the same person who set up the first two tableaus.'

Daniel frowned, not sure what to say. 'Right, okay. What makes you think that?' he asked finally.

'Two things. First, there are a number of indications that the body parts were cut by someone who is left-handed. They're messy, so it's difficult to be certain without Samson taking a look back at the morgue, but the first two victims were definitely cut up by a right-handed person.'

'Shit,' Daniel said.

'Also the symbols around the remains are slightly different. Not the work of the same person. Some of the symbols from this effigy also appeared on the previous one, but the way they have been rendered shows inconsistencies with last time. Line weight, loops, neatness, that sort of thing. All vary too much from the last scene, and I have my doubts that it's the same person.'

If the first reason had not been enough to convince him, the second one was. Daniel took a step back, pulling in a deep breath. Were they dealing with multiple people working together? Or a copycat?

'Daniel!' Charlie called from behind him, then bounded over, red-cheeked. 'We're needed back at the office. We have a suspect, and someone has come in with some very interesting information on the case, apparently.'

'Thanks, Emi, speak to you soon,' Daniel said before following Charlie quickly out of the playground, his heart pounding.

'Okay, so let me get this straight. You were seeing this man, Richie Tseng, for a few months, and when you ended things he became aggressive, even choking you in your flat. You reported him, an officer gave him a warning but said nothing else could be done without evidence. And that's when you went to see a witch.'

Daniel looked up from his notes at Angelica Okeke, who was sitting, wide-eyed, across the table from him. Above them the strip light flickered. Angelica glanced up at it, as though she thought that whatever magic she had messed with was following her and tampering with the electricity.

Making eye contact with Daniel again, she nodded. 'Yes.'

There was a pause.

'Look, I know it sounds fucking stupid. Sorry, I shouldn't be swearing at you. But that's what happened. I went to see this woman who claimed to be a witch because I thought maybe it would help calm me down, give me some sense of karmic satisfaction or something. At least give me back a feeling of control. Like I said, I don't believe in magic and all that, but my mum maintains that there are too many stories about witches and magic and ghosts in the world for it to all be total fiction, and I guess – I don't know, call it a moment of madness, I thought, why not? I'd give it a go. Make the universe warn Richie off. It's not like the police could do much, is it? I didn't think that anything would come of seeing her, not really.'

Angelica dropped her hands in her lap in a 'there you have it' gesture, acknowledging that she was fully aware that they were talking about a weird situation more suited to an episode of *Supernatural* than real life.

'You said this woman was called Cally Buchanan, correct? And you met her at a women's business and lifestyle centre in Deptford called Enchanted Women London.'

'LDN, but yes. My friend Sarah dragged me along to an art workshop there. She's here with me if you want to talk to her about the place.'

Daniel nodded, thinking that wasn't a bad idea. 'Buchanan mentioned she did these... let's call them spiritual treatments, so after the incident with Richie you reached out to her and visited her house. Can you describe what she did while you were there?'

Angelica nodded, but took a moment to find her words. What she described to Daniel sounded like something out of a cheap horror movie.

'The lamb's guts were real?' he asked partway through her description, revolted by the thought. 'She said they were from a lamb?'

Angelica's eyes widened. 'Oh God, are you suggesting they might not have been?'

'It's possible, I suppose,' he admitted.

'They were definitely real. They smelled pretty ripe. She said she used them to connect us to the earth. She balled up the T-shirt I gave her, Richie's T-shirt, wrapped the guts around it, and then she stuck a skewer, like a kebab skewer, right through it. She pinned the photo of Richie on it as well, then dropped it all into a metal bucket and set fire to it. And she chanted something – I don't know what.'

Daniel raised an eyebrow. 'Miss Okeke, this is quite a story. And you say that Richie disappeared just after this?'

'Yes. I know it's ridiculous, but... I saw that image of his tattoo on the news and I just knew. It has to be her, surely. She must have killed him.'

'Let's say for a moment that you're right: this apparent witch took your money for a ritual, then afterwards she hunted down Richie and killed him. Why would she do that? What would be her motive?'

It just wasn't adding up for Daniel. Ridiculous as the story sounded, he did believe that Angelica Okeke had visited this woman and paid for her to do some bizarre ritual, but after that nothing made sense. He didn't believe in witchcraft. And there was zero motive for this woman, Cally Buchanan, to have killed Richie Tseng. The man had done nothing to Buchanan, surely.

'Miss Okeke, you said that Richie Tseng was aggressive and scared you, and that the police officer who came to speak with said he was powerless to do anything more than warn him without evidence, correct?'

Angelica nodded.

'And you decided to visit this self-identifying witch as a way to gain some sort of closure or control over things, over your own feelings.'

Again she nodded.

'It seems to me that you wanted Richie out of your life and that this woman, this witch, may have presented you with an opportunity to do just that. Did you hire Cally Buchanan to kill Richie Tseng?' He knew the question was blunt, but he wanted to see Angelica's reaction. People often gave away their true feelings or intentions when caught off guard, and telling Angelica Okeke that she was a suspect when their entire conversation had painted her as a victim and witness was sure to do just that.

Angelica looked stunned, her mouth open. 'I... no! My God,

no! I didn't ask her to kill him – that's insane!' she stammered, eyes moist with the start of tears, her voice cracking.

'Any more insane than this story of visiting a witch to conduct a ritual to free you of your ex?' he pushed.

Angelica slumped in her seat, tears properly coming. She tried to talk through the sobs. 'I know it's insane! This woman... Look, you have to believe me. I didn't want Richie *dead*; I just wanted him to leave me alone. He scared the shit out of me, but I'm not a killer. I didn't do this. And I didn't ask her to either, I promise you!'

Daniel did believe her – at least, his gut did. Nothing about the woman crying across from him suggested she was lying. He'd seen plenty of crocodile tears in his time, and suspects had tried to fool him in a number of ways. Angelica Okeke seemed to genuinely be innocent. He thought it was bizarre that she had paid for the ritual she had described, but her description seemed genuine. And she had come to him, after all. Granted, some people tried that as a tactic to remove themselves from the suspect list, but that didn't feel right in this instance either.

'Okay, Miss Okeke, I do believe you. Of course, you will have seen on the news that there has been a spate of ritualistic murders, and we believe that Richie Tseng was one of the victims, so the fact that you visited a witch, real or not, means that we need to talk to this woman and see if she is in any way connected. I'm going to get an officer to take your official statement, then I need you to give me as much detail as you can about Miss Buchanan and this women's group in Deptford.'

Angelica nodded, wiping her eyes, looking calmer, although clearly still very upset. Daniel wasn't surprised. She had paid to have some random woman perform a ritual to remove her ex from her life, then just a short time later he was dead. He could only imagine how guilty she must feel. He thanked Angelica for her time and for coming forward with what she knew, then called in Sergeant Amelia Harding to take her statement. Then he called Charlie, who he knew would be as eager as he was to go and see a woman about some witchcraft.

CHAPTER EIGHTEEN

The concrete sky looked ready to crack and shower the city as Molly Goodings trekked from Finchley Central Tube station to her flat. Finding herself distracted at work by too many students taking advantage of her open-door policy, she had gathered up the books she needed to help Daniel on his case and had left the university.

Her backpack pulled on her spine from the weight of the books and essays inside. Molly felt the first spots of rain landing on her cheeks as she reached her front door. Swinging the backpack off her back, she dropped it on the porch step and dug in its front pocket to retrieve her keys.

Unlocking the door, she rolled her eyes. The bottom lock had been left off again. She knew it would be the students who lived above her. They never locked the front door, left endless piles of post in the hall, and listened to music way too late into the night. She hoped they would move soon. It was only a few months until the end of the academic year, and they were final-year students. If they didn't move she thought she might, although she was loath to leave the flat. She had lived there for almost three years and felt settled.

Unless I moved in with Daniel...

Surprised at the thought, she shook herself and stepped into the hallway, shutting the door behind her, bolting the bottom lock and rifling through the envelopes.

Way too early to be thinking so far ahead!

She found a gas bill with her name on it, then unlocked her own front door. She spotted a smudge of something black and oily near the lock and wiped it off with a finger before rubbing her finger clean on her jeans. They needed a wash anyway.

The flat was cold; the heating wasn't due to come on for another three hours, when she would normally be home. She dumped her backpack in the living room, then headed into the kitchen to flick on the boiler, which rumbled happily. Minutes later she had a cup of tea and could feel some heat starting to come through from the radiators.

She began to leaf through the first book, a text on the representation of sex in ancient iconography. She was looking for any of the symbols that had been used at the crime scenes – the ones she hadn't recognised, anyway. The main problem was that she didn't know where the unfamiliar symbols came from. It was evident that the killer Daniel and his team were looking for had taken inspiration from different cultures and sects, which made it hard to know where to start. Hence the stack of books.

Molly stopped when she came to a symbol of Scandinavian origin. Vertical in shape, it looked approximately like the letter V but was rendered with four lines instead of two. It also had one horizontal line cutting across it. According to the book, it had something to do with strength and had been found to relate to life in some contexts. It looked very similar to a symbol found at the second murder, but not exactly the same. She wondered if it had differing forms. She made a note on her pad, then continued her search.

It wasn't until after she had finished her tea and looked up from the book that she realised something felt wrong. She looked around the living room, which was silent except for the small clock ticking away on her bookshelf, a gift from her father, and the gentle patter of rain on the window behind her.

Something felt different, not quite as she expected, but she couldn't figure out what. She got up off the sofa and moved to the middle of the room. Standing with her hands on her hips, she scanned the room. Nothing seemed out of place, exactly, but it felt as though someone had picked everything up and then put it back where it was supposed to be, only not quite exact enough. The clock seemed slightly further to the right than normal, no longer placed symmetrically. The picture of her and her best friend Stacy from their trip to Ibiza a few years back seemed to be angled differently.

An odd feeling washed over her. She was sure she must have moved things herself and not realised, but she couldn't shake the feeling that someone else had done this, that someone else had been in her flat and moved things around.

She thought back to the unusual dirt on the door, then looked down at her jeans. Was it car oil? Who could have left that there? She didn't think she could have. She didn't own any oil. And now she thought about it, the lock on the front door couldn't be locked if you pulled the door shut from outside and didn't have a key. Perhaps it hadn't been the students after all.

'Shit,' she whispered, trying to keep calm. Urgently, she quickly checked the other rooms, starting with the kitchen. Everything looked approximately the same, but something key had changed there too. The magnet holding up the family photo on her fridge – hadn't it been the plastic ladybird? Now it was held in place with a picture of Niagara Falls, and the ladybird was off to the side.

She sped to the bedroom, and instantly knew she had not left the dresser drawer open. 'Shit, shit, shit!'

Last she ran into the bathroom. Her breath choked in her throat. There was writing on the mirror, written in her eyeliner, the tube discarded on the sink.

She read the message just once.

STICK WITH GRAVES AND YOU'LL END UP IN ONE YOURSELF!

Underneath was a drawing of a coffin.

She took a photo on her phone, then grabbed her coat from the hall, checked she had her wallet and keys, and left the flat. She was dialling Daniel before she had even reached the pavement, as the rain hammered around her.

'I'm calling it,' Charlie said. 'Cally Buchanan is definitely involved in the murders. Witch or not.'

'Well, she seems to have vanished into thin air, that's for sure,' Daniel said as they stood in the almost empty sitting room. 'Maybe she magicked her stuff right out of here and jumped on her broomstick,' he added with a smile, despite the situation.

They had raced to the address Angelica Okeke had given them. Her friend, Sarah Boyd, had not provided any more useful information other than a few snide comments about their new suspect, and they didn't want to waste any time in meeting Buchanan. Things hadn't gone to plan, however.

The front door of the house was unlocked and all personal effects had been removed. There were still some bits of furniture, that Daniel assumed had come with the place, some random kitchenware as well as two battered old chests of drawers, a bed frame with an old mattress and a broken wardrobe upstairs, but nothing that looked like it had recently belonged to anyone.

'Maybe she did. I don't understand how she could have got out of here so fast otherwise,' Charlie said. 'She must have had help. But how the hell did she know?'

'Maybe she was watching our witness? Realised Okeke had come to us.'

Charlie nodded. 'Okay, I'm calling Patrick and his team. Maybe she was caught on a few street cams. If she used a moving van, we can likely follow her and see where she went.' He pulled out his phone and dialled. 'Hey, Patrick, glad I caught you,' he started.

Daniel tuned him out and took another tour of the vacant house, hoping he would spot something useful. He found nothing, and sat on the stripped mattress in the main bedroom.

He considered the timeline. Angelica Okeke had gone to see Cally Buchanan on Saturday morning for the ritual she had described to them. Richie Tseng had apparently been murdered in the very small hours of Sunday morning. His body had been found this morning, Tuesday, and just hours after that Okeke had come in to speak to them. It wasn't a big window of opportunity. It meant that Cally Buchanan must have moved within the last two days, if she had been watching Okeke. It was possible, but weird. When had she moved? Had she ever actually lived in the house?

He thought back to what Okeke had told him. Buchanan had met her at the front door and taken her straight to the living room. Buchanan had also made tea, so the kitchen must have had a kettle and some essentials. However, Okeke did not see the rest of the house. The other rooms could well have been empty the entire time, and Buchanan could have simply packed up what was in the living room and left. They would check with neighbours, but it seemed to indicate that the house had been empty beforehand and this had all been planned in some way. Daniel didn't think that Buchanan would have known about Richie Tseng before she met Angelica Okeke, but she had arranged their meeting a day in advance, and had clearly been able to quickly stage the house to suit her needs.

'Dan?' Charlie called from downstairs. Daniel got up from the bed and headed down to his partner.

'Patrick is on it. He'll get back to us by the end of the day, hopefully.'

'Great...'

'You seem distracted – what are you thinking?' Charlie asked, an eyebrow raised.

'About how our suspect could have vacated so quickly. I think this whole set-up was staged. The living room was dressed up for the ritual, then cleared out as soon as Okeke left. It's the only thing that makes sense.'

'Okay, yep, that's possible. But how did Buchanan get in here in the first place?'

'She must have had help. Perhaps either she or someone she knows has access to empty houses. Letting agent, perhaps?'

'Yes, that would work!' Charlie exclaimed. 'Let's find out who owns this house!' He whipped his phone out again and tapped the screen a few times. Daniel waited. The house felt eerie, as though it too was watching them, curious to see what happened next.

'The house is up for rent, letting agent is Petersons. This is starting to come together, Daniel, my good fellow. Let's get down to their offices and find out who has access to this property.'

'Agreed. It's time to nail someone for this,' Daniel said. He felt his phone vibrating, pulled it out from his pocket. His heart skipped a beat when he saw it was Molly.

'Meet you at the car,' he said to Charlie.

Charlie grinned and winked back. 'Gotcha!' He left Daniel alone.

'Hey, what's up? Missed me?' Daniel started.

Molly cut him off. 'Daniel, someone broke into my flat. Can you meet me? They threatened me.' She was speaking fast, breathless. Her words clawed through Daniel's skin.

'Shit, are you okay? I'll get a team over to your flat straight away. And of course I'll meet you. Where are you?'

'I'm okay, just scared shitless. I'm getting the Tube now. Where should I come to?'

'I'll text you the address of my offices.'

'Okay, I'll meet you there. Listen, though, Dan, it wasn't just a regular break-in. I'm texting you a picture. I think someone is after you.'

His phone buzzed and he lowered it to check the text. His blood froze. 'Shit, he's back.'

'Who?'

'I'll tell you everything when I see you. Just get to the station, okay? And be careful.'

Molly promised she would, and ended the call. Daniel was already running back out into the cold day.

'Slight change of plan,' he said to Charlie. His heart was pounding harder than it had in months.

CHAPTER NINETEEN

After Daniel and Charlie returned to the office, Charlie had taken point on the estate agent lead, setting out into the unwelcoming afternoon gloom to find out who had access to the empty house.

Daniel was trying to stay calm, not let his world unravel.

Molly was sitting next to him in the small café in Daniel's building, her hands wrapped around a steaming mug of hot chocolate. Her hair was tied up in a messy ponytail and she looked shaken, but certainly calmer than Daniel felt.

'So this person, who you're assuming is Greg Armstrong, the man who dated your sister, broke into my flat to warn me off you because of the death of that woman in your old case? A woman who was a killer? And he's been messing with you on and off for months? And almost killed you in a car crash?'

Daniel nodded. 'That's about the size of it.' He looked down at his coffee, watching a swirl of frothed milk turning lazily on the surface, but didn't take a sip.

Nothing had happened for three months, not since he had been run off the road by the Range Rover. Not since his sister Amanda had revealed that the man she was falling for also happened to be someone with a secret vendetta against Daniel. Yet here he was again, feeling like his every move was being watched from the shadows. He was back to feeling incredibly on edge. This man had been slowly and methodically tormenting him over time, and had now threatened the first woman Daniel had grown close to since Jenny Cartwright had been murdered almost a year ago. Murdered as revenge. It was all too familiar.

Armstrong sure knew how to reduce Daniel to a wreck. The note on the mirror was a shrewd move that had shattered Daniel's feelings of relative safety in record time.

'Okay. I get the revenge part. Even considering that the woman he's avenging was a murderer. This is strange behaviour, though – him popping up to torment you, then disappearing again, only to rear his head a few months later to threaten you, and now me too. It's abnormal.'

'He's having fun. Tormenting me when he sees fit. Clearly he enjoys putting me on edge so I never know what he might do. Who he might hurt.'

'Well, at least he doesn't want you dead right now. That's... something,' Molly said, though there was no way to put a positive spin on the situation. Even if Armstrong didn't plan on trying to kill Daniel yet, the alternative wasn't much better.

'It's... it's just scary. He's so unpredictable. Nothing for months, then he threatens you. It means he's watching me, that's for certain. Waiting for something he could use to get to me.'

'And I'm that something,' Molly said, sipping her hot chocolate. 'Wish this had Baileys in it. This is not quite how I expected our first week of dating to go.'

Daniel gave her a smile, but there was no cheer behind it. He was waiting for Molly to cut her losses, leave him, thinking it was all too much hassle.

'You'll need to be put under guard. And you can't go back to your flat,' he said, not wanting to address his thought out loud.

'Okay.'

'And I've sent a team to your house to do a full crime scene sweep.'

'Okay, sure.'

His next words took even him by surprise. 'I think you should stay with me for now.' He swallowed.

'Okay,' Molly said again without even a hint of hesitation before twisting in her seat and leaning in, kissing Daniel and pulling him closer to her. She broke the kiss and held his face in her hands, looking into his eyes. 'I know what you're thinking, but it's okay. It's scary but it's okay. We have something here, Daniel, I know we do. And I think being in your house, with my own very handsome detective watching over me, sounds perfect.'

He smiled and kissed her again, shocked but happy, even given the circumstances. 'You're right, this is a nightmare. I thought you'd run for the hills when you knew what was going on, when you knew that being with me puts you in danger. It's only been a week.'

Molly shrugged. 'What can I say? I'm tough. And although we've not known each other long, something tells me that you might be worth it, Daniel Graves.' Molly sat back but held Daniel's hand. It was somehow everything he needed. The situation was terrifying but now he knew for sure what Molly felt, he felt better, more empowered.

He was going to find Greg Armstrong and put an end to his sick plans for revenge.

'Thanks for having me along, DI Palmer,' Amelia Harding said as they drove through the city in the direction of Petersons Letting Agency in Limehouse. She was staring out of the passenger window, watching a Docklands Light Railway train high above them transporting strangers on their way to Lewisham.

She wondered what would happen if the elevated tracks suddenly fell down onto the roads and buildings they passed. She was surprised at the dark thought. It wasn't like her. She suspected it was reflective of her current mood, which was rather melancholic. She was supposed to be happy that she was working the ritual case with Palmer, getting directly involved rather than simply assisting back at the office, but she couldn't get rid of the doubt that had been winding its way through her since Daniel had told her off the week before. At the time she had been upset, of course, but she hadn't expected it to stay with her. Normally she was pretty resilient and didn't take constructive criticism to heart. In fact, she usually welcomed it, knowing how valuable it could be. Not this time. It was like a mental splinter hooked in her brain that she couldn't pluck out, but if she didn't it would only dig deeper and deeper and start to fester.

'Happy for the help, Amelia,' Charlie said. 'DI Graves had to be elsewhere urgently, so it's good to have your company.'

She turned back to look at him and he flashed her a smile before looking back at the road, indicating around a bus and taking them away from the DLR line.

'It feels good to finally be involved again,' she said.

'That sounds pointed.'

'Oh, shit, I didn't mean any offence. It's just... I've not worked on this case that much. Did DI Graves mention that he had a word with me the other day?'

Charlie nodded, a wary frown appearing on his face.

'He warned me about being too pushy and taking credit away from Ross, even though I was just trying to work hard, show the effort I've been putting in. I mean, I'm not saying he was wrong, I'm not... I just mean...' Amelia suddenly felt flustered and embarrassed. She knew how close Palmer and Graves were, and now she was complaining about one to the other. She felt like she had suddenly dug a hole without planning her route out of it. She could feel herself trembling, and flexed her fingers in response.

'Hey, hey, calm down. Take a breath,' Charlie advised.

She did as he said. 'Sorry, yes, I'm okay.' She didn't feel okay, but at least outwardly she looked calmer.

'Good. Now tell me why has this bothered you so much. You're normally so confident. This isn't like the usual unflappable Sergeant Harding,' Charlie said.

Amelia was not surprised that she could hear genuine concern in his voice. He was that type of man. She felt bad for starting this conversation with one of her superiors, yet also relieved to be speaking about her worries to someone who would understand. She had chatted to a few of her friends and her mum about it, but not to any colleagues.

'I don't know. I think... I'm just... it upset me more than I thought.'

'Was Graves rude to you? Did he cross a line?' Charlie asked, concern clearly written on his face.

'Oh God, no. He was good about it all, constructive. He wasn't mean or anything. And he was right. I think... I'm just disappointed. In myself, I guess. More so than normal, clearly.'

'Well, I know how driven you are, how determined you are to progress and stake your claim. And I know it doesn't feel good to be told you're doing something wrong at work, trust me.'

Amelia felt her cheeks flush. She was fully aware of how driven she was, how keen to go up in the ranks. Having Charlie say this to her, however, made it feel like that was all she was known for. Was she just the pushy one at work who annoyed people?

'Yeah, it's horrible. And I know I can be a bit much; I was just brought up that way. Always wanting to impress people and do well – my dad, mainly.'

'You do impress, Amelia. Constantly. You know that, right? Graves would say the same too.'

'Yes. Most of the time I do, to be honest. But now... I'm doubting that. I really want to be promoted, but I guess that isn't going to happen any time soon.' Even as she spoke, she realised she was not behaving the way she should, not with a DI. She was veering into rant territory and felt she was dangerously close to saying something she would not be able to take back. She was also aware that something inside her didn't want to stop it from happening, as though she was curious to see what the outcome would be.

'So that's why it's affected you so much. Have you tried to reframe what Graves fed back to you in a way that would allow you to learn and grow from it? Actually help your career path?'

That stumped her. Now she thought about it for a second, she had to admit to both Charlie and herself that in fact she hadn't. She had been so focused on reading the situation as her being a failure who had screwed herself over that she hadn't paused to see how she could turn it around in her favour.

'If you want to progress, then you need to be able to take criticism in a way that allows you to continue to develop. Graves was probably trying to push you to challenge some of the ways in which you work to benefit *you*, not just for his or Junior Sergeant Hayes' sake. We want a great team around us, and perhaps that was something you needed to hear to further yourself.'

'Wow... you're good at this. I feel like I've just had a mini therapy session,' Amelia said with a nervous laugh as her earlier frustration and melancholy gave way to an awkward sense of relief. 'I think you may be spot-on...'

'Glad to be of help. Graves wants you, all of us, to succeed. Always.'

Amelia smiled, feeling foolish but better nonetheless. She knew Daniel Graves well after he had opened up to her about his troubled teenage years – perhaps better than most other people at work knew him, if not Charlie. Graves was not a mean person, not difficult or aggressive, and had always been nice to her, apart from a few incidents where he had become snappy while under stress. He'd always apologised afterwards. He was a kind, mature person, a good boss and someone worth looking up to. And just as passionate about his work as she was.

'Thank you. For snapping me out of that. Very efficiently too. Don't tell Daniel about this, will you? I'm already mortified.'

'I won't say a word,' Charlie promised. She knew that he wouldn't.

Amelia stared out of the window again, her thoughts already brighter. Then she spotted the sign for the letting agency. 'Petersons!'

'So it is. Good spot.' Charlie quickly pulled into a quiet stretch of road. 'Let's find out who might be working with Buchanan, shall we?' Charlie's confidence rubbed off on Amelia. She felt something inside herself click back into place, as though the real Amelia Harding was back. It was empowering. She felt good again and more determined than ever.

The window was filled with lit-up listings for rentals and sales in the area but the offices beyond were dark, with little light getting past the signage.

'Maybe they knew we were coming,' Amelia said, pressing her face to the window in an attempt to see inside.

'I suppose they could have, but I'm not sure how. I think it's more likely that they're just closed,' Charlie said as he tried the front door. It was locked, as he had suspected. 'Dammit.' He moved to look at one of the house listings and found a phone number for the agency. He pulled out his phone and dialled it.

'Hear that?' Amelia asked. The faint but unmistakable sound of a phone ringing came from inside the building.

'No one is picking up,' Charlie said. 'They must be closed.' He heard a click, then the line went dead. 'That was odd. Sounded like it connected, then hung up.'

They turned back to the window. Again Amelia peered through the glass, her hands cupped around her eyes. 'I can't see anything.'

'But maybe someone can see us. Come on.' Charlie made a big show of looking at his phone again and huffing before walking off out of view of the agency window. Amelia followed. Once out of view Charlie had a look around, surveying the building.

Petersons was in the middle of a short line of shops, all a little battered and worn. On the far side was a small newsagent. On their side, the store they were standing in front of used to be a café but was now closed down, the windows painted white and a *For Lease* sign pinned above the door.

'What are you thinking?' Amelia asked him as he started towards the end of the shops.

'I think someone is in and was tipped off somehow, but I have no idea how. I think they're pretending to be out. I think they panicked when we rang, and picked up and put down the receiver quickly.'

They reached the end of the building, where they found an alley blocked by a high wooden gate that led to the rear of the shops. Charlie stood on tiptoe to see over the top. 'And I think we might be able to catch them trying to leave the back way.' He tried the gate. It was stiff but not locked, and it swung open with a judder to reveal the alley, dotted with bundles of flat-packed cardboard and a few bin bags.

Stepping over some loose rubbish, Charlie reached the rear corner of the building and peered around it. Behind the shops was a small strip of gravelled ground with more bins and just enough space for a battered Fiesta and a dark blue delivery van, penned in by a tall wooden fence that ran along the back, parallel with the building unit. It looked like the only way to get out was either the way they had come, up the alley, or the exit from the other end, which vehicles were clearly able to use. He couldn't see any gaps in the fence.

No one was around. He stepped out from the corner, heading to the rear of the agency. Amelia followed close behind.

A grey metal fire escape door was the only feature on the back of the unit, other than a small closed window approximately two metres up, which had a rusting grill over it.

'Let's see if this is open, shall we?' Charlie reached for the door handle and flinched when it opened without his aid. He had just enough time to see a person in a dark hoodie standing, wide-eyed, in front of him before the door was slammed in his face. Instinctively he kicked out to stop the latch catching, and heard a grunt from the other side of the door and the sound of hastily retreating footsteps.

'Shit! Harding, call for backup. I'm going in. Go around the front!'

Charlie hadn't brought a gun with him; he rarely did. They

were not often needed. He did have a baton, though, something he was rarely without. He pulled it from his belt and, keeping low, pushed the door open.

The building was dark inside, and his gut told him not to charge in. His brain told him he didn't have a lot of time. If the person he had surprised got to the front of the building before Amelia did, they would be gone, and it would be hard to track them down. He paused to check his surroundings. The short hallway he was in didn't reveal much. It was a typical back-of-house corridor. A noticeboard was nailed on the wall on the left; a fuse box was on the right. A fire extinguisher stood in one corner, and a stack of boxes against one wall. The corridor took a right turn only a few metres ahead of him, and he could see two doors. One led to the toilets, given the symbol on the door. The other had a cheap plastic plaque on it. As he approached slowly, listening for any sounds, he saw the word *Kitchen* was written on it. A break room for staff.

He wasn't convinced whoever he was chasing would hide in there. It would make much more sense to leg it out to the front of the shop and be gone. That was what he'd do, anyway.

Baton raised and ready, Charlie took the corner. The light from the back door had faded. He shivered at the thought of someone waiting in a shadow to pounce. He hoped he was ready if things went that way.

As he took the corner, he realised how small the building was. He was already at the back of the main shop floor. Grey daylight seeped through the windows, creating as many shadows as it dissolved, but he could make out six desks, three on each side. There were a few tall potted plants, some cabinets, a large printer and not much else. Nowhere for anyone to hide.

Edging forward into the open space, he ducked low to scan under the desks, half-expecting someone to be crouched beneath one. There was no one.

Charlie stood straight, baton still in hand but his grip more relaxed. 'Shit...' he muttered. Had he missed them? Could they have been that fast? Amelia wasn't even at the front of the building yet. They might have had enough time to get out the front of the property and be halfway down the street by now.

Then he saw the small bronze bell above the door to the letting agency, an old-fashioned piece of decor, there to ding whenever a customer entered. And presumably whenever one left too. He hadn't heard a bell in the last minute, and surely he would have. Even in the back corridor he should have heard it. Could the door be opened without it ringing? He supposed it was possible, but would the runner have taken the time to do that, since they knew he was on them?

His fingers tightened around the handle of the baton and he turned back to the small corridor. A figure lurched at him from the shadows, and a guttural scream tore through the silence. He raised the baton instinctively, quickly, but not quickly enough. Something heavy and cold connected with his forehead, and everything went black.

Dodging the rubbish in the alley and charging through the gate as fast as she could, Amelia skidded onto the pavement, thankful that there were no pedestrians around. As she sped towards the front of the estate agents, she realised she couldn't see anyone else at all. No one emerging from the building in a hurry, no one halfway down the road, bolting. Not even any cars. Surely they couldn't have been so fast that they had cleared the vicinity before she could get back to the street? The end of the road was a decent distance away, surely too far to have reached the corner and got out of sight so fast. And if that was the case, then whoever they had seen at the back was still in the building – with DI Palmer. She knew the detective was perfectly capable, but that didn't stop a dagger of panic slicing through her.

Breathing heavily as she reached the front door to the letting agency, she went to open it before realising that of course it was locked. With her nose pushed up to the glass as she had done earlier, Amelia attempted to see into the interior. She saw bits and pieces of furniture but no people. No Charlie.

Fuck, what do I do?

Quickly, she considered her options. She could go around the back again, hope that Charlie was fine and that he had captured their suspect. But that would take her precious minutes that she wasn't convinced she had. What if Charlie wasn't okay? Or what if their runner was trapped, but her going around back opened up an escape route?

No, she couldn't let that happen.

She took a step back, glad she had heavy-duty boots on, and aimed a kick squarely at the lock of the door. It shook, didn't give way, but it looked flimsy. She took a deep breath and tried again, putting as much weight and momentum behind her foot as possible. The door swung in with a crunch, the windowpane cracking, and she stumbled forward. Quickly righting herself, Amelia called out for Charlie. No answer came, and she felt a knot in her throat. She pulled her baton from her waistband and entered the property, holding the weapon out, ready to strike. She had only made it a few metres inside when she saw the fire extinguisher lying on the floor. Dark circles dotted the beige carpet. She knew it was blood. Not a lot, but enough.

'DI Palmer! Can you hear me?' she yelled, panic flooding through her.

Then she heard tyres screeching on gravel. Instinct took over and she shot through the letting agency, barrelling down the small corridor that led to the back of the building. The back door was wide open. As she ran out into the cold daylight, she could just make out the back of the van, disappearing round the end of the shop units.

She called for Charlie again but knew he was gone, that he was in the back of the vehicle. Knew that it had been his blood.

'Charlie!' she screamed, but she was too late.

DI Palmer was gone.

CHAPTER TWENTY

S arah and Angelica sat in silence in Sarah's living room. It had started raining outside, the dark afternoon already segueing into an even darker evening. It was as though the weather had read the room and adapted to match it.

They had cups of tea on the table in front of them. Both drinks remained untouched, already cold. But the whisky Sarah had bought for her dad but had never got around to giving him, that was going down well. Angelica held her glass as if it was the only thing in the world keeping her alive.

Sarah stared at her friend, taking her in. Angelica was always confident, overly talkative. She always had an opinion but was nevertheless stubbornly positive too. And there was rarely a problem to which she couldn't suggest a solution. Looking at Angelica now was like looking at another person entirely. Sarah thought she looked absent, as though her inner self had drifted away and left the shell of her friend behind.

Angelica wasn't mute; the shock hadn't taken away her ability to speak. Her desire to, however, had vanished. Since they had left the police station she had barely said a word, responded to Sarah with grunts or one-word answers. It was an

Angelica that Sarah didn't know how to deal with. It was unsettling.

Sarah felt guilty. Some of this was her fault. If she hadn't joined that stupid women's group, none of this would have happened. Sure, technically she'd had nothing to do with Angelica going to Cally Buchanan's house to perform that weird ritual, but she had made Angelica go to workshops at EnchantedWomenLDN, and if it weren't for that, then they would never have met Cally.

A small voice in Sarah's head was trying to tell her that this wasn't her fault, wasn't about her, and that the women's centre was not responsible either. Only Cally was. But of course it was always the small voice that got ignored, shouted down by the one that chose blame instead. Sarah felt horribly responsible.

There was also another voice, one she had not heard before, that had started questioning whether witches were in fact real. Whether magic really did exist. The logical side of her brain told Sarah that this woman had something to do with Richie's death. She didn't just swish a wand or sacrifice a chicken and have a man drop dead as a result. Not this new voice, though. It was whispering to her that maybe the ritual that Angelica made Cally perform had actually done something. Sarah shivered.

Her phone buzzed, and she grabbed it from the table. It was Mike, and she felt relieved for the distraction. She had told him the basics and he was checking in. She couldn't believe how good he was being. He genuinely seemed to have changed since the first time they had gone out, even though she still half-expected him to vanish again. Once burned and all that.

Not wanting to chat over text, Sarah got off the sofa to head into the kitchen so she could speak to Mike in private. As she stood she glanced at Angelica, who took a sip of whisky but didn't even seem to register that Sarah had moved. Her eyes were glassy, staring into nothing. It sent another shiver down Sarah's spine.

She left the living room and dialled Mike's number.

'Hey, gorgeous, how are you holding up?' Mike answered. She felt a physical relief at the sound of his voice.

'I'm okay. A little shaken still. This whole situation is so fucked up.'

'And how's Angelica? Did she really do it – attend that witchcraft ritual thing?'

'She must have. She told the police everything.'

'It's like something out of *American Horror Story*,' Mike said. 'Who does that? Who goes to the house of some crazy woman who's claiming to be a witch? I thought Angelica was more sensible than that.'

Sarah had thought that too not that long ago. 'Richie must have really done a number on her.'

'That's the dead guy, right?'

'Yes. The third victim, I think, according to the press, presuming it's related to those other ritual killings. It's terrifying to even think about it. This isn't supposed to happen to people you know.'

'Look, I'm stuck at work until about seven, but do you want me to come over after that?'

'Ange is probably still going to be here. She doesn't know we're back together yet.'

'She has to find out some time, Sarah. I know she hates me at the moment, but she'll come round. Anyway, there are more important things happening.'

Sarah thought about that. In her current state, Angelica probably wouldn't even notice Mike standing in front of her waving in her face. But even if she was annoyed, Mike was right. She would be fine after a while, especially once she saw that Sarah was happy. She was a good friend. And maybe she wouldn't even care, not after what she had been through in the past few days.

'Okay. But can you bring some food? And some wine? I think we'll need it.'

'Of course. Text you when I'm leaving work.'

They said goodbye and Sarah hung up, her body sagging against the kitchen counter. Outside the rain continued to pound down, tracing watery snakes down the window and the glass pane in the back door to the garden Sarah shared with her upstairs neighbour. She glanced outside, chilled by the overt coldness of the world, before turning away and heading back to the living room. She needed another sip or two of whisky herself.

She didn't notice the small parcel that had been pinned to the window frame on the outside. Rainwater ran off it. If she had, then maybe she would have seen that the parcel seemed to be made out of skin. Maybe she would have spotted that it was bound and entwined with hair. Human hair.

Amelia Harding had only just stopped crying by the time Daniel met her at the office. Just an hour ago, he thought his day had got as bad as it was going to, what with Molly being threatened and the apparent reappearance of the man who had been taunting him for months. But Amelia had destroyed that notion with one phone call. Charlie was gone, and no one knew where he had been taken.

'We'll find him, Amelia, you know we will,' Daniel said, trying to sound reassuring even though his mind was racing and his heart pounding with fear and confusion. 'And it's not your fault. You know that, right?'

Amelia nodded, wiping her eyes, but he knew it would take

more than that for her to believe it, to accept that it really hadn't been her fault.

Daniel left Amelia in the good hands of a woman called Abigail who worked in their HR department and specialised in counselling people in the armed forces. He suspected that Amelia would need a few sessions to come to terms with what had happened, although of course time would help too. He had benefited from similar in the past. Therapy had saved him when he was younger, after the incident with Adam Spencer, the one that had altered the course of his life. His sister's too.

He was sure Amelia would feel better soon. She was strong and had a lot of heart: he knew she'd bounce back. He held on to that feeling as he left her with Abigail, knowing he couldn't focus on her, not with everything else that was happening.

Patrick Siadatan, who led the IT forensics team, had already gathered CCTV footage from the Limehouse area. Daniel hurriedly made his way down to the tech department. As soon as he saw Patrick, he launched in. 'Have you found him? Have you found the van? Do we know where it went yet?'

'Breathe, Daniel, okay?' Patrick said. If it hadn't been for the concern on Patrick's face, Daniel would have snapped at him, but he knew Patrick was a good guy and wasn't being condescending. He also knew he looked manic. At least he knew that Molly was safe.

'Yeah, sorry. I'm trying. But please tell me you have something.'

Patrick pointed to one of the monitors behind him. On the screen was a van. It was a dark blue, no branding anywhere on it that he could see. The picture was blurry, making it impossible to get a clear view of the licence plate.

'That's our van. We have a few other shots of it moving through Tower Hamlets, but none yet where we can see the plate. Looks like it was heading towards Bromley. We don't know where it went yet, but we've put out requests to expand CCTV access. As soon as we have something I'll let you know.'

'Shit. Not what I wanted to hear. Thanks, though. I appreciate your hard work.'

Patrick simply nodded, offering a sympathetic smile. 'He's one of us, Daniel. We won't rest on this, I promise you.'

'I know. But still, thank you. While I've got you, did your guys manage to dig up anything on Cally Buchanan?'

Patrick smiled more widely. 'Actually, yes. I was waiting until Shaun had pulled a full report together, but seeing as you're here... Shaun!' Patrick called across the office floor before instructing Daniel to follow him. They stopped at a cluttered desk, where a man who looked no older than twenty-three sat, surrounded by bottles of Lucozade, an empty bag of sweet chilli crisps, and other wrappers.

'Shaun, come on – clean desk, clean mind,' Patrick said, stooping to retrieve a bin next to the young man. He swept a hand over the desk, and the rubbish fell into the bin.

'Sorry, sir. I just get sucked in.'

'How's the report on the Buchanan woman going? This is Detective Inspector Graves – he needs to know what we do.'

'Graves? Really?' Shaun said before blushing and apologising.

'I know – ironic, isn't it? Let's move on, shall we?' Daniel said briskly. 'Buchanan?'

'Right, yes, of course. Sorry. I'm not quite done, but I have a lot already. I got all of her data from that women's workshop place – amazing how willing they were to give me it all. But it was mostly fake. She gave them a fake address, contact details and all that. She wasn't that smart, though. She paid with her actual credit card so I tracked her that way instead, and man, did that open up some interesting stuff. I got her real address, her bank details, her phone number. Also the address of her parents in Derby. But, better than that, I got into her Facebook account. She doesn't post anything, hasn't in years, it looks like, but you know how social media is connected to everything these days? Like for logins and cookies and stuff? So dodgy. God, even WhatsApp listens to you, then uses what you've said to show you targeted ads. Proper Big Brother shit. Helpful for me. Turns out she is a full-on witch. At least, she thinks she is.'

Daniel had to admit he was impressed – both with what Shaun had already found out and also by how much information he could impart in a single breath. Clearly he really had been sucked into the project.

'Yep, that fits given what we know. Go on,' Daniel urged.

'Great. So obviously witches are bullshit, right? I mean, we're not in an episode of *Charmed* or *Buffy*. But the point is, she believes it, and it tracks through everything she does. She's a member of loads of so-called covens on Facebook, and her search history – what I can access, anyway – is all about rituals and spells. But better still, her spending is all witchy stuff too. She's bought all these herbs and books and pots and crap off the internet, all visible on her banking records. Woman is full-on hocus-pocus. Only thing she hasn't bought is a broomstick.'

Shaun laughed at this and looked at Patrick and Daniel for approval. Neither of them gave him what he was hoping for, just stern looks, so he carried on. 'Once I found all this stuff out, I started running a bespoke algorithm to try and connect it all, to build up a web of all of her interests and behaviours, and that's where it gets super-interesting.'

'That is?' Daniel asked, surprised that Shaun considered everything that had come before to be mundane.

'Yep. See, us knowing she's a witch, not that helpful, right? We already figured that out based on her profile and the crime scenes and stuff. But see, witches belong to groups.'

'Covens, like you said?' Patrick stated.

'Yes, exactly. But Buchanan doesn't keep it all online. She's a member of a real coven. They have a website and everything. It's password-protected but naturally that didn't stop me. The site and the actual coven are called the Devil's Mark. Turns out that's one of the ways people used to identify witches in the olden days. If a woman they thought was a witch had a mole or birthmark, they'd claim it was the mark of the devil, then burn her or drown her. This coven seems to have kind of reclaimed the term, taken back ownership of it, if you get what I mean.'

Shaun looked down at his desk and began searching through the notes and papers scattered across it. He grabbed one and brandished it at Daniel. It was a list of names.

'That's everyone who's a member of her coven. I don't know if she set it up or not, but she's certainly one of the more active members – and yeah, all these people think they're witches.'

'Holy shit... Shaun, this is amazing. Our other suspect could be on here. The one who took Charlie. We know Buchanan can't have been working alone. God, any number of these people could have helped her. Can you find any info on them?'

'Already started, although I don't have much yet. I'll let you know if I find anything helpful.'

'Great, thank you.' A thought struck Daniel as he scanned the list of names on the printout. 'Can you tell if any of these people work as estate agents?'

Shaun rolled his eyes, as though Daniel had just asked him if he knew how to breathe. He turned to his computer and began to tap at the keyboard. A box popped up on the screen with flowing code that Daniel couldn't read. Then another.

It took Shaun all of two minutes. 'This one does. Natalie Hastings.'

'In Limehouse?' Daniel asked, his heart pounding.

Shaun nodded. 'Petersons.'

'Our second suspect! My God, it must have been her.

Natalie Hastings must have been the one who kidnapped Charlie!' Daniel exclaimed. He turned to Patrick, and was surprised to see that Patrick didn't look excited by the news. Rather, he looked like he had tuned out.

'Patrick? Come on, this is what we needed. You can track Charlie with this, surely.'

'Hmm? Yes, sorry, it's fantastic. Well done, Shaun. It's just... that surname. I've seen it somewhere else recently.'

'Hastings? Are you sure?'

'Actually, I have as well,' Shaun said. Again he tapped at his keyboard, but this time his results were even quicker. 'Here it is. Beatrice Hastings.'

'Who's that?' Daniel asked.

'The woman who set up the business place in Deptford. EnchantedWomenLDN,' Shaun answered.

'Fuck me,' Daniel muttered, as puzzle pieces started to fall into place.

The woman behind the reception desk looked terrified when Daniel demanded to speak to Beatrice Hastings in relation to a murder investigation, but his stern approach worked. Daniel, Amelia, another sergeant called Amrit Malik, who Daniel knew of but had never met before, and four other officers had paid a visit to the EnchantedWomenLDN building. Even though the centre offered numerous evening workshops and meets, it was quiet, which Daniel was glad about. This case had drawn a huge amount of press attention over the past fortnight, and he could do without the press finding out that a detective inspector had been kidnapped. Nonetheless, he and his team had to work fast. If anything happened to Charlie, he would never forgive himself.

Beatrice Hastings was in her office, smoking, despite numerous signs around the building instructing people not to. Daniel watched her for a few seconds through the large window. The woman was tall, elegantly dressed, her long red hair perfectly styled. She looked like the type of person who was always well put together and always in control, but the smoking and her worry lines suggested some cracks in her composure. Daniel hoped he could make them bigger to find out what the hell was going on.

'Malik, you good to stay out here? I don't want any interruptions.'

Amrit did a quick captain's salute. 'Sure thing, sir!'

'Amelia, I want you in the room with me.'

Amelia nodded. She seemed to have recovered from the events of just a few hours ago, and Daniel was glad she was there. He told her she could take time out if she needed to, but she had refused. She said she needed to work, needed to help him find Charlie. He had been concerned that she wasn't ready, but he knew he would do exactly the same. In a way, he was. He had been desperate to go on the hunt for Greg Armstrong, but had forgotten about that the second he had heard about Charlie.

'Let's do it.'

He and Amelia entered Beatrice Hasting's office. She stubbed her cigarette out. 'Sorry, horrid, I know, especially indoors. But as I'm sure you can imagine, you wanting to talk to me about a murder is a bit of a shock.'

Daniel offered a quick smile of understanding. He would be professional, of course, but he just wanted to get to the point. Beatrice sat down behind her desk. Daniel sat opposite while Amelia remained standing, her arms crossed as she looked over the office.

'I know we've told you we're here about a murder investigation, but let's get to the details.'

'The ritual murders, am I correct? I read the papers, watch the news. I've seen your name in a few stories. How can I help?'

It took Daniel by surprise that she knew who he was, but he imagined that a lot of people in London had heard of him and Charlie if they paid any attention to the news.

'I'm afraid so. I won't go into details of the murders, but your name came up in relation to your daughter. Natalie Hastings.'

Beatrice sighed and sat back in her chair, her posture not so much relaxed as resigned. Daniel had expected more shock. It didn't come.

'I did wonder, despite the thought making me feel ill. I honestly don't know where I went wrong with that girl. She's... difficult, for want of a better way to put it. Always has been. In fact, to tell you the truth, although I feel horrible about this, her father and I have pretty much washed our hands of her. We've tried our best, but it's exhausting trying to help someone so committed to doing the opposite of everything you say all the time. But... murder? Really?'

Despite the question, something about Beatrice's expression led Daniel to believe that somehow she had long ago resigned herself to the inevitability of this conversation.

'Your daughter seems to be involved in, well, witchcraft, and our main suspect seems to be part of the same coven. They call themselves the Devil's Mark. The ex-girlfriend of the latest murder victim comes to workshops here, so you can imagine why we're interested in talking to you. You don't seem as surprised as I would have expected. Why is that?'

'I'm sorry, I know Natalie is involved in... that sort of thing – the dark arts and such. It's nothing new. It's caused us some problems in the past. She made voodoo dolls of one of our neighbours and hung them from the tree in our front garden once. She bullied other girls at her senior school, and drew satanic symbols and wrote quite horrid quotes on their desks and lockers. She's even been arrested a few times. She's quite the militant feminist, if I'm allowed to say that – hates pretty much all men. And the types of protests she has joined in, vandalism she has committed, have all been quite extreme. It's a miracle she's never been charged with anything before. Hence I'm not surprised that you're here,' she said. 'But she doesn't come here – she has no involvement with EnchantedWomenLDN. She once told me that I should study witchcraft myself if I really wanted to support women, called this place stupid. Didn't care how insulting that was. Still... even with all that, murder? Who is she in a coven with? God, what a ridiculous question to have to ask. And who is the woman who knows the victim?' She frowned.

'I can't tell you the member's name, but our suspect and apparent fellow witch is Cally Buchanan,' Daniel answered flatly.

'Oh.' Beatrice said, her mouth pinching. Daniel clocked the reaction immediately. It seemed that Beatrice wasn't a fan of Buchanan.

'So you know her, then,' Amelia said.

'That's her on the wall there,' Beatrice said, pointing to a framed photo to Amelia's right. 'She's the small one in all the purple and black. I should have guessed right away who it was when you said Natalie was in a coven with someone here. It could only be Cally.'

Amelia stepped over to the photo to get a look at their suspect.

'Can we take that?' Daniel asked.

Beatrice nodded. 'So you think Cally and my daughter are behind the ritual murders.' Her voice was low, and vibrated with stress.

'Yes, we do, and we have plenty of evidence against Buchanan too.'

'I just... can't imagine why either of them would murder anyone. Not even Cally, as odd as she is. Why on earth would they want to? Even given their belief in all that supernatural nonsense. Belief is one thing, but acting on it like this... are you sure?'

'We are sure, I'm afraid, yes. What I really need from you is information. Your daughter's whereabouts, anything pertinent about her or Cally Buchanan, and anything you can tell us that may lead to motive, whether you think it relevant or not.'

Beatrice looked away while she thought about it. She tucked a strand of red hair behind her ear and got a notepad and pen from her desk drawer. She scrawled something on it and handed it to Daniel. 'I don't know much about their relationship, or actually much about Cally as a person, but this is Natalie's address. I've never been there, but this is where I send birthday cards.'

Daniel thanked her.

'As to why either of them would do it... Maybe money? Lord knows she isn't getting a penny more from me, not after she wasted so much while treating me and her father the way she does, with utter disdain. As for Cally – maybe the woman genuinely thinks she is a witch. I don't know. Even with their... quirky ways, murder just seems so...'

It wasn't much to go on, but the address helped. Daniel didn't think he was going to get much more from the woman. He passed her a business card. 'Thank you. We'll be in touch. And if you hear from either Natalie or Cally, I want to know about it. Come on, Sergeant Harding.'

They left the office and pulled the door closed behind them. Glancing through the glass Daniel saw Beatrice lighting another cigarette.

'Malik, can you organise some surveillance on Mrs

Hastings? I'm not convinced she's involved, but you never know.'

'Yes, of course,' Amrit said.

'Let's go, Amelia. We need to go to this address.'

As they were heading down the metal staircase towards the entrance of the building Daniel suddenly cursed.

'What is it?' Amelia asked, stopping on the stairs and turning to him.

'I need to phone Kelly Malone, let her know.'

'Oh. Shit.'

'Yep.'

As they headed for Natalie Hastings' address in Stoke Newington, Amelia behind the wheel and another squad car behind them, Daniel plucked up the courage to call Kelly. He was against the very thought of talking to her, but he knew he had to. Just because he couldn't stand her, that didn't mean she was any less important to Charlie.

'Hello, you're speaking to Kelly Malone, *City Post*,' Kelly said.

Daniel cringed and took a deep breath. 'Hi, Kelly, this is DI Graves. I work with Charlie.'

'For God's sake, Daniel, don't be so formal. We've met, I know who you are.'

Daniel rubbed a finger and thumb over his forehead, already frustrated with her, though of course she was right. 'Yes, yes I know, my apologies.'

'Look, I'm pretty busy, what is it?'

He could hear rustling in the background and suspected she was barely even engaged in the call. 'It's about Charlie.'

'What about him? If you're calling to tell me to break up

with him, you can stop right there, Daniel. It's none of your busi–'

'He's missing, Kelly.'

There was silence. Daniel looked at Amelia.

'You have to tell her,' Amelia whispered.

'The case we're working on... it's got pretty serious and...' He was struggling to find the right words.

'Please, Daniel, just tell me what's going on. What do you mean, he's missing?' Kelly said, her voice much softer, shaky. He could hear the panic.

'He was going to question a possible suspect. Something went wrong and... he was kidnapped.'

'Oh my God!' Kelly exclaimed, her voice cracking. 'What... I just... Oh God, Charlie!'

'I know, I know. I'm as shaken as you are. But we'll find him, Kelly, I promise.'

'Shit... thank you, thank you, Daniel,' Kelly said.

She was crying, and his heart physically hurt for her.

'I'm... shit, this is horrible... I'm sorry I was so rude. I know what you think of me and...'

'Don't worry about that. I'll bring him back. I won't stop until I do.'

'Thank you. Please... keep me updated, okay?'

He assured her he would and hung up, wiping a tear from his eye. 'That was...' he muttered.

'We'll find him, Dan, we will,' Amelia said. 'We have to.'

He nodded, hoping she was right. He couldn't even think about the alternative.

CHAPTER TWENTY-ONE

'Fuck me, it's horrible out there,' Mike said as he hustled through the front door, handing Sarah Boyd a wet plastic bag full of food. He took his soaked leather jacket off and hung it up, wiping a hand over his forehead. His normally blond hair was dark and matted to his head.

Sarah leant in to kiss him, and a few drops of water landed on her nose. She didn't mind one bit. 'Thanks for coming.'

'I bought two bottles of wine – hope that's enough. Where is she? Is she going to flip out that I'm here?' he asked Sarah, peering behind her. He looked nervous and she was taken aback, not used to seeing him be anything other than irritatingly confident. This was not like the old Mike at all, who had been quite happy to trade barbs with Angelica the previous two times he had met her. The old Mike had bordered on obnoxious at times, too arrogant for his own good. She liked the change. It made him even more attractive.

'Honestly, I don't know what she'll do. She's in the living room, so I guess we'll find out.' She went to move, then stopped. 'You know, she has every right to not like you.'

Mike's face dropped and his shoulders sagged. This really

wasn't the same Mike. The old Mike would have laughed at the thought that he might even vaguely care. 'I know. Listen, I know we didn't really talk about it other than me saying sorry but... fuck, I was such a shit to you. I feel horrible. Really.' He took her hands in his, rain still dripping down his forehead. 'I was a dick. I mean, I was going through some things, family stuff and work. And that whole douche persona, that's not really me. No excuses, though. I was a total dick and I'm so sorry. I won't fuck up again.'

His eyes were wide, and Sarah thought she saw tears in them.

She smiled at him, squeezed his hands. 'Thank you. I appreciate that. You're right, you were a total dick, so don't do it again, yeah?' She went up on tiptoes to kiss him. 'Now, tell that to Ange too and hopefully you're golden.'

Sarah led Mike into the living room and took a deep breath. Angelica really didn't like Mike, and she was not someone to hold back her opinions. When she wasn't in shock, anyway.

'Ange, don't be mad, okay? Mike's here. He brought food and wine!' Sarah put the bag of takeaway food down on the coffee table and Mike pulled one of the bottles out from his bag.

'Ta-da!' he said with an awkward smile, brandishing a bottle of Sauvignon Blanc as though it were the answer to all life's problems.

Angelica glared up at him, then at Sarah. 'Really?'

Sarah almost laughed, filled with a sudden burst of relief to see some of the real Angelica for the first time since that morning.

'Really. He knows he was a dick, I do, you do. But yes, we're back together.'

Angelica shrugged but fixed her gaze on Mike again. 'Hurt her again and I'll track you down and kill you.' She clapped her hands to her mouth when she realised what she had said, and without warning the tears came thick and fast.

'Oh my God, I'm evil...' she sobbed. Sarah rushed to her side, dropping down on the sofa and wrapping an arm around her. 'Oh, babe, no, no you aren't! Come here.'

Angelica collapsed into Sarah. Over her shoulder, Sarah nodded at Mike, mouthing the word 'wine' at him. He took the hint and left them alone.

It took a minute for Angelica to calm down again, but calm she did. She rubbed a sleeve over her face. 'I'm so glad I'm here, not at home.' She sniffed.

'Of course. Stay here as long as you need – you know you can, right?'

'Even with Mike? Aren't you two all... you know?'

'I'm sure we can contain ourselves. And I have the spare room. I mean, it's full of laundry but there's a single bed with your name on it.' Sarah smiled before hugging her friend again, pulling her tight. She jumped when Mike appeared at the living-room door.

'You know your back door was open? There's water all over the floor.'

Sarah frowned. 'What? Are you sure?' She wriggled free of Angelica.

'Yeah, I just shut it. Want me to mop up?'

Sarah stood up, still confused. When had she last been in the kitchen? She swore the door had been shut. She and Angelica had been in the living room for at least the last half hour. She raised an eyebrow at Angelica.

'Not me. You know I've barely moved from this spot,' she said, wiping her nose.

'Weird,' Sarah muttered and nudged past Mike. She needed to see for herself. As she entered the kitchen, she felt water on her bare feet. Mike was right – the floor near the door was soaked and footprints were everywhere. 'Fuck's sake.'

'Sorry, I trekked it through the flat a bit,' Mike said, resting his hands on her shoulders. 'I'll clean it up, don't worry. Then I'll bring you wine and some plates and stuff. Where's your mop?'

'It's in the bathroom. I'll get it. I don't understand how the door was open, though. I swear I didn't leave it like that.' She padded out into the hallway, surprised that she hadn't noticed the flat getting colder. She was stepping into the bathroom when the lights in the flat went out, plunging them into a thick darkness.

All three of them cursed from their respective rooms.

'Is there a storm out there? Maybe that blew the door open,' she called to Mike. She could barely see her own hands in front of her; her eyes hadn't adjusted yet. There was a small window in her bathroom but it didn't let in much light. She cursed as she smacked her knee on the rim of the toilet. She could hear the rain battering the window, and was glad it was shut.

'It was pretty bad, maybe the weather took out the power,' he shouted back. 'Where's the fuse box?'

She paused to think. She rented, and her landlord was great so she rarely needed to worry about stuff like that. 'In the cupboard in the hall, I think. Next to the kitchen.'

Sarah blinked and saw that she could just make out the shapes in the bathroom, thanks to a glint of moonlight reflecting off the glass of the shower unit. She knew the mop was next to it and reached out.

She wasn't a fan of the dark. 'Hurry up, Mike.'

She flinched when she stepped in a puddle, and pulled her foot back. There were evidently wet prints everywhere, and she was annoyed that Mike had not taken his shoes off.

She heard a strange noise, like the sound of a struggle, then a scream charged through her. Guttural, it was like nothing she had ever heard. A thud followed, then a weak groan, then the flat went silent.

'Mike?' she called, the mop forgotten. Her heart pounded as she waited for him to answer.

'You okay, Mike?' she heard Angelica ask. Carefully, just about able to see the door frame, Sarah turned and went back into the hallway.

'Mike? Did you hurt yourself? I stacked a lot of stuff in there, sorry.'

Slowly she stepped forward, one hand trailing along the wall. Her foot came down in another puddle – sticky this time. It was warm too.

'Oh shit, Mike. What the hell happened?'

Something grabbed at her ankle and she screamed and yanked her foot back. She skidded and stumbled forward, landing hard on the floor. Her hands went out instinctively to save her. One landed in more warm sticky liquid. The other landed on fabric, a body. Even as Sarah struggled to figure out what was going on, she heard Angelica scream.

'Fuck, Sarah, there's someone in here!'

Another thud, followed by the sound of a glass shattering.

'Ange?'

'Sarah, help! No, get away!'

Someone grunted, then the sound of furniture being shoved aside groaned through the dark. Sarah pushed herself off the floor, tears streaming down her face as she registered that it was Mike lying in front of her. There was blood everywhere and she fell forward again, feeling it smearing up her arms. She could smell it now too, and fought to stop herself being sick.

'Oh God, Mike, please make a sound,' she whimpered.

Angelica screamed just metres from her, then fell quiet.

'NO!' Sarah yelled. She managed to stand up and staggered

to the living-room door, feeling the effects of pure fear mixed with the afternoon's whisky in her veins. Someone charged at her, slamming her against the wall behind her. Hot breath washed over her face and she fell sideways, tripping over Mike. Sarah scrambled across the laminate, the blood under her hands making her slide. She was just a metre from the front door when something heavy connected with the back of her head, knocking her out cold.

CHAPTER TWENTY-TWO

Three squad cars had accompanied Daniel Graves and Amelia Harding to the address of suspect number two, Natalie Hastings. Red and blue filters spun over the street with the energy of a carnival as inside the house Daniel and his team ransacked each room. Superintendent Hobbs had granted a search warrant immediately. Things moved much faster than normal when one of their own was in danger. Daniel was eternally grateful that he hadn't had to wait around. Finding Charlie was his top priority.

Natalie Hastings was not home when they arrived. After six people had hunted through the small terraced house for almost an hour, they had still found nothing of use to the investigation. Daniel slumped on the sofa in the living room, trying desperately to convince himself that he still had hope.

'I thought for certain we'd find something. Beyond a few fake skulls and black candles, anyway,' Amelia said from across the room, where she was perched on the windowsill. Outside, the night was thick and oppressive.

'Me too. After what Shaun found out, I have no doubt

Natalie Hastings is involved with Cally Buchanan, and it had to be Hastings you saw at the estate agent.'

'What I don't get is why they're doing this. Either the murders or why they took DI Palmer.'

Daniel could hear the worry in Amelia's voice, and knew it only too well. His inner voice sounded exactly the same. He also thought she was likely still blaming herself.

'I figure they took Charlie because they panicked. He saw someone, presumably Hastings. We hadn't identified her yet but suddenly we knew what she looked like. She hid, attacked him to avoid being arrested, then panicked when she saw she had an unconscious detective in front of her.'

'I guess that pans out. She must have struggled, given Charlie's size, but yeah, the panicking makes sense.'

'But the murders? I don't know. Angelica Okeke went to Buchanan for revenge. Stupid magic bullshit, sure, but that was why. Clearly Buchanan and Hastings decided to follow through with what their ritual claimed to do.'

'So they told Okeke that magic would get rid of Richie, then – what? Killed him to follow up on their promise?' Amelia asked. 'That's... I don't know what that is. Psychotic.'

Daniel stood, watching one of the assisting officers search the drawers of the bureau next to the dining table, knowing he'd already looked in there once.

'Clearly one or both of them is unstable – mentally, I mean. Either they believe they are witches, like actual servants of darkness, or they're simply murderers who use the witch stuff as a cover-up.'

'Fucking weird cover-up.'

Daniel laughed, a nervous, scared sound. It was all so strange. If these women really did believe they were witches, it would explain a lot, especially the ritualistic crime scenes. It didn't entirely explain why they were killing, however. Every victim so far had been male, and Daniel still thought that the murders might revolve around a hatred of men or as revenge against bad men, but that remained conjecture.

Each of the victims so far had also been less than pleasant, but all in very different ways. The first had been involved in something dodgy concerning money, although who had commissioned the women to kill, and how they had known about such a service, was unknown. The second might have been a cheat – not ordered for death but killed by Hastings and Buchanan anyway. The third had been abusive. Maybe it did all fit. Maybe that really was it. There had been a lot of talk in recent years about men owning up to all the shit they had been able to get away with previously. Were these women simply taking things a step further? It was extreme.

He thought about the possibility that the witchcraft angle was just decoration. He couldn't see why anyone would choose to use it to cover up killings, though. It didn't ring true. Either these killers thought they were witches, or they were using witchcraft to make a point.

His mind filled with mental images of the crime scenes, the blood, the exposed bones and chunks of flesh, and he gagged at the thought of Charlie ending up the same way. 'Okay, this is doing us no good. Right now, why they're doing this is not important. The fact is, they are, and they have Charlie. We have to find him quickly.'

'But how?' Amelia asked.

He was about to answer with a frustrated shrug when a picture on the wall above the bureau caught his eye. It showed a woman dressed in black standing on a misty moor, looking out over the countryside. Above her, a storm was coming. The painting was bleak and moody. It fit right in with what they knew about Natalie Hastings.

'Oh my God, of course!'

Amelia frowned. 'What? What did I miss?'

'Think about it. These women are obsessed with witches, correct? They have been copying symbols and rituals, and their online footprints show they read up on everything related to witches. They named their coven after an old way to identify witches. And what do we know about witches?'

'They were hunted. Burned at the stake. They fly around on brooms, love cauldrons. How is that helpful?'

'Well, it's not, not those bits anyway.'

Amelia shrugged. 'Then I don't get it.'

'Molly told me that the UK had just as many witch trials as America. And in London, there were witch hunts for years. Right in the centre of the city. If you were a witch now, in modern-day London, and a murderer, and you had already begun to escalate your murders, what would you do?'

Amelia's eyes lit up as she realised what he was getting at. 'Oh shit! They kidnapped Charlie and they know we're getting closer. If they think they're going to get caught anyway, then there's a good chance they'll go out with a bang. Something big and symbolic.'

'Exactly. The second crime scene was pretty public, and the third was even more so. If I'm right, then this time...' He grabbed his phone from his pocket to make a call. 'Molly! I need a favour as fast as possible. I need a list of all the most famous spots in London related to witchcraft. The big ones. Fast as you can.'

He thanked her and hung up, saw Amelia's face filled with determination. His heart soared. This was it, he knew it. Maybe he didn't know why these women were doing what they were doing, but if he was right then maybe he could end things once and for all. He prayed he wasn't making a mistake.

Molly had initially felt awkward being in Daniel's flat without him there. It was odd, weirdly intrusive. The fact that she was there for her own safety and there was a policeman sitting in a car right outside didn't make it any better. She had been at loose ends. As soon as Daniel had called, though, her worry was out the window. She suddenly had a task, one that distracted her and that was right up her street.

There was not one book in Daniel's flat that would help her. She knew the campus library would be better suited to the task, but there was no time to waste. At least she had his computer and a decent internet connection. She could do the research right there.

Sitting at the desk in his living room, Molly gathered everything she needed. A notepad and pen, a bottle of white wine she found in Daniel's fridge, plus some Brie and crackers. She hoped the wine and snacks would help calm her nerves. She had initially considered not taking anything, but then dismissed her worry. The way she and Daniel were, the instant closeness they had, she figured she was basically his girlfriend already. Plus she was in his flat alone, helping with his case. If nothing else, that deserved some wine and cheese. She just wished he was with her.

Securing her hair in a messy but efficient bun and sipping her wine, Molly started to think about everything she knew about witch trials in London. She knew a fair amount, but it wasn't her speciality. It turned out the internet could tell her a whole lot more.

Witches and sorcery in general had been a big deal in the mid-sixteenth century after Henry VIII had passed a Witchcraft Act, effectively giving permission for witch hunts to take place, but records went back as far as the tenth century. Trials had occurred across the country in all sorts of places.

London, as a hub of activity, had seen its fair share. This included some of the most famous incidents.

There were numerous websites that discussed witches in London, some going into extensive detail, and as Molly started to dig into each story, taking notes as she went, she quickly compiled a list of reports that included almost every central borough.

'How the hell am I going to narrow this down?' she said. She slumped back in her seat and took a bite of the Brie, barely even tasting it.

There was so much riding on her assisting Daniel, she could really feel the pressure. His partner had been kidnapped and she had to help figure out where he may have been taken. This was an entirely new experience for her. The most pressure she'd faced before was either passing her own exams or ensuring her students passed theirs.

She got up, wine in hand, and began to pace the living room. What had started as a simple assist on the case a fortnight ago had led to a boyfriend and the hunt for two killers. It was all so wildly out of the norm, yet Molly had to admit there was something about the pressure that she quite liked. She was getting a kick out of the adrenaline. She wondered if Daniel got that too, assumed he must. He was passionate about his job.

'Okay, Detective Molly Goodings. It's your turn to find the killers,' she said before taking a seat at the computer again. After a few minutes of silence, her thoughts going nowhere, the buzz had started to dissipate.

'Shit, this is hard,' she muttered. She continued her research, discovering more about witches in the city, hoping something would stand out, focusing on some of the higher-profile stories.

A woman and her son had been thrown into the Thames near London Bridge as punishment for supposed witchcraft. In

Southwark a man had been found with a skull and a severed head, was accused of practising spells but had not been charged. A man had been stoned to death at St Paul's, accused of rape and the invoking of demons.

Molly circled St Paul's on the pad. That one was pretty big. Something about it didn't feel right, though. For one thing, it was a man who had been killed, and she knew the suspects were women. Also, despite the demonic association, did it fit into witchcraft? She was sure it could be argued as such, but she trusted her gut and kept looking.

It wasn't until half an hour – and another glass of wine – later that she stumbled across something harder to ignore, a name she had heard of but didn't know anything about.

Margery Jourdain had lived in London in the 1400s and had been called a witch her whole life. Nicknamed 'The Witch of Eye' due to her fortune-telling, Margery had officially been charged with being a witch in 1432 for carrying out rituals of divination. The charges were dropped and she was released on bail. That was not the end of the story, however. Nine years later she was charged with using magic and witchcraft in an attempt on the life of Henry VI, working alongside four others. The combination of treason and her history of apparent sorcery were enough for her to be charged.

For Molly, there was one detail of this story that proved to be the kicker. Burning witches at the stake was not something that had happened in the United Kingdom. As it turned out, Margery Jourdain was the exception. After being found guilty of both treason and practising witchcraft she was sentenced to death by burning – one of the only people ever accused of the craft to be killed in this way. It made her unique.

Molly quickly scanned the website she was on, absorbing every detail until she spotted what she needed. She phoned Daniel.

'Oh thank God – please tell me you have something,' he said.

'I think you should look at Smithfield Market,' she said. 'And Daniel, you need to be fast. I think they may try to kill Charlie by burning him alive. At the stake.'

There was silence for a second. Molly thought the line had been cut. 'Daniel? You still there?'

'Sorry, yes. Listen, Molly, are you sure? We don't have much time.'

'Sure? No. God, I don't know, Dan. I can't say for certain. After all my research into famous witches in central London, it's the most likely option I could find. These women would definitely know of the story if they're as steeped in witchcraft as we think, but... I'm sorry I can't be more sure.'

'Don't be silly. It's really helpful. And it's our only lead, location-wise. Thank you.'

'Of course. Good luck, Dan,' she said. The call ended, and she knew Daniel was already off to try to corroborate what she had said.

Again she sat back and ate some cheese, but this time she felt more worried than anything else. What if she was wrong? What if she had sent them on a wild goose chase and something happened to Charlie? She wasn't a detective, after all.

'Fuck, how do you do this for a living, Daniel?' she groaned before taking a gulp of wine.

She jumped when a knock at the door broke the quiet of the flat.

Wine still in hand, Molly got up and headed to the front door. There was a peephole and she peered through, conscious that she had to be careful, reminding herself that just a few hours earlier someone had broken into her flat and left a clear threat for her. One she had ignored.

'Hello?' she said, seeing the warped shape of a man standing on the other side. He was soaking, his clothes dark and glistening.

'Hi there. My apologies, it's Officer Baker. Sorry to bother you, but could I use the bathroom? I had too much coffee in the car and it's gone straight through me.'

'Oh yes, of course. One sec.'

Daniel's alarm system was set and Molly knew she needed the code, otherwise the alarm would go off when she opened the door. He'd texted it to her earlier in the day, so she skipped back into the living room to grab her phone. Something made her pause, and she leant around the desk to look out at the street. The rain was heavy but she could still make out the police car, empty now that Officer Baker was on the step outside.

She unlocked her phone, found the code and headed back to the alarm system. She was about to punch in the first number when she hesitated again. She turned back to the door.

'Sorry, just being cautious, but could I see your ID?' she asked, peering through the eye hole.

'Of course. There's no need to apologise,' Baker said. He put his hand in his jacket and pulled out his ID, held it up to the door.

Molly couldn't see it properly. There was very little light and the photo seemed faded, but it did kind of look like the man on the other side of the door, as far as she could tell. Soaking wet, at night, and through a peephole, it was hard to be certain. She hadn't paid much attention to what the two officers who had driven her home looked like, and was angry with herself for not being able to remember him for certain.

He smiled then, hopping a bit on the spot.

'Sorry, I don't mean to be rude but I'm really desperate. I'll only be a minute.'

'Shit,' she whispered. She didn't feel happy letting him in, but then who the hell else could he be if not the policeman who had been watching the flat all evening? She would feel terrible making him pee outside in the pouring rain.

'Okay, sorry, hang on.' Molly thought quickly, ran to the kitchen and grabbed a knife from one of the drawers, putting her wine on the counter. If she was wrong, then great, but on the off chance the man was not who he claimed, then she was prepared. It was a compromise, sure, but better than nothing. She returned to the front door and entered the alarm code.

With a deep breath, one hand holding the knife behind her back, she twisted the latch and opened the door, stepping back as she did so. The look of relief on the man's face was clear.

'You're a lifesaver, thanks so much. Would you mind pointing me in the right direction?' Baker asked, shaking himself as he stepped over the threshold and into the flat. Keeping her distance, Molly offered an understanding smile.

'Sorry I'm so wet. What a horrible night, huh?'

'No worries. Just down the hall on the left.'

He grinned and hotfooted it in the direction she had pointed. Seconds later she heard the toilet seat go up, and she pushed the front door shut to stop any more cold and rain from coming in. Remembering her wine, she headed back to the kitchen, quietly moving past the bathroom. She heard a flush and had just entered the kitchen when Baker emerged.

'Thank you – so much better!' he said with a smile. 'Promise I won't bother you again.' He offered her a thumbs-up and she smiled back, watching him head towards the front door before turning back to retrieve her drink. She sighed with relief when she heard the front door shut. Taking a gulp to calm herself, Molly brushed off any residual nerves, let her shoulders drop and put the knife back in the drawer. Research done and Baker back outside, she could relax – as much as possible under the circumstances, anyway. Back in the living room, she put her wine down on the coffee table and was about to turn on the television when she remembered the alarm system.

The code still in her mind, Molly went back to the alarm unit and pushed the digits in order. The system gave a satisfying beep and blipped green to signal that it had been reset. The flat was secure again.

'Sorted,' she said, turning around.

Baker loomed over her, grinning wildly, stealing her breath. The knife flashed through the air and found flesh as it came down, puncturing its screaming victim.

CHAPTER TWENTY-THREE

The air felt bitingly cold, but Charlie wasn't sure if that was what had woken him. It could have been the sound of rain hammering down on a roof high above him. It sounded heavy and aggressive, almost alive.

When Charlie came to, he shuffled into a seated position. His head was pounding. He tried to touch a finger to his skin to find the source of the pain, then realised that his hands were bound behind him. His mouth had also been taped up. He felt a flash of panic.

A sharp bolt of pain lanced through his skull.

Maybe that's what woke me up, he thought.

Trying not to lose his shit, Charlie racked his brains for an explanation for his current situation. He seemed to be in some sort of cage, bound and gagged. It was night-time, freezing cold, and clearly pissing it down, although he wasn't wet.

He recalled being rushed. Someone had attacked him, hit him with something.

At the estate agent.

'Shit,' he mumbled behind the duct tape.

The suspect he had been after. Clearly they had attacked

him and kidnapped him. But where the hell was he? And where had they bought the cages? They looked like ones he'd seen holding tigers and other big cats on TV before.

His vision was still hazy, and there was little light in the immediate vicinity. He blinked a few times, trying to focus. As his sight adjusted, he started to make out some details.

The cage he was sitting in was in a wide-open space. Indoors, under shelter, but open to the elements on two sides. Despite the sheets of rain pounding down outside he could see a few streetlights, the outlines of one or two buildings.

He could also see fencing and walls. The entire space was walled off, closed to any passers-by, with sections of fencing inside and also blocking off the sides open to the night. It didn't make sense at first. And then he registered the stalls. Some were covered with tarpaulin sheets, while some consisted of just a table built into a box-like frame, but he knew now what the space was. A market. At least, during the day. At night and in the middle of a rainstorm, it was deserted. Except for him, sitting in a cage.

Charlie heard a muffled whimper. There was someone else! He wasn't alone. He felt his heart rate rise.

The noise had come from behind him, and he twisted awkwardly, the metal bars pressing painfully into his shoulders.

Just a few metres away were two more cages. Both had occupants. He couldn't see the person in the furthest cage, but the woman in the cage closest to him was familiar, he knew. But how?

As though on cue, a memory flashed into his brain. A photo in an email. Daniel had sent him something. A picture of a woman.

'Miff Okeke?' he tried to say. His words were muffled. The woman locked eyes with him. She nodded, and he thought he saw a glint of tears on her cheeks.

'Uck me,' he mumbled, as the reality of his situation came all too clearly into view.

Evidently the suspect he had chased had panicked, and that was why he had been taken. Either that or they really were psychotic and wanted him out of the way.

As for the woman, as far as Charlie could recall, her ex-boyfriend had been one of the victims, chosen after she went to Cally Buchanan to hold some insane ritual. Clearly they hadn't liked that and had kidnapped her too. He presumed the third person in a cage, beyond Angelica Okeke, had also either pissed them off or at least got in the way.

Now the big question was, what the hell would happen next? Three people in three cages in the black of night. A rainstorm keeping everyone indoors. A space absent of passers-by and surrounded by fencing, but that would be full of people again by the early morning. Added all together, Charlie could only come up with one answer.

He, Okeke and whoever else had been locked up with them were to be the next victims, and they only had a few hours. The thought made him sick and he felt faint. He willed himself not to pass out, took a few slow breaths through his nose.

'Ink, Arlie, ink,' he muttered. The first thing he needed to do was free himself a little. He needed to get his hands out from behind him. He knew it was possible, had seen plenty of people do it on television and in films. He pulled his legs up towards him, his knees touching his chin, then worked his hands down under him until they were under his knees. Then he tried to get his feet through the loop of his arms. His wrists caught at the heels of his shoes. Despite all the time he spent at the gym, Charlie wasn't that flexible and he groaned with discomfort as he tried again, his forehead pounding.

'Um on!' he hissed, pulling his knees up as much as he could. His wrists moved past his heels and he sighed with relief when his hands were finally in front of him. His shoulders ached and he rolled them, trying to stretch the muscles.

He pulled at the duct tape over his mouth, hissed again as it tore away from his skin, then turned to Okeke, who was watching eagerly from her cage.

'I'm Detective Inspector Charlie Palmer. Are you okay? Are you hurt?'

She mumbled something back. He thought she said she was a little hurt but okay overall.

'Okay, great. I don't know how yet, but I'm going to get us out of this. Copy me, okay? So you can get the tape off your mouth.'

She did as he instructed, getting her arms in front of her more easily than he had, allowing her to remove the tape with her fingers.

'Oh God, what do we do?' she said, panicking again now that she could talk.

'I'm thinking, but we have to stay calm, okay? Do you know who the third person is? In the other cage?'

'It's my friend Sarah. They broke into her house and attacked us. I think they killed her boyfriend. God, there was so much blood. And they knocked her out.'

'Do you know how you got here?'

Angelica nodded. 'In a van. They gagged me and said they'd slit my throat if I tried anything. Dumped us in a van and drove here. Maybe an hour ago? One of them was the woman who did the ritual – I think she's called Cally. They must have been following me, knowing I went to the police.' She wiped tears from her eyes, but Charlie was impressed by how well she was keeping things together, all things considered.

'Do you know where we are?'

'Somewhere near Farringdon, I think. I saw a pub I recognised when they pulled us out of the van.'

'And do you know how many of them there are?'

'Three that I saw.'

'Are you sure?' Charlie asked, and she nodded.

Three killers. It just kept getting better. Cally Buchanan, then the person who had attacked him, and another person. If by some miracle an opportunity arose to put an end to this, it was going to be much harder against three.

And what if there are even more of them? What if there's a whole fucking coven? Charlie sagged, suddenly feeling less hopeful. But he had to try.

'Okay, three of them,' he said, trying to inject some confidence in his voice, for himself as much as for the poor woman just metres from him. 'We need as many advantages as possible. Can you free your hands or feet?'

'I'm not sure. Let me try.'

For the next few minutes they both did just that. Charlie pulled at the rope around his wrists with his teeth but achieved only an aching jaw and rope burn. He tried to free his legs too, to no avail. The ropes were just too tight and the knots too well done.

'Dammit.' He groaned. At almost the same time, he heard a yip from Angelica.

'My hands are free!' she whispered.

He watched her try the bindings on her ankles.

'Can't free my legs.'

'Hands are a good start. Can you stand? Try the lock?'

Angelica shuffled to her feet, then slowly stood. She hop-jumped over to the door, where Charlie could see a very solid-looking padlock. She inspected it.

'No good. This thing is sturdy.'

Think, Charlie, think! 'Okay, do you have anything you could try picking it with? A hair clip or anything?'

'No, sorry, not when I wear my hair in an afro. I don't need them.' Angelica hopped again, looking out from each side of her cage. 'There's nothing around I can use either. Just some rubbish bags.'

'What's in them?' Charlie asked.

'I don't know, I can't tell.'

'Can you reach any of them? If you stick your arm out?'

'Maybe...' Angelica crouched and stuck an arm out. She couldn't reach, so she got down on her front and tried again.

'Yes!'

'Well done! See if you can find anything that might help to get that lock open.'

He watched Angelica tear open the bag and start rustling through the rubbish.

'Nothing – it's all just paper and cardboard.'

'Are there any other bags?'

'Loads.'

Charlie didn't need to ask. Angelica was already on her front, fingers stretched out to grab another one. She pulled it to her, tore open the side and started rustling through it.

'Will a wire hook work?' she said, turning to Charlie and holding up the piece of metal.

'It might. Give it a go. Even if not, it's a weapon. If the time comes, don't be afraid to use it,' he said. Angelica's eyes widened and he saw the sheen of tears again. 'I'll do everything I can to keep you safe, but if I can't then you need to be prepared, okay?'

He saw Angelica slump a little. He felt inclined to do the same. A hook was not much against at least three people who believed they were witches and who were definitely killers. He knew he had to stay strong, had to have faith that Daniel and the team would somehow find them before it was too late. It seemed hopeless but he wasn't dead yet, and nor were Angelica and her friend. He would do everything he could to keep them alive.

'Now try that lock, okay?'

Angelica was on her feet again quickly. He could just hear the scratching of the wire against the lock when a muffled noise stopped her in her tracks.

'Sarah?' Angelica whispered, leaning in the direction of the third cage. Charlie could see the other woman moving, wriggling and trying to scream again.

'Well, I see you're all awake,' a voice said just inches from him. Charlie swore in shock, turning to see a woman peering in at him. For a second he couldn't see her body, then he realised that she was wearing a black cloak. From what he could tell her hair was black too, and she had dark lips and eyeliner.

He backed away slightly but kept a firm gaze on the woman.

'I see you've been busy, Detective,' she said. 'You took your gag off, and your hands are now in front of you. Trying to escape. Don't blame you. Clearly we should have been keeping a closer eye on you. I guess we'll just have to speed things up before this little mouse gets out of his cage!' She grinned as she wagged a finger at him. 'And what a treat we have in store for you. There's a certain poetry – an irony, maybe – in what we're setting up. Sod witches being the victims. No, this time it won't be us. I think we're having crispy roast pork tonight!' She laughed, her eyes wild, before turning away and disappearing into the shadows.

Charlie swallowed hard. He heard a commotion from somewhere within the market. It sounded like logs being dropped onto the smooth concrete floor, and with a sinking heart he knew what she had meant. It wouldn't be the witches being put on display and punished as once they might have been. The trio were building stakes. And he knew who was going to be burned alive on them.

CHAPTER TWENTY-FOUR

For the last hour Daniel had felt more on edge than he ever had before, which was truly saying something. Shaun Simmons, the young tech whizz who had helped Daniel previously, was feeling the brunt of his anxiety. He looked mildly terrified as he worked, and Daniel knew he'd probably have to apologise to him later. But he didn't care. The only thing he was interested in was making sure that he didn't send a whole team of officers to the wrong place.

'For God's sake, is this as fast as this bloody thing goes?' he snapped as he watched code scrolling down all three of Shaun's monitors.

'I'm afraid so, sir. It's the best – it will find what we need, I promise.'

Daniel huffed at him, his patience whittled down to nothing. 'I thought Patrick told you to keep your workspace clean?'

Shaun looked panicked and quickly started to clear his desk. He threw away all the empty wrappers and two empty bottles of Sprite before nervously popping a can of Red Bull and taking a swig, as though the drink would calm his nerves.

'Sorry, sir!' he stammered, his other hand tapping nervously on the edge of the desk, willing the software to go faster.

'Got another one of those?' Daniel asked, indicating the can. Shaun nodded almost wildly and bent down to look under his desk. Daniel did too, and saw the mini fridge plugged in by Shaun's feet. Shaun offered him a can and he took it.

'Thanks,' he said, smiling. He knew he was freaking the poor guy out, and felt a little guilty, but his nerves were frayed to shit. He couldn't help it. He'd snapped at Amelia too, and felt pretty hypocritical considering he had admonished her previously. Fortunately she didn't seem to notice him not practising what he had preached. She was also caught up with the task of finding Charlie. He'd sent her to prep the team they would take once they had locked in the location. She needed to be active as much as he did.

The computer beeped.

'Okay, erm...' Shaun muttered, scanning through the data that the computer had pulled up.

'Well?' Daniel asked. 'Does it confirm it?'

'There's a lot of places they searched, but...' He clicked through a few boxes, looking back and forth between his three screens. 'Cally Buchanan definitely searched Smithfield recently. Facebook has been advertising the market to her, fresh meat and stuff. It's not the only place, however. It's not one hundred per cent the place we're looking for.'

'Shit. Patrick!' Daniel yelled across the office, unbothered by the looks of surprise on a few nearby faces, that popped up over screens like meerkats. The only person he was looking for was Patrick, and he spotted him instantly. Patrick came running over, clearly feeling the same sense of urgency.

'How's the hunt for the van going? Has anything been picked up near Smithfield Market yet?'

'We're downloading all the footage now. The computers are

already scanning but it'll take a while, maybe another half an hour to an hour.'

'Shit!' Daniel ran his hand through his hair.

'I know. I'm sorry, Dan. The team are going as fast as they can, but the footage files are big and there's a lot to scan. We pulled video from every camera we legally have access to. If they went there, we'll find them, I promise.'

'Isn't that what you said about tracking the van from Limehouse? And you lost it. What if that happens again?'

Patrick's face fell and he swallowed. Daniel could see the pressure his colleague was under.

'We did lose it that time, and I'm sorry. The footage just wasn't there. They managed to avoid a lot of cameras. But at night, with this much rain, the roads are a lot quieter and we know – we think we know, anyway – where they're headed so we have more info to work from. We'll get them, Dan.' He put a hand on Daniel's shoulder.

Daniel nodded, trying to calm himself as best he could. 'Sorry, I know. It's just...' He trailed off but Patrick nodded back.

'Mate, I know. I feel it too. Half an hour, okay? An hour tops.' He turned and headed back across the floor.

'Sorry I couldn't help more, sir,' Shaun said, his voice vibrating with worry. He looked like he was preparing to be told off again.

'You did great, thanks, Shaun. Honestly.' Daniel smiled even though he didn't feel like doing so, but was glad when Shaun returned his smile and appeared more at ease.

'Keep searching, okay? If you can find anything at all that locks in the location, let me and Patrick know.' With that Daniel headed towards the lifts, intending to check on Amelia. He trusted her and didn't really need to go and see what progress she had made with preparing a strike force, but he couldn't just stand around and wait for the tech team to give him what he needed.

As he waited for the lift, he checked his watch. It was almost ten. Charlie had been missing for nearly seven hours. Daniel couldn't help wondering how many hours he had left.

The confirmation still hadn't come half an hour later. Patrick had tried to apologise to Daniel, but he hadn't wanted to wait around to listen. He needed to act.

He called Superintendent Hobbs. 'Sir, I can't wait around any longer. I need to go for it and hope we're right,' he had said, dreading what Hobbs would say.

'Graves, how sure are you that the location you have is correct? And I want an honest answer.'

'Maybe seventy-five per cent? Eighty? Look, it has to be enough. It's Charlie we're talking about.'

'I know, Graves, trust me. Listen, we both know that I can't authorise a whole strike team to be sent out without enough evidence to back it up. The whole department would be in shit for the cost alone if we're wrong here. And God help us if the press got wind of something like that. But–'

Daniel didn't wait, instead jumping in to finish the sentence. 'But I could go, take a smaller team. Harding and two other officers, firearms specialists. And if we're right, I can call in for the full team immediately.' Daniel realised he was gabbling, barely taking time to breathe, but he also knew that Hobbs would agree to his suggestion.

After a brief pause, Hobbs confirmed it. 'Okay, you have my permission. I agree, we can't just sit on our hands. If anything happened to Palmer because we waited around – well, I don't honestly want to finish that thought. But listen, Graves, the second you can confirm either way, I need to know. We need to act fast. And the team need to come up with an action plan right now in case the location is wrong.'

'I have the whole tech team on it. Patrick won't rest until they have confirmation, same as me.'

'Okay. I don't love this, Graves, but get going. And please bring back our man.'

'I won't return without him,' Daniel said, hoping with his whole heart that he could keep the promise.

Less than five minutes later, he and Amelia were hustling into his car, both equipped with handguns. He'd made the mistake of not being sufficiently armed before, but not this time. He signalled to the two other officers who would come with them, and then they were off. The rain beat down on them like an angry monsoon the second the car was clear of the underground garage.

CHAPTER TWENTY-FIVE

C harlie felt few glimmers of hope as he watched them finishing their preparations, but one positive was that Angelica had been right. There were three of them. This didn't make his heart leap with hope, but at least no others seemed to be present. That was something. Unfortunately almost everything else made him worry.

His phone had been taken from him and he wasn't wearing a watch, but Charlie guessed it had taken them around twenty minutes to build the three stakes. Although it was dark, he had learned a few things in that time. The first was that he definitely couldn't remove his bindings without assistance. Whoever had tied them had done a good job. Angelica, on the other hand, had succeeded in freeing herself entirely. She pretended still to be tied up whenever one of the so-called witches looked their way, but that was good. She could run, maybe, and get help, or injure them, or even free him. Something. And she still had the hook. The witches hadn't really checked on them since starting their build. That told him they might have opportunities for action.

The second thing was that one of the three women didn't seem entirely as keen on her task as the others. Though he couldn't make out any real details as they worked in near total darkness, sucked up into the shadows thanks to their long black cloaks, he could tell from the glimpses he got of her face that she was nervous and uncomfortable. She kept looking around, at him and the other caged women, and at least once she had seemed upset. She had paused in what she was doing and the one Charlie knew was Buchanan, the shortest of the three women, had hustled her back to work, quietly but firmly. Charlie had seen a blade appear briefly from inside Buchanan's sleeve. It very much looked like, whoever this mystery third woman was, she wasn't participating in murder of her own free will.

The third thing, and the most depressing, was that the area around them was deserted. Charlie wasn't surprised. The market was, of course, closed and the rain was the worst he could remember. No one with any sense would be out in it. In the time the women had been assembling the stakes and pyres, he had not seen a single set of headlights go past either entrance to the market.

One woman picked up the lamp, and his breath caught in his throat as the light shone over what the witches had crafted. Three stakes, each two metres high, held in place by supports on either side. Each one surrounded by enough kindling to keep a fire burning for a week. And symbols had been painted in glistening red all over the floor. He couldn't make any of them out from where he was, but that didn't matter. He knew what they looked like, had seen them already, at the three previous crime scenes. He presumed that once again they had been drawn with blood, and wondered if it had been from one of the previous victims.

The first crime scene in Hyde Park had been hidden, a private ceremony for those involved. It had been found by accident. The second had been laid out more publicly but still in a quiet spot. That one had been discovered more quickly. The third, in a playground, was no longer subtle or hidden in the least. And now he had watched the fourth being created before his very eyes. These women's behaviour had escalated – and fast. They were ready for their biggest show yet. Charlie was terrified right down to his soul that his corpse would be found in the morning, his name on the news. He would be the latest victim in the string of ritual murders that had shocked the city. And maybe he wouldn't even be the last.

Cally Buchanan was next to him again. Once more he shuffled away from that side of his cage – not that it made any difference. The cage wasn't very big. In one hand she held a knife, twelve centimetres or so long, clearly razor-sharp. In her other hand was a wooden stick with a cloth wrapped around one end.

'It's time, Detective,' she growled. 'Are you ready to play? I know I am. But here's the bit I love the most. You don't get to go first. Oh no. You get the pleasure of watching. I hope you enjoy the show!' She stepped back, grinning insanely again, brandishing the knife and torch above her. 'Natalie! Let's begin!'

One of the women moved to the cage furthest from Charlie. She grinned just as Buchanan had. Whoever Natalie was, she was equally unhinged. The third woman stayed back, almost shrinking into the shadows. Charlie shouted for them to stop, pleaded with her to help them, but when Natalie dragged Sarah Boyd from her cage, the woman stayed put. The third witch was too far in. She was going to let this happen. The fires were about to be lit, and there was not a damn thing Charlie could do to stop it.

Everything had been a haze, a blur of sounds and occasional glimpses of shapes. It felt like she was under a thick duvet, swamped in fabric that was shielding her from danger. Nothing had really broken through that barrier. Not until the clink of a lock and the rough grab of fingers in her hair yanked her into full consciousness.

It was as though previously her mind had been protecting her and now it wanted her on high alert. It had been keeping her in the dark deliberately, padding her world so that she would not have to deal with the truth. That was no longer the course of action required, however. Her brain needed her to wake the fuck up and kick in as much adrenaline as possible. With a brutal surge of clarity, Sarah Boyd fought and screamed as much as her bound and gagged body would allow.

'Stop bloody wriggling!' the woman who had grabbed her hissed. This only spurred Sarah on even more. As she was dragged from the cage she kicked out, hooking her feet as best she could around one of the bars. The metal was freezing and her bare toes already felt numb, but for a second it seemed to be working. Only a second, though. Another swift tug from her assailant and she was moving again.

Her surroundings were drenched in darkness. Sarah had no idea where she was, but it didn't really matter. What she did know was all she needed to. She was in grave danger, it was a bitterly cold night, she was almost frozen to her bones, and whatever was happening to her was also going to happen to Angelica.

As she was pulled across the floor, still struggling, her heels scuffed on the concrete. The pain barely registered. Instead she was focused on breaking free by any means necessary. That was, until she was dropped onto her side, her head bouncing with a jolt off the floor, and she saw the sticky red symbols. She instantly recognised them. Like a whoosh of cold air bursting through a newly smashed window, the truth of what she was facing hit her. She was about to be killed – and, worse, it would be in some horrific ritual. She was going to end up like the victims she had seen on the news. Like Angelica's ex-boyfriend.

And there, right in front of her, was the reason. She and Angelica had gone to the police, put themselves in the firing line, and now it would be their remains that were discovered by someone in the cold light of morning, ready to be broadcast to the country as part of the breakfast news cycle. For a split second she felt furious at Angelica for bringing this into her life, but the fury faded as fast as it had arrived. There was no time for being angry at her friend. There was only time for trying to get out of this. Face down on concrete, however, she was struggling to work out how to do this.

She could see pairs of boot-clad feet and the hems of black skirts or capes milling around her, and she tried to pull her hands down from behind her to loop her feet through. One of the kidnappers noticed and gave her a swift kick in the stomach. Sarah groaned.

'Stupid bitch. You can't get away. Stop trying.'

Sarah had only time to flinch as she saw the black shoe kick out again, this time at her face. It connected with her cheek. The pain was sharp, like a bite, and she cried out. She heard someone scream for them to stop, heard two voices. One was Angelica's. The other was a man. Was it Mike? She assumed he had got in their way, and that was why he had been stabbed at her flat. Could he still be alive?

Not for long.

The thought came before she could stop it, but through the new pain in her right cheek she squeezed her eyes closed and attempted to shake off the negativity. She knew she couldn't give up. She lay still, her eyes open again, scanning for anything that would help. She saw nothing before she was abruptly hauled to her feet by two of the women. She was pulled backwards, lifted over a load of wood, and then her hands were suddenly free. Immediately she broke free of the grip of one of the women and lashed out, started to fight. The woman brandished a blade in front of her face and hissed at her to stop. Sarah froze, couldn't help it, and stayed motionless long enough for them to get her back under their control. Her hands were pulled harshly behind her, behind a wooden pole this time, then she was being tied up again.

Something in her brain began to talk to her, to tell her that these women were not just psychotic killers, that there was something else she had to pay attention to.

They were witches. Witches out for revenge. And everyone knew what happened to witches. They were drowned or hanged or... burned at the stake.

She started to wriggle again, furiously this time, trying to force her way off the wooden beam she was tied to. Something splashed all over her legs, over her stomach, and the strong smell hit her like another kick to the gut. Lighter fluid. Her eyes were circles of horror as she registered the bloom of flame in front of her – and the three pairs of eyes glinting in the light of the flame, ready to watch her burn alive.

———

Molly Goodings could smell blood. Was dismayed to realise that it was her own. That wasn't the worst thing, though. The rumbling of the engine, the constant bumps and the tight, dark space she was in were much worse. It was also freezing cold. From somewhere she could feel water dripping onto her face. She knew it was raining. Could hear it as the car she was trapped in drove to wherever that psycho policeman was taking her.

She knew instantly what was going on when she woke up. She remembered Officer Baker, remembered his smiles and his lies, and of course she remembered the knife plunging into her shoulder. She had passed out from shock and pain. And then she had been bundled into the boot of a car.

Molly knew Officer Baker wasn't a policeman. Or, rather, he was, but the real Baker was probably dead and dumped in a hedge somewhere outside Daniel's flat. No, the man who had stabbed her was not a crazy rogue cop. He was Greg Armstrong. It was the only explanation. He had warned her pretty clearly to stay away from Daniel, but she hadn't, and now she was facing the consequences.

She wondered if she was in Baker's car – a police car. That would make sense. She figured he'd occasionally need to check in over the radio to report that everything outside Daniel's flat was quiet and there was nothing to worry about, but otherwise he could do whatever he wanted without being disturbed.

That led her on to her next topic. What the hell was he planning on doing with her? Would he just kill her and send a piece of her to Daniel? He'd done it before, apparently. Which part would he send?

'Stop it, Molly,' she hissed, her voice a strange echo in the confined space, made almost inaudible by the rain and the car engine. She had considered screaming when she realised he hadn't gagged her, but the rain and the car engine would no doubt muffle the sound. Also she feared that if he heard a peep from her he would pull over somewhere dark and quiet and kill her right there. She didn't want to run that risk.

The car bounced over a speed bump or similar and jolted Molly. She whacked her head off the underside of the boot, and her shoulder throbbed. She raised a hand to the wound. It was sticky, still bleeding. She felt woozy but not too bad, considering. She figured she wasn't bleeding out just yet. It just hurt like a total bitch.

Once the pain subsided a bit, she started to think again. She wasn't dead – that meant something. Armstrong could have easily killed her. Could have left a gory mess for Daniel to discover on his return home from work. Yet here she was, in a car boot, being driven through a rainstorm to a destination unknown. Armstrong was planning something, he had to be. He was up to something more dramatic than just leaving her body for Daniel to find. While the thought terrified her, it also gave her hope. If he didn't want to just kill her, then maybe there was a chance she could survive the night. Maybe.

The screams and shouts didn't seem to be working. Angelica knew that no one would be out for a casual walk, given the weather and time, but the mad women didn't seem to care either. In fact, they were ignoring her. Angelica realised she had an opportunity. Retrieving the hook that she had moments before hidden on the floor outside the back of her cage, she started again to try to pick the lock.

The detective had been shouting too, still was, but they were ignoring him too. It was helpful, though. His voice covered some of the noise of her prodding the wire into the heavy padlock.

She heard a click. Hope soared inside her, but the lock hadn't opened.

'Fuck, come on!' She grimaced. Her fingers were aching already and she was about to give up when she looked up. What she saw made her blood chill to ice. The smaller of the three cloaked women had lit her torch and was brandishing it at Sarah, who was tightly roped to one of the stakes. Tears flooded down Angelica's face and bile rose into her mouth. She spat into the corner of the cage, coughing, her throat burning.

Then the women started to chant, mostly in a foreign tongue, although the words 'witch' and 'goddess' were audible in English. She knew that her time was rapidly running out.

'Angelica, you have to keep trying,' Charlie whispered. She knew he was right. She felt dizzy and weak but she couldn't stop. She wiped her face and went back to the lock, her hands shaking.

The foreign words snaked in the air around her, making her skin crawl. She glanced at the witches and saw them slowly circling Sarah. All three of them held torches. The space was illuminated, the symbols painted in blood glistening under their feet. It was terrifying.

She forced her focus back to the lock, jamming the wire hook into it and wiggling it in every direction. There was no skill involved; she had no idea what she was doing. She couldn't even see the padlock properly. She knew it was hopeless, that it would never work.

And then it did.

The padlock hit the concrete with a thud.

Angelica ducked backwards away from the cage door, her eyes locked on the witches. None of them looked her way.

'Angelica, listen to me – you need to run. Get out of here and send for help,' Charlie urged her as soon as the lock fell.

She turned to him. 'What? I can't leave! I have to stop them – I have to save Sarah!' Her hands were shaking again.

'No, listen, you can't take on all three of them. Please, you have to go and get help!'

'Where? Where, Detective? You've seen the rain. No one is going to be out there. I don't have a phone, don't have money for a pay phone even if I could find one. We're on our own, and Sarah only has...' Angelica couldn't finish the sentence, but she didn't need to. She knew she was right. She could run into the middle of the street and be bloody lucky if she even found a taxi or bus – maybe then she could call for help, but it would be too late. Sarah would be dead and maybe he would be too.

'Okay. Shit! Okay, you need to get me out of here too. Then you run, or at least find a better weapon. Deal?'

Angelica nodded and stepped to the cage door. She rested her hand on one of the bars, then looked at the women, entranced by their sick ritual. Saw Sarah's face, horrified, lit up as though it were already on fire as the torchlight danced over her cheeks. It spurred her on.

The gate opened silently. Seconds later Angelica was wriggling the hook in the next lock, her pulse hammering through her. It clicked and she was in. She couldn't believe it. She ducked to Charlie and started pulling at the rope on his wrists.

'I can't get it off – the knots are too tight!' she squealed.

'Use the wire.'

She did as he said, jabbed the blunt end of the wire under the rope and sawing it back and forth. Something snapped, and she saw a thread. It felt like it took forever, but then suddenly Charlie's hands were free. He immediately started on the bindings on his ankles.

'Angelica, go now, okay? Find a weapon, something heavy, and get around them. We don't have much longer.'

She didn't want to leave him; it felt wrong. She also didn't want to run into the dark market by herself. The building suddenly seemed huge, full of shadows that loomed above and around her. But she didn't have much choice. She turned and bolted out of Charlie's cage, heading for a covered stall.

Then two things happened.

The chanting stopped and the torches were lowered. The witches lit the wood at Sarah's feet.

That was the first thing.

Headlights whipped through one of the entrance gates to the market, then a car pulled up.

That was the second thing.

Seconds later, two people were screaming.

One of those people was Sarah. The other one someone new.

CHAPTER TWENTY-SIX

Cally Buchanan could barely contain herself as they reached the end of the incantation and she lowered her torch. Everything was coming together on this night: this perfectly Gothic storm on the site of one of the most famous witch killings in English history. Her sister in spirit, Margery Jourdain, had been taken from the world in the most vicious of ways, and it was time for someone to honour her death by repaying it in kind.

Cally had always thought she was a witch, at least had an affinity with the craft, even when she had been small. It wasn't until she joined the women's centre in Deptford a year ago, however, that she found her kin, Natalie Hastings.

Natalie was a true witch in Cally's eyes, a woman who lived and breathed the calling of dark arts, and it was through her that Cally had begun to get in touch with her own inner spirit.

The coven Natalie belonged to had welcomed Cally with open arms. To begin with, their weekly meets seemed like a natural extension of the workshops at the centre, which she sometimes attended. They talked about the history of sorcery and witchcraft, which she found fascinating. They studied ingredients found in the natural world that had long been used for their healing or mystical properties. They even practised minor incantations, creating potions and such, though Cally wasn't sure that anything ever came of the spells or concoctions. It was fun, something different, and while in the back of her brain she felt that maybe she did believe, she knew that she enjoyed it.

But Natalie was interested in doing more. It wasn't long before she had become closer to Cally than the other women in the group. Sometimes Cally felt as though she'd been chosen deliberately. She started talking about doing more, of using the craft to achieve more in life – something beyond friendly sisterhood and meetings about crystals and flowers.

Together they started to study darker practices. They read books about summoning demons, about punishing spells and sacrificial rituals. Cally thought it was all interesting, and she enjoyed Natalie's company. Natalie brimmed with energy and passion, and Cally found it infectious.

It took just four months for Natalie to suggest they tried something for real, something much darker than anything the coven would dare to discuss.

There was this guy, Evan. He and Natalie had dated, though from her description of their relationship, Cally didn't think 'dated' was quite the right word. They hung out, fucked and did drugs, by the sounds of it. And then one day the police had caught Evan with heroin in his jacket pocket. Natalie had told Cally that she'd had no idea he had any, that she didn't think he touched the stuff, although she had admitted that she'd seen him do coke and the occasional bit of MDMA. She was with him when he was arrested, and apparently he – the shit – tried to blame it all on her. Told the police she was a dealer and she had sold the heroin to him. That led to her arrest too, and endless questioning. In Natalie's tale, the police finally discovered that she had nothing to do with it, gave her a warning, and told her to steer clear of people like Evan in future. She figured that would be the last of it, but the police wanted to find out where Evan had got the heroin from, so they let him go. Natalie was not happy about that – not after what he had done. It was unsatisfying. She told Cally she wanted revenge. He needed to be punished. That was when she decided that scaring the shit out of him would go a long way towards making her feel better about it all. Cally was more than happy to help, considering what her friend had been through.

The plan was simple. Natalie would meet up with Evan, get him high, then convince him to go with her to a party. They knew it would work. Even off his face, Evan also liked to drink. Natalie would tell him they were going to Hackney Wick, to a warehouse party. And that's where they would go. A warehouse in Hackney Wick. Only there would be no party.

Cally had arrived at the abandoned site earlier in the evening and set up everything. She had painted a pentagram on the floor, surrounded by symbols, and placed a fold-out table in the centre of the pentagram. Then she had lit clusters of candles to add some ambience before finding a hiding spot.

Natalie had shown up with Evan not long after. He was barely coherent, thanks to the pills she had convinced him to take along the way, mixed with heroin, to make sure he was nice and pliant. He hadn't even complained that there was no party; he had no idea where he was. Natalie and Cally strapped him to the table, dressed in black cloaks and masks, and had a few beers while they waited for him to wake up. He had to be more alert if they were going to scare him properly.

Messing with him was fun. They chanted behind their

masks, they threatened to cut him open on the table... everything was going according to plan. Evan was scared shitless, even pissed himself, and Natalie was as happy as Larry. Mission accomplished. All they needed to do was set him free and let him run away in his soggy boxer shorts. He'd never be able to prove that it had been Natalie behind one of the masks, getting her revenge.

But that wasn't how things went. They had underestimated Evan. As they freed him, brandishing knives, threatening to kill him if he didn't run away, he had seized an opportunity that they hadn't anticipated. He ran from the table, grabbed a long steel rod that had been left leaning against the wall of the warehouse, and came back.

'You fucking bitches!' he spat. 'Think you can kidnap me and get away with it? You're trash, Natalie, cos yeah, I know it's you. And you, whoever the fuck you are, you're just as bad! I ain't scared of two little whores and their knives.'

He had swung for Natalie first. She dodged, jumping backwards. He swung again, missed again, but she fell, the knife spinning away from her. Evan didn't miss a third time; the bar came down hard on Natalie's shin.

That was when Cally panicked. As Natalie screamed out in pain and tried to crawl across the dirty warehouse floor to escape, her psychotic ex swinging for her, Cally had charged. She plunged her knife into his back. As he roared, she pulled it out and stabbed him again before she could stop herself.

Evan didn't say anything else, simply dropped to the floor with a groan. The blood came fast, puddling under him in seconds, and he stopped moving.

Natalie was still on the floor. 'Holy shit, Cally, what the fuck?'

'I don't know! He was... he was going to kill you!'

'Yeah, but fuck...'

They remained motionless for a few seconds, Natalie on the floor, Cally standing over the body. Then Natalie spoke.

'How did it feel?'

Cally had already thought about it, and was surprised by the answer. 'Amazing. It felt... incredible.' She looked down at the knife. 'Powerful.'

Natalie had laughed then, the sound echoing around the ramshackle building. 'If that isn't witchcraft, I don't know what is!' She grinned. 'Power! God, I'm so... I'm jealous, Cally.' Natalie had got to her feet, flexed her leg and looked at Cally. 'Can we do it again? I want to try.'

They had cleared everything up, hidden the body under some sheets in the warehouse. Three days later, after no news reports about a man's body being found in the warehouse and no police banging on the door and questioning them, they knew they had got away with it.

And that was how it started.

The rules were simple. They had to choose men that no one would miss, men that were total fucks, men that the world could do without. Men with few connections. They had to leave no traces of themselves. And they were never to discuss what they did with anyone else.

Two men later, however, the rules changed. A woman called Jessie Hoskins had joined the coven, and it wasn't long before she mentioned to Cally her plans to make money out of the whole witchcraft thing. Jessie had a business plan. She wanted to target women who were feeling desperate, out of control, and charge them to carry out a ceremony involving spells and rituals – nothing too dodgy, just a good old-fashioned con that would also help people to feel better. Win–win. Cally could see the con working nicely alongside their own more nefarious plans. It was kind of perfect, but Natalie wasn't convinced.

For starters, Jessie had access to empty houses through her job as an estate agent, so they had a perfect way to carry out ceremonies and so on without leaving a trace, as long as Jessie never met the punters. Jessie hadn't loved the idea of being kept out of the witchy parts of the plan, but she knew they could charge a decent amount for ceremonies, and the thought of the cash managed to persuade her. The best thing for Cally, however, was that this plan would give them a supply of men. That had perked Natalie up.

Their rules stayed the same after they had brought Jessie into their plan. The men still had to be deplorable. The customers handing them names needed to truly want rid of the men, so they wouldn't be concerned if said men vanished from their lives. It didn't matter so much if other people would miss them, as no one would ever connect the dots between their death and a fake witchcraft service, just as long as the men were never reported missing by the women who had paid to wash their hands of them...

They decided to keep Jessie out of the murder part of the service. That was just for Cally and Natalie, and it needed to stay that way. She was, naturally, also to be kept in the dark when they decided to seek an extra adrenaline rush, leaving ritualistic scenes outside in playgrounds, for example. Cally knew that it was extremely risky leaving a crime scene, even a well-hidden one, but the high that she and Natalie got from doing it was second to none. And for a while it had worked. They were getting revenge, on behalf of the people who had come to them, and felt like truly powerful women – powerful witches. Then the scene they'd left in Hyde Park had been found.

Cally had panicked badly, and so had Natalie – they were angry at themselves for choosing somewhere so central when they could easily have picked a far more out-of-the-way location.

Then it was all over the news and the hit of adrenaline had been huge. They had killed someone, left behind a brutally violent scene and got away with it – still. It was too good. It made them feel unstoppable, an intoxicating experience. And anyway, they were killing bad men so they were also doing the world a service. It was perfect.

The second time they left a ritual behind, Natalie suggested they make it more public, and the rush had been even better, like being on cloud nine. It was a high stronger than anything either of them had ever experienced from narcotics, and they knew they were on to something. They were earning money, helping suffering women, tapping into their mutual love of the dark history of witches, and they felt more powerful than ever. As long as they continued to be careful, then they could keep doing it.

Then Jessie connected the dots.

One of their customers did too.

It didn't take long for Cally to realise that everything would come crashing down around them. Natalie was forced to admit that too, but she didn't want to stop. Instead she had another idea. If the fucking woman who had gone to the police was going to bring them all down anyway, then why not go out with a bang?

Natalie also knew how to protect them from Jessie blabbing too soon and ruining their big finale. Jessie had helped them find victims, both to con and to kill. She had helped them cover their tracks. If Natalie and Cally went down, then Jessie would too. They were very clear about that. All three of them were culpable.

That was enough to keep Jessie from going to the police. The threat of prison time for involvement, combined with Cally's threat to slit Jessie's throat, kept the trio together. They just needed one last victim, to finish things properly. To make a statement, before they were inevitably caught.

As it turned out, they got more than one – and even better, the victims chose themselves. Angelica Okeke had gone to the police and run her mouth; she was an obvious choice. Sure, she didn't fit their pattern – she wasn't a bad man – but Cally and Natalie no longer cared. Her friend Sarah knew too much as well. Cally figured it would be fun to take her out too. Sarah Boyd had been rude and dismissive, and Cally had seen enough of that in her lifetime. Boyd could die too. Why the fuck not?

And their prime piece of meat for the slaughter was Detective Inspector Charlie Palmer, one half of the tenacious duo that was after them. When Palmer had come looking for Jessie at the letting agency he had unwittingly offered himself up, a cherry on top of one hell of a cake.

What better way to go out than by burning alive one of the detectives trying to bring them down?

'Who knows?' Natalie said. 'If we kill him and the women before we get caught, then maybe we can get away with this too!'

Cally was less confident, and had reminded her of Jessie.

'So maybe she won't make it out alive either,' was Natalie's response.

Everything had led up to this moment. Now, fire in hand, it was almost too much for Cally to handle. They were doing it. They were getting revenge against the world for how it treated women, getting revenge for what had been done to their fallen witch sisters over time – even for all those people who had been murdered who didn't even identify as witches. And on top of that, they were getting rid of numerous witnesses.

It was perfect. They were leaving their mark on the pages of history. They would be legends, talked about for years, if not decades, to come. Best of all, though, for Cally anyway, they were tapping into something primal and powerful, the taking of human lives at will, which beat everything else. If she was arrested that very night, or even killed, she believed it would be worth it.

The flames of her torch touched the logs. She beamed from ear to ear as the flames leaped around Sarah Boyd's feet.

'Still don't believe in witches?' Cally sneered.

Then someone else screamed. Not one of their prisoners. Someone new. Cally turned to the source of the noise and was shocked by what she saw.

It seemed they weren't the only ones with murder on their mind.

CHAPTER TWENTY-SEVEN

Greg Armstrong had a rough plan. Not precise exactly, but he figured it was good enough. He wanted to see the look on Daniel Graves' face. Then he'd shoot the fucker. Simple.

At first it had been fun tormenting Graves, he had to admit. Murdering the bitch who had got Cassandra Vega killed – *his* Cassandra – had been an excellent start. It had certainly helped with his own grief.

No one had known about him and Cassandra – how they had been getting closer, how she had just found out she was pregnant. They had discovered a way to get a shit ton of money and life was going to be great. Then Daniel fucking Graves got involved and it all went to shit. A stupid little woman called Jenny Cartwright had got involved in their business. She had become a liability and they had agreed to take her out, but the bitch survived the attack and told Graves everything she knew – which, as it turned out, was more than enough. She led Graves straight to Cassandra, who had been shot and killed. Greg had got away, as the police hadn't known about him, but he had lost everything except his freedom. Cutting out Cartwright's heart and sending it to Graves as revenge had felt amazing. It was delicious, in fact, but, shortly after, Greg realised that he could do more, that the heart could be the start of a lot of fun.

It took him a while to figure out a plan, to decide what he would do, what would be most enjoyable, but after a few months he was ready.

Breaking into Graves' house and leaving a threatening message had been a laugh. Chasing him through traffic and making him crash had been even better. Dating his sister Amanda – well, that had been excellent too, for a while anyway. In the end Amanda Graves had proven too good at winding him up, but she was good in bed and she kept giving him info on her brother, so he got what he wanted from her.

Greg had grown bored with tormenting Graves from a distance. It wasn't enough. His plan needed to evolve.

After some back and forth, Greg thought he had decided on the next step. He'd come close to killing Amanda. He thought that would be a brilliant way to fuck Graves up, but then he'd discovered that the siblings weren't very close, so killing Amanda might not have that much of an effect on Graves. It was an option he could fall back on if needed, but it was predictable, and he wanted something better. Problem was, Daniel Graves was kind of boring. The man was always at work, and he didn't have many close friends. There was only really Detective Inspector Charlie Palmer as an alternative for maximum impact. But Greg didn't want to risk fucking up with Palmer. The man lived in the gym and was huge, much bigger and more muscular than him. If Greg took a wrong step, Palmer would end him quickly and abruptly, so targeting him seemed like a much more difficult option.

And then, just as Greg was starting to circle back to killing Amanda, due to a lack of better options, Danny boy had gone and got himself a girlfriend. A pretty, smart girlfriend who, after a bit of casual stalking, Greg could tell Daniel cared for a lot.

And she wasn't a cop. She was exactly what he had been looking for.

So he needed to get on with it and make Graves pay for Cassandra, make the fucker apologise for her death, once and for all. No more games. Greg wanted Graves to cower and beg, and then he would put a bullet through the man's skull.

How to go about things, though, that was the problem. Greg knew he could just follow Molly Goodings around until an opportunity arose. He could break into her house at night and take her. Or kill her. Then he could leave Graves a message, lure him somewhere and confront him before taking him down. Still, the plan lacked something. Greg wanted a little more from it all. Then it struck him. If he scared Graves again first, *then* got him on his knees and begging, oh man, *that* would be even more satisfying!

So Greg had broken into Molly's flat and left her a little message, then he'd watched her and Graves from afar. He could tell that she was terrified. After she'd gone to Graves and told him what had happened, the look on the man's face had been pure gold. His new love had been threatened. Greg savoured the expression of fear that was written all over Graves like a fine wine. He had him nervous again, on edge, looking over his shoulder. If he could get to Molly and take her after that, then Graves would truly feel vulnerable. Greg would have him right where he wanted him.

So he had continued to follow Molly until – bingo, opportunity.

The policeman had been so easy to kill. The man had been a fucking simpleton, way too trusting. Greg pretended he needed help, had jabbed him with a sedative, pulled him behind a large hedge and stripped him of his clothes. To finish, he stabbed him in the neck, happy that no blood would get on the uniform. Then Greg had put on his uniform and, just like that, had become a man of the law. Piece of piss.

The girlfriend had been less trusting. That almost did his plans in – but still, the power of a uniform was a wonder to behold. Molly had been cautious, but not cautious enough, and too nice for her own good. After he'd used her bathroom and pretended to leave, she'd turned her back on him. Moron. He'd shut the door and hid in the hallway cupboard. She basically walked into the knife.

Now it was time to strike. He had his bait. He had Graves on the edge. He was about to get what he wanted. He just needed a nice dramatic way to end this whole thing. A quick snoop around Graves' flat had given him just that. The notepad, the circled location, all those exclamation points. He had checked the girlfriend's call history. She had phoned Graves just minutes earlier. Clearly it was urgent that Graves got to that location. It was perfect – so dramatic, so serendipitous.

Greg knew about the ritual killings that had been happening in London. Everyone did. They were constantly on the news. He also knew that Graves was working the cases. The fucker's face had been flashed all over the place – Palmer's too. And now Greg knew where Graves was heading to find the killers, on this wet and windy night straight out of a horror film. How shocked he would be when Greg rocked up, gun and knife in hand, and Molly ready to be slaughtered in front of him.

Graves would suffer. Then Greg would kill him. After that, he didn't really care what happened. Greg didn't have an escape plan in mind, but as long as he saw pure terror and vulnerability in Daniel Graves' eyes before it was over, then he would be happy. Satisfied at last. It was long overdue – almost a year in the making.

The drive to the location had been a breeze. The roads were extremely quiet because of the rain, and Farringdon was often close to deserted at night anyway compared to most central London boroughs. It was as though the world was helping him out. As Greg dragged a screaming Molly Goodings from the boot of poor Officer Baker's car and into the rain, he could feel his blood pumping. There were no other police vehicles in sight, so he had some time, but he knew they would be there soon. He couldn't wait. It was all about to happen. He would finally end what Graves had started.

Thoughts spiralling in his head, focusing on the task in hand, Greg was surprised by what greeted him at Smithfield Market. Three women, dressed in black cloaks and wielding fire, were ready to burn another woman at the stake.

Nothing Greg had envisioned could have prepared him for what happened next.

CHAPTER TWENTY-EIGHT

Charlie Palmer didn't hesitate. He launched himself into action out of pure instinct. He practically threw himself out of the cage as the first torch was lowered to the kindling surrounding Sarah Boyd. The fire leaped into action as fast as he had, whipping around Sarah with terrifying speed.

Charlie registered the headlights almost simultaneously, prayed that it was Daniel with backup, and didn't stop running. He was about to collide head-on with Cally Buchanan when the scream tore through the warehouse. He turned, just for a second, his eyes barely registering the two people who had entered the fray, when the woman Cally had called Natalie charged him.

The flaming torch rose above Charlie, swinging fast, and he ducked, the heat roaring past his face. He brought a fist up, connected with Natalie hard, knocked her back. He let his motion carry him. Hands outstretched, he pushed her back further, slamming her into Sarah Boyd, who was still screaming. Fire licked at his feet as he stepped onto the burning logs and he yelled, jumping backwards, the heat biting at his legs. He looked down, saw he was not on fire, breathed a quick sigh of relief.

Natalie had also leaped out of the flames. She swatted furiously at the bottom of her cloak as tongues of fire tried to take over.

Charlie's mind swam. He knew Cally was close and knew she had a knife. Then there was Natalie, just seconds away from being ready to fight again. The third woman was somewhere unknown; he couldn't see her. Another as yet unknown woman was still screaming from across the warehouse. Angelica Okeke was hiding in the darkness somewhere. And last but most certainly not least, Sarah Boyd was still strapped to a stake and about to go up in flames.

'Fuck!' he yelled and lunged forward. He shoved Sarah and the pole as hard as he could, felt it give a little.

'No, you don't!' came a scream of pure anger. He spun just in time to see Cally Buchanan's knife slicing through the air towards him. He grabbed her arm and, using her momentum, practically threw her into the stake. Her body ricocheted into the shadows off to the side. The stake splintered at the base and fell backwards, sending a huge, booming crack through the warehouse. Kindling and flames leaped in every direction.

Charlie fell sideways, straight into the fire, rolled as fast as he could. He could smell burning hair, knew it was his, but he was out of the heat again, unable to believe his luck.

More screaming. Sarah. She was on her back, fire all around her legs. Charlie staggered up, ran round to her head. He grabbed the top of the wooden pole and pulled with all his strength. The fire billowed around the base of the pole, and Sarah's feet. She was free of the worst of it, but it had caught the bottom of her jeans. Her feet were on fire.

As fast as he could, he darted around to Sarah's legs and began patting the flames, desperate to put them out, barely worrying about burning his hands. That was when Natalie lunged again. She grabbed the back of his shirt, yanking him backwards. He fell painfully onto his side, rolled again. A plank of wood slammed down next to his face, missing him by an inch.

'I will fucking destroy you!' Natalie screamed, then brought the wood down again. The end splintered as it hit the concrete. Charlie twisted, pulled up his legs and kicked her as hard as he could. Natalie flew backwards, landing hard on the kindling, which was still very much on fire. Her cloak lit up quickly. The flames enveloped her in seconds, blazing through the fabric of her robe. She shoved herself up off the floor, her yells of agony and terror ripping through the building. She made it just a few metres across the market before she dropped to the floor and fell silent, her body almost invisible among the flames that ate at her.

Not waiting to see if she got up, Charlie pushed himself up. Cally Buchanan was standing next to the second stake. He flinched, flexing his hands into fists. Then he registered the fear in her eyes. Charlie could see a blade at her neck. Angelica Okeke was just behind her, holding Buchanan in place.

And to the right, the third witch, the mystery woman, knelt, untying Sarah Boyd, tears pouring down her face. He had been right; she was there against her will.

'I should never have joined them. Oh God, I'm sorry, I'm so sorry,' she whispered over and over again.

It was over. Cally was at knifepoint, Natalie was likely dead, and the third woman was surely going to give herself up. Sarah's legs were badly burned, but she was alive, and Angelica had made it out unscathed.

He took a deep breath, letting oxygen fill his lungs, even though the air was smoky and hot. Then a gunshot broke the sudden silence. He jumped.

'DI Charlie Palmer. That was quite the action show you just put on. You're like Indiana Jones,' the man said, his voice carrying through the air like poisonous gas. 'But I'm afraid your night isn't over yet. Tell me, where's your partner Graves?'

'Who the fuck are you?' Charlie asked, exhausted. The man grinned. Charlie thought he looked familiar but couldn't place him. Then he realised who the bloodied woman kneeling next to Greg was. The other woman whose screams he had heard.

'Molly?'

She looked up through drenched, matted hair. Even though she was soaking wet, Charlie could tell it was her. And that meant the man was...

'Greg Armstrong. Fuck me.'

This is not how it was supposed to go! Cally Buchanan screamed internally. The blade of her own knife was being held against her throat. She stood perfectly still, nervous of being cut, but also because she didn't know what else to do.

Although she tried not to, she couldn't help glancing at Natalie, who lay unmoving. She was still on fire. There was no doubt that she was dead. The smell of burning flesh was unmistakable. Cally sighed, couldn't help noting the irony of Natalie dying by fire on the same night they were, as a coven, attempting to reclaim the act of burning at the stake. She felt mixed emotions too. It was tragic that Natalie was dead. She had inspired Cally and, in many ways, had allowed Cally to reveal her true self to the world. Cally hadn't realised that up until recently she had been living such an inauthentic life. Natalie had completely changed that, so to see her burn to death was a loss that Cally felt deeply. That didn't stop her inner voice piping up again.

Better her than me.

Cally had not known exactly how the night would end. She

thought she'd be arrested, or killed. Now, faced by Natalie's death, she found herself hoping that she'd be arrested. She wasn't as prepared to die for the cause as she had thought. If it was a case of staying alive but locked up rather than being burned to a crisp, a life behind bars with her skin intact seemed like a clear winner. Her name would still be known across the country. She would still achieve the accolade of being a nationally known witch – maybe even globally known. Her name would go down in infamy, forever tied to the craft.

Given her current circumstances, arrest seemed inevitable. This stranger, however, the man that DI Palmer had just called Greg Armstrong, was very much an unknown element. Especially as he had brought his own victim with him. The look on Palmer's face suggested the chaos wasn't over just yet.

Cally decided that the only sensible thing to do was to stay still, wait and see what happened. At least that way she wouldn't end up like Natalie.

A few minutes later an opportunity presented itself, however, and Cally took it without hesitation.

'Detective, what on earth have you got involved in? Filming the sequel to *The Witches of Eastwick*?' Greg Armstrong laughed as he gestured with his gun to the stakes and the burning woman. He made sure he didn't let go of the woman crying on her knees next to him.

Charlie Palmer did not return his laughter.

'Oh, come on, that was funny. I mean, look at this place!'

Again Charlie stayed silent. Greg assessed the situation. While he couldn't figure out exactly what had happened, it didn't seem to him as though Palmer had full control over it all. To Greg's left a very nervous-looking woman held a blade to the neck of another woman – clearly one of the women responsible for the fire. Then there was the woman on her back still strapped to a wooden pole while a fourth woman, dressed in black just like the other little witch, attempted to untie her. And now Greg, and Daniel Graves' girlfriend. It was a lot for one detective to stay on top of.

'A lot of plates seem to be spinning here, Detective. I wonder which one will fall first.'

'Shut up, Armstrong,' Palmer snapped. 'Backup is on the way. This is over.' He stepped forward.

'I wouldn't move if I were you. And I have no doubt that Graves is on his way here as we speak. I planned for it. I'm ready for it. This is not over just yet.'

'What do you want, Armstrong? Really.'

Greg laughed at the question even as he glanced around the confused faces watching him in the darkness, their eyes lit up like glittering gems in the firelight.

'Graves in a grave, of course! You know that.'

'I thought as much. But that doesn't involve any of these people.' It was Palmer's turn to gesture, waving a hand at the women. 'This is between you and Daniel and, like you said, he's on his way. Just let me deal with this, okay?'

Greg thought that Palmer sounded desperate, pleading. That wasn't a surprise, really, given the circumstances. The man must be shitting himself at the thought of more dead bodies. Greg considered the request.

'How many of them are innocent?' he asked.

'What?'

'These women. I count four. Two seem to be of the witchy persuasion. The other two, not so much. Are they innocent?'

'Yes. Correct.'

'So the witches here, they'll be arrested?' He looked at the women in black. The one helping the injured woman off the wooden pole looked terrified. The other one, who had a knife to her throat, seemed to be paying very close attention to what was happening.

'Yes,' Palmer answered. 'Why? What does that have to do with anything?'

Greg smiled.

'I'm just thinking, Detective. Until Danny boy gets here, you have six people under your watch, if you include me. One person is already dead. That's a lot of pressure.'

Charlie watched him like a hawk, his brow furrowed.

'Tell you what. I'll ease your workload.' Greg raised the gun, aimed at the woman in black crouching next to the fire, and pulled the trigger. The shot exploded in the relative quiet of the building and the woman screamed as she fell backwards. In fact, everyone screamed except Palmer, who looked horrified, frozen in place.

'Down to five. Already easier. You're welcome!' Greg laughed again. This was fun! He was enjoying himself immensely. He had only planned to kill Graves and maybe the girlfriend, yet now that he had multiple lives in his hands, he realised the power was intoxicating.

'Shall I make it four? That one is already injured, anyway. I could put her out of her misery,' he said, raising the gun again. Palmer raised his hands, clearly about to beg him not to shoot someone else, when the sound of a car pulling up outside changed the game yet again.

'Let them go, Armstrong!' came a shout. Greg turned to see Daniel Graves running towards him, three other officers close behind him.

Shit! Too many of them.

He had what he wanted, Graves in front of him, ready to pay, but he needed it to be one on one. He tightened his grip on Molly Goodings' hair and pulled her backwards, away from

Palmer and the other women, holding his gun against his captive's head.

'Everyone but Graves needs to leave, or I'll shoot her!' he shouted, glancing between Graves and Palmer.

Graves skidded to a halt, his face a picture of fear and panic.

Not everyone froze, though. The witch with the knife at her throat clearly had other plans. She jammed her elbow into the stomach of the woman holding her. The knife dropped to the floor. She swooped down and grabbed it, then she was off, speeding towards the exit. She was soon swallowed by shadows. When Graves nodded to the officers behind him, all three took off in hot pursuit.

'Palmer, take those two, the burned-up blonde and the black woman, and get out. I'm feeling charitable. Graves, buddy, you stay right where you are.'

Palmer was already moving to the woman who had been gut-punched. He helped her up. The others watched as Palmer and Angelica headed towards the police cars, carrying Sarah between them, her arms over their shoulders. The market was silent again, save for the rain still hammering down above them and the soft whimpers of Molly Goodings, who Greg still held hostage.

He waited until Palmer had left with the women, then locked eyes with Graves.

'So much better! Any last requests?' he said, lifting the gun, aiming it squarely at Daniel Graves, his finger hovering over the trigger.

He was close to getting everything he wanted.

CHAPTER TWENTY-NINE

The downpour was like a slap to the face as Sergeant Amelia Harding charged through the open gate and out into the night after Cally Buchanan. She was forced to pause to get a bead on the runner and in seconds she was drenched, her hair matted to her head. She saw movement to her right, clocked Buchanan. Pushing her fringe out of her eyes, Amelia sped after her.

The rain was worse than she recalled ever seeing in London, and she pounded through a river that had formed in the road. As the rain hit her face she found herself squinting, droplets blurring her vision. It made it hard to keep track of the woman she was chasing, but Buchanan was facing the same conditions – and at least the roads were deserted. Amelia ran right in the middle of the street.

Buchanan took a left up ahead and Amelia tried to pick up her pace, fearful of losing the witch. She reached the road, saw Buchanan ahead of her, and checked to see if the other officers were still with her. One was.

'Where the hell has Martin gone, Steve?' she yelled as she slowed.

'He went the other way when we left the market, looping around in case he can get her from the other side.'

Amelia immediately knew that wouldn't work. It was too far around the block. She had to stay on Buchanan. If she lost her, she would never forgive herself. Amelia charged off again, not waiting to see if Steve was keeping up. She didn't care.

I can take this bitch myself!

Spurred on by anger and determination, Amelia barrelled down the road after the suspect. All the shops, delis and bars were closed, their insides hidden in shadow, and only a few streetlights fought to illuminate London through the oppressive rain and darkness, but Amelia could still see Buchanan. The woman had got further ahead, but not much further.

I can catch her...

Amelia saw a lit-up sign for Farringdon train station, and for a second her heart almost stopped. If Buchanan got on a train before Amelia caught up with her, then she would be gone. Then it dawned on Amelia that the station was closed, and had been for an hour or so. Obviously Buchanan had had the same thought. She had stopped, was desperately looking around her for a plan B. She saw Amelia in pursuit and legged it again, taking a right down the road that ran parallel with the station. Amelia knew there was a main road somewhere nearby, thought she had a better chance if she could herd the witch that way. Less chance to lose her if she could get off the side streets, and maybe there would even be a few cars or buses around, some witnesses, someone to block Buchanan's route.

Amelia reached the road Buchanan had taken, barely slowing to take the corner, when she realised she could no longer see the woman.

'Shit!' she yelled. A few seconds later Steve was next to her. 'Fuck!' she shouted, again wiping water from her eyes.

'Where did she go?'

'If I knew that, I wouldn't be fucking standing here chatting to you,' Amelia snapped. Steve looked taken aback but didn't say anything, for which she was glad. She didn't have the time or inclination to apologise. Steve would cope.

Jogging down the road, Steve keeping pace, Amelia scanned the terraced buildings on their right. The train station was on the left and offered no options. There didn't seem anywhere that Buchanan could have gone. She had just vanished.

Hopped on a fucking broomstick?

Amelia spotted the entrance to the station on their left, ran to the door and tried it. It was locked, as she had suspected. Buchanan hadn't broken into the station, then, at least not this way, and the wall was too high to scale without equipment.

'She couldn't have reached the end of the road already; I was too close behind her. I would have seen her,' Amelia said, as much to herself as to Steve. She continued jogging up the street.

'Is that an alley?' Steve asked.

'Where?'

He jogged past her. 'Here. Shit. Come on!'

Knowing he had to be right, Amelia didn't hesitate. She ran after him and together they sped down the shadow-filled alley. After about twenty metres, the space opened up into a small courtyard, and Amelia realised it hadn't been an alley at all. It was an entrance to a private parking area, with only one car parked there. Buildings rose up on all sides. It was a dead end.

'Shit!' Amelia yelled again. She checked around the back of the car, under it. Nothing. 'Now what?'

'There!' Steve said, taking off down a second, much more narrow, alley almost entirely hidden in darkness. It led out of the courtyard. He was gone in a flash and Amelia took off after him, worried that she would lose him too. She could only just make out his silhouette. Up ahead she could see a bit more light, and when she caught up with Steve they stopped. They were standing in a small park. The path went two ways.

'Bollocks. Which way?' Steve asked.

'I don't know. Fuck, we don't even know she came this way!' Amelia said, her anxiety building, her mind screaming that they had to find Buchanan fast or that was it, they would lose her entirely.

'She had to have. Where the hell else could she have gone? You go right, I'll go left. Deal?'

Amelia nodded reluctantly. When her adrenaline had kicked in, she had not been even slightly bothered whether or not Steve had followed her. Now, with trees towering over and around her, barely any moonlight breaking through and the rain still hammering down, the thought of splitting up terrified her. She knew they had no choice, though. She swallowed hard, removed her baton from her belt. Steve did the same. Then he was off, jogging down the path to their left, swallowed by the darkness within seconds. She felt incredibly alone, as if she were suddenly the only person left on the planet.

Amelia went right, jogging slowly, trying to take in every shadow around her. Could one of them be Buchanan? Would she hide, rather than keep running? Amelia was breathing heavily from chasing her, yet she was fit, worked out regularly. She wasn't sure about Buchanan. It would be just her luck that the woman ran marathons every other weekend and was now long gone.

The wind picked up, as if to add insult to injury, and the rain thrashed around her, whipping the trees into a frenzy. Amelia could barely see anything, and wiped frantically at her eyes again as she followed the path. Just a minute later, she reached a gate. It was closed and she pulled at it. It rattled but didn't budge. On both sides was a fence topped with sharp spikes slick with water, high enough to pose difficulty and an actual threat to anyone trying to climb over. Ducking down, she checked to the left, looking for gaps in the fence. It was unbroken. She checked the right too, and found it to be intact also. Amelia stood up and turned back to the path. If Cally Buchanan had come this way, she would likely not have got out of the park. She was a small woman and Amelia didn't think she could have clambered over the fence. That meant she was either hiding or had gone the other way, unless they had lost her back when they had stopped next to the station.

But she must have gone this way! She didn't just vanish in the middle of the street!

Amelia's heart sank. They had messed up. *She* had messed up. Buchanan was clearly gone. In this weather, at night, there was no way they would find the woman. She hoped that either Steve or Martin had found her, but knew it wasn't likely. She couldn't believe it.

We've lost her... I've failed...

With less conviction, Amelia started back in the direction Steve had taken. The park seemed much smaller now that her adrenaline had started to level out again. She still kept an eye on the shadows among the hedges and trees, but nothing jumped out at her and no human-looking shapes seemed to be among the leaves and branches. As she reached the junction where she and Steve had separated she called his name. Her words were buried by the downpour. She doubted he would hear her anyway; he was likely long out of earshot.

It was so dark she could barely make out anything as she continued further down the path Steve had taken.

Then she heard something. It sounded like a scream.

Amelia stopped, held her breath, trying to listen through the steady rhythm of the rain and wind and rustling branches overhead. It was impossible. She couldn't hear anything, and after a brief pause started to jog again. Then she heard the sound once more.

Amelia surged on, spotted the open gate exiting the park. A rusted padlock lay on the ground. She emerged onto another small road, swamped with darkness apart from one pathetic trickle of light coming from a Victorian streetlamp that had not been replaced with a more modern version. Her breath caught in her throat when she saw a figure lying motionless in the street. Cautiously she approached, the baton gripped tightly in her hand.

'Steve!' She rushed to his side, saw trickles of blood mixing with the rain under him.

'She... jumped out...' he muttered.

Amelia, glad he was alive, quickly inspected the wound on his head before checking around her. 'Where is she?' she whispered.

'I... I don't know...' Steve tried to sit up. Amelia helped him to his feet and walked him to the shelter of an overhang on the building next to them, out of the rain. He slumped down onto the ground again, wiping his face.

Amelia scanned all around. There were three roads apart from the one she had just come from. Three escape routes, each as likely as the next. That was it. Buchanan really was lost now. She had taken the chance to put down one of her pursuers to buy some breathing room and had vanished.

With a painful sigh of disappointment, Amelia turned back to Steve. 'Are you okay?' she asked, crouching to get another look at the cut on his forehead, not really able to see the level of damage in the low light.

'I think so. Dizzy, a bit anyway. I think I blacked out for a second. She tried to stab me but my vest blocked it. My head is pounding but I'm okay...' he answered, taking a few slow, deep breaths. 'I'm sorry I lost her.'

'It's not your fault.' Amelia sighed again. 'I'll radio in, get an ambulance to come get you.' She was reaching for her radio when Steve shouted.

'Behind you!'

Amelia spun round just in time to see Cally Buchanan swing a tree branch at her. It slammed into Amelia's shoulder and she screamed in pain as she fell sideways, her elbow cracking off the hard ground.

'You fucking bastards!' Buchanan spat, her voice overflowing with hatred, her eyes wild and rabid. She swung the branch again, and it hit Amelia across the face. Amelia screamed in pain, felt blood in her mouth. The witch didn't pause, heaving the branch up above her. Amelia rolled backwards, heard the branch splinter as it hit the pavement.

She scrambled back, pushing up onto her feet. Her shoulder and jaw rippled with agony as she locked eyes with Cally Buchanan. The woman held up the broken branch, ready to strike again. She was inching closer, looking for a chance. Amelia knew she would take it too.

The baton!

Amelia went to grab it from her belt, found it was missing. She must have dropped it somewhere. She looked around, risking taking her eyes off Buchanan. The branch swung again, whistling past her face. She jumped back in surprise.

'You need to stop this, Cally,' Amelia said as she tried to keep a distance from the woman. 'It's over. You must know that.'

'Over? I don't think so. He's no challenge and you don't have a weapon. I kill you both and *voilà*, I'm gone into the night.'

'No one else has to die!' Amelia pleaded. 'Haven't enough people been hurt?' She thought she saw her baton on the ground behind Cally, but she couldn't be sure. The street was one big puddle. She couldn't take the chance and go for it if she wasn't certain.

'Oh, really? You're not going to let me go, are you? I almost got away already tonight. Two more bodies and I can. If I don't take you down while I have the chance, what hope is there for me? This is my story and I will show you how it fucking ends!' Buchanan laughed, her voice high-pitched and manic.

'You're not a real witch, Cally – you know that, right? There's no way to magic yourself out of this.'

'Oh, I don't know. I'm sure it would feel like magic to cave your head in!'

Amelia could tell there was no reasoning with the woman. Cally Buchanan had nothing to lose except her freedom. That made her extremely dangerous. Amelia saw that Steve was trying to stand, but clearly it was a struggle. Buchanan risked glancing at him, following Amelia's gaze. So fast that Amelia barely registered the motion, Buchanan jumped at him and cracked the branch across his head. He slumped onto the pavement, more blood flowing from his forehead.

'No!' Amelia shouted. She charged at the so-called witch. Had to. *She* had to end it, not Cally Buchanan. Amelia slammed into the woman and they fell, landing on the concrete with a thud and a splash. An elbow lashed out and connected with Amelia's jaw and she felt a tooth loosen, her mouth filling with blood again. She struggled to free herself from the tangle of flailing arms and black cloak, the material soaking and heavy, threatening to smother them both.

Buchanan howled in rage, staggered up to a crouch, and swung the branch. This time Amelia grabbed it just before it hit her again. Her hand throbbed at the impact, but she pulled. The resistance evaporated suddenly and Amelia fell back, the branch spinning out across the street behind her. Buchanan leaped up and threw herself onto Amelia, grabbing at her hair and slamming Amelia's head onto the tarmac. Buchanan twisted Amelia's head sideways and pinned her down, trying to drown her. Spluttering as water flooded into her nose and mouth, Amelia punched out as hard as she could, using everything she had left in her. Buchanan yelped in pain and fell off her.

NOW!

Amelia shoved herself up. It was her turn to pin Buchanan down. She leaped on top of the woman, knees keeping her in place, and punched her hard in the face. Even in the rain Amelia saw blood spray from Buchanan's mouth. The woman thrashed underneath her, bucking wildly, but Amelia punched her again. She couldn't stop, couldn't fail, not now. She punched again as hard as she could. She felt something in her hand crack, and she bellowed in agony. And yet still she punched again. And again.

'Amelia, stop!' Steve called, his voice rough and weak. It was enough to break the trance.

Amelia looked down at the woman beneath her, at her mangled face, her crushed nose, the unmistakable shape of a broken jaw pushing against skin. Buchanan's face was a mess, blood trickling from it as the rain tried to wash it clean. The witch didn't move, didn't thrash. The fight was over. Amelia stared down at her and felt her breath catch again. She scrambled backwards, falling off the woman. Off the body. The body that was not moving, that lay deathly still. Amelia looked more closely.

Cally Buchanan was dead.

CHAPTER THIRTY

He couldn't believe it had all come down to this. He felt sick, physically weak, as he stared into the black barrel of the gun. He was already anticipating the flash, the pain, the end. Months of worry and torment, ending with a bullet to the face.

'Please, you don't have to do this,' Molly pleaded, pulling Daniel's attention back to her. The woman he had fallen for was being held hostage right in front of him. He couldn't give in, not yet. It wasn't just his life that was at stake.

'Shut up!' Greg Armstrong snapped, kicking Molly in the thigh. She hissed in pain and fell silent. He grinned at Daniel, looking pleased with himself.

'Didn't you hear me, Graves? Pay attention! Any last requests? Surely you can think of something witty to say in your final moments?' Greg laughed. Daniel stayed quiet, knowing that whatever he said wouldn't make a difference. Greg had no intention of letting either of them go, no matter how much Daniel begged.

Daniel looked down at Molly. Her tears and pain cut through him. She looked defeated too, yet there was no blame in her eyes, no anger at Daniel for what was happening. He couldn't believe it. This incredible woman who had just a few weeks ago appeared from nowhere to change his world had chosen him. Even after all that she had suffered as a result, she felt no hatred for him. He felt tears running down his cheeks: his feeling of utter failure was hard to bear.

Molly mouthed something at him then. Three words. Three unmistakable words.

Daniel felt his heart catch as he struggled to process what he had heard. Then he mouthed it back.

'What was that, Graves? Couldn't hear you.'

Greg still held the gun out, his expression one of anger, all sense of joviality gone. 'You know what, fuck it. I don't care what you said. We're done here.'

'I said hit the crotch,' Daniel responded.

He lowered the gun slightly, his aim faltering. Greg raised one eyebrow in confusion.

'Crotch!' Daniel yelled.

Molly swung her right arm, her fist tightly balled, and punched Greg square in the crotch. He fell backwards in pain that he had not been prepared for. Molly was free and she didn't waste a second, scrambling to one side.

Daniel charged forward, ploughing into Greg. Together they hit the cold concrete floor. Daniel tried to pin Greg to the floor, one of his knees on the man's arm. He punched hard, his fist connecting with Greg's jaw, and Greg roared, the gun still in his hand.

'Dan!' Molly screamed from off to Daniel's left. He saw the gun come up, rolled sideways as a shot fired. The sound was deafening, an explosion that made his ears ring and bright spots dance in front of his eyes. As he struggled to recover he felt Greg wriggling under him more. He punched again, but with little effect.

The gun went off again and Daniel jumped, panic filling him. Greg jerked up one knee underneath Daniel, pushing him off to the side. Greg was free and suddenly they were both scrambling to their feet.

Shit!

Daniel knew another shot was coming, and he hadn't unclipped his own gun. He stumbled backwards, putting as much distance as he could between him and Greg Armstrong.

Sure enough, the gun came up.

This is it...

A scream came then. As Daniel looked down the barrel of the gun for surely the last time, Molly charged Greg, swinging a plank of wood into his arm.

Greg dropped the gun and the weapon skidded across the floor away from them. Without hesitating, Greg spun and elbowed Molly hard in the chest. Her momentum was stolen and she yelped, falling backwards.

'You piece of shit!' Daniel spat. He went to unclip his gun, but Greg was ready. He lunged forward and kicked Daniel. Daniel stumbled into the wall behind him. Greg kicked again but hit the wall with a thud; Daniel had jumped to the side and was already bringing up a fist, punching Greg's upper arm.

'Just fucking die, Graves!' Greg hissed as he hopped back, his eyes red with fury. Daniel registered him reaching behind his back and suddenly a glimmering knife was slicing towards him. He ducked back, felt the air ripple as the blade missed his chest. Greg didn't pause and the weapon came back, eager for blood.

Instinctively Daniel raised an arm, then screamed in agony as the knife plunged through his left forearm. He staggered backwards, feeling blood trickling down his wrist. He looked down at his arm, saw the knife stuck there. It looked almost comical, fake, but the pain was very real. Greg laughed. Kicked out again. This time his boot hit Daniel squarely and he felt his breath escape him as he catapulted backwards, hitting the floor hard.

He heard Molly yell out and rolled his head to the side. He saw her on the floor not far from him, one hand clutching her chest, the other reaching for the wooden plank she had hit Greg with. She wasn't giving up either, but she was struggling. Daniel looked back to Greg, who loomed over him.

'Oh, Graves, it's been good fun, I have to say. And you put up a decent fight. I couldn't have asked for more.' He kicked Daniel hard in the side. Daniel growled in pain as the impact reverberated through him. His body ached and his arm felt somehow hot and ice cold at the same time.

'Time to snuff you out and send you to your namesake,' Greg said with a smile. Suddenly he was on top of Daniel, his face close to Daniel's. His breath was hot and his eyes gleamed. As Daniel stared up at him, Greg smiled. Then his hands were around Daniel's throat.

'Fight him, Daniel!' Molly begged as she tried to get to her feet. Greg saw her move and tightened his grip. Daniel started to choke. Black spots began to form around his vision and he realised that the last thing he would see was the grinning face of Greg Armstrong. He felt his body sag as his oxygen supply faded.

Then suddenly Greg's grip released. Daniel gasped, sucking in air, his lungs burning as he tried to understand what had happened.

Molly stood there, plank in hand.

'You stupid bitch,' Greg spat at her, one hand to his head as he moved to get up off Daniel, blood trickling between his fingers.

Weak and dizzy, Daniel spotted his chance. He gripped the handle of the knife that jutted out of his arm, and pulled it out.

He hissed in pain. He flipped the knife in his grip, pushed up off the floor, ignoring the pain in his bleeding arm, and stabbed the blade straight into Greg Armstrong's neck. Greg's head snapped back to Daniel in shock, his eyes wide, a stark white of horror. Daniel wrenched the knife through a forty-five-degree angle, slicing through flesh. Blood spurted everywhere – an artery had been severed. Without hesitation Daniel pulled the knife free and stabbed Greg again, the knife slicing through his already red police shirt into chest muscle. Daniel felt it connect with bone. Again he pulled it out and stabbed once more, using every ounce of his remaining strength.

Blood poured from Greg's mouth and neck, covering Daniel's face, arms and chest. Then he was gone. His body fell back.

Daniel slumped onto the floor, supporting himself with his good arm, looking at the knife in Greg's chest.

'Holy shit...' he managed.

Molly hurried over to him as he fell backwards. She was the last thing he saw before he passed out.

CHAPTER THIRTY-ONE

Sitting in the task force room, Daniel watched Charlie, Amelia and Ross take down the photos, notes and pins from the wall, depositing them in various folders and binders.

He grabbed the box of painkillers on the table in front of him, popped two out of the packet and swallowed them with a gulp of Red Bull.

'You know, you can help us,' Charlie said with a frown.

'Nah, the doctor said I shouldn't use my arm for at least another three weeks,' Daniel answered with a deliberately smug smile.

'Your left arm, yes. There's nothing wrong with that one,' Charlie said, nodding towards Daniel's right arm.

'But you're doing such a good job, Charlie. I don't want to deprive you.'

'Fuck off.' Charlie laughed. 'It's probably for the best. Got to save your energy for tonight.'

Daniel groaned.

'What's tonight?' Amelia asked. Neither Daniel nor Charlie said anything for a second, then Amelia gasped. 'Oh my God, your double date!' She giggled. Both men groaned at her.

'What's so bad about that?' Junior Sergeant Ross Hayes asked. Before Daniel or Charlie could answer, or stop her, Amelia was explaining everything.

'Well, Daniel hates Charlie's girlfriend. You know Kelly Malone, the reporter?'

'Oh shit...' Ross muttered.

'Exactly. But Graves has decided to give her a chance. And since Superintendent Hobbs had agreed to ease Kelly's ban from attending most press conferences, in light of her good behaviour and poor Charlie here having been kidnapped, I expect they'll have lots to talk about! Oh, to be a fly on the wall.'

'You're categorically not invited,' Daniel said.

Charlie laughed again. 'It'll be fine, you'll see. And if you're a dick, at least Molly will surely be a pleasure.'

Daniel couldn't help laughing too. He really didn't want to chat to Kelly, in all honesty. He had not forgiven her for her numerous indiscretions, but for some reason his friend seemed to love her, so he was willing to make an effort. Plus, now that she was allowed to attend official police press conferences again he knew he would be seeing more of her, so it would be better if they could at least be civil. He just prayed she had learned her lesson, that she would no longer be the ruthless hunter of headlines that he knew her to be.

'I can't believe they thought they were witches,' Amelia said as she looked at one of the photos. 'I mean... witches. Were they just delusional? And why did all those women pay for bogus rituals to try and make themselves feel better? Alistair Watts' ex-girlfriend is stunning and successful. What did a woman like her need to feel better about? And Antoni Kowalski, that drug dealer and wannabe crime boss who used Buchanan and Hastings to kill the first victim, the one who owed all that money – what was he thinking? That witchcraft would be a good cover, keep him out of the conversation?'

'I guess, like Angelica Okeke, most of the people who sought out our trio of killers wanted to gain some control, and these women offered them a way to do that. You'd be surprised what people will believe when they're desperate. Only Kowalski knew that he was signing a death warrant, having already had dealings with Natalie Hastings' ex-boyfriend and sleeping with her occasionally too. Given his history, she apparently thought it was okay to tell him what she and Cally were planning, and he saw an opportunity. He admitted that Gallagher's murder was financially motivated. He thought the witches would distract so much his name would never come up. But he's been charged with good old accessory to murder. As for our killers, I think both Cally Buchanan and Natalie Hastings were very disturbed women. They fabricated this whole narrative around being witches to excuse their behaviour, to give them a justification for killing, although it seems that Sarah's boyfriend Mike just happened to get in Natalie's way. For every other victim they used that, and the perverted belief that they were delivering justice, to allow themselves to tap into primal, frankly horrible desires. Beatrice Hastings has suggested they were actually using EnchantedWomenLDN to try and find possible new women to point them towards new victims. Natalie and Jessie were never at the centre, but she said she'd seen Cally talking to several women there. But maybe they did buy into the witchcraft thing too. Certainly Buchanan seemed to have. I mean, the flesh bag she left at Sarah Boyd's house to show Natalie which was the right property to attack? That was sick. Apparently witches used charm bags, but clearly Buchanan thought of a fun new twist on that. Novel and gross, all in one. And trying to burn people at the stake at Smithfield, the site of one of the most famous witch trials in London? That was designed to send a huge message.'

'A pretty disgusting message,' Ross said. 'I didn't realise people could be that... messed up.'

'They sure can. You saw all the crime scene photos. The rib effigies to connote man, the mix of symbols to signify their own strength or the downfall of their victims. Molly said it seems they were literally picking from numerous different dark crafts to compose each scene, to suit their own narratives,' Charlie responded, sitting next to Daniel and taking one of the cookies Amelia had brought in.

'Sure your gym routine allows for that?' Daniel smiled.

'I got in a workout this morning, I'm definitely allowed.' Charlie ate the cookie in three swift bites.

'Wow. I guess I'm in for a treat, then,' Ross said as he plucked a printout from the wall.

'Comes with the job, I'm afraid. You'll never get used to it but you will, in a weird way, come to understand some of these people. Not sympathise, of course, not usually, but with some of them, you'll get why they do what they do,' Daniel said.

'Does that apply to Greg Armstrong?' Amelia asked, doubt on her face.

'My feelings on him are a little more complex, I suppose, but he also wanted revenge. I do understand that.'

After all, I killed him so he couldn't hurt Molly again. But Daniel knew the thought wasn't the whole truth. It really wasn't that simple, and he felt guilty every day that he had been forced to take a life, a repeat of the horribly familiar feeling he'd experienced when he was a teenager. He also knew that Molly was at least partially the reason he had refused to let Greg Armstrong get away. Something primal in him that night had refused to let the man escape with his life. Not unlike Buchanan and Hastings. It was a dark realisation, and Daniel had decided to keep it pushed down as far as he could.

'Revenge. Classic,' Amelia said.

Twenty minutes later, the room was clear. Ross and Charlie had already left but Daniel asked Amelia to stay behind for a minute.

'What's up?' Amelia said as she took a seat, a stack of folders in front of her ready for final processing.

'I wanted to check how you're doing. After what happened with Buchanan. I read your report. And Steve Sharp's too. I know how tough, how intense, it must have been.'

Amelia slumped back in the chair. 'It was horrible. And it's been keeping me awake at night. I lost control, I know I did. And I know Steve thought so. I've never... that's never happened before. It scares me, thinking that I did that, that I was capable of it.'

'You did stop a serial killer, Amelia.'

'I know. But I killed her. I... I didn't need to do that, and I shouldn't have done it. I certainly didn't intend to.'

'Steve's report said that Buchanan tried to kill him, and you. That he was certain she wouldn't have stopped either. If you hadn't prevented that by putting her down, then maybe we wouldn't be having this conversation.'

Amelia nodded but didn't respond.

'Look, I know what you're going through. Honestly, I feel the same about what happened with Greg Armstrong. But our job comes with a lot of risks, a lot of danger. There's sometimes a need for self-defence. Sometimes that means violence to end violence. I hate it. Nothing about it makes me feel good. You know what happened with my sister. I feel the same about Armstrong in many ways. But if you had tried to arrest Buchanan instead, or I had tried to arrest Armstrong, they might have killed us instead. I know Greg Armstrong wouldn't have hesitated. I knew he would kill Molly, and others too.'

'I know. It's just... if they had been arrested instead, we wouldn't have...'

'We're not like them, Amelia. We're not cold-blooded killers. It's horrible, I know it is, living with what we had to do, but I believe we had to do what we did. We both stopped vicious murderers who were trying to kill us. They can no longer hurt anyone else. Try to hold on to that. And of course talk to me whenever you need to. And make use of the counselling team. I know I will.' Daniel smiled, hoping that his words would ease at least some of Amelia's guilt and pain – perhaps his own too.

'Thanks, Graves. I will.'

'Oh, and one more thing. I'm going to put you up for promotion.'

'What? Are you kidding? After what I did?'

'You risked your life to save another officer. To stop a killer. Maybe you don't feel like your actions deserve it right now, but you're an incredible sergeant. Own that, okay? And anyway, you'll need to have a few interviews, get an evaluation after what happened with Buchanan. I'm recommending you, but you'll still need to prove yourself to a few others to secure it. But I know you can do it.'

'I... thank you. I'm not sure what to say.' Amelia let out a deep sigh, got up and hurried out of the room with her files.

Daniel sat back, taking a moment for himself, thinking over everything that had happened during the past few weeks. He knew it would be a while before he or Amelia came to terms with what they had done, even if there were many more reasons to support their actions than to condemn them. It was hard, emotionally and mentally, with few black-and-white scenarios. All they could do was their best.

As he looked around the empty room, he allowed himself some time to feel proud. The room was empty because he and his team had solved a case. Three killers had been stopped, prevented from taking any more victims, because of him, Charlie, Amelia and the wider team. Angelica Okeke and Sarah Boyd were safe. So was Molly. In fact, so was Charlie. Many more lives could have been lost.

He stood up, looked down at his arm, at the bandage wrapped around it to keep the knife wound from opening up again. Underneath it were a staggering number of stitches. He would have a permanent scar to remind him that if he hadn't killed Greg Armstrong then he himself would be dead and buried.

His phone buzzed. It was Molly. She was having lunch. With his sister Amanda.

He smiled, couldn't help it.

Amanda had come to London again, wanting to reconnect with Daniel and eager to meet Molly. Since Greg Armstrong's death, she seemed to have regained some of her old fire. The fear that had been pinning her down had begun to fade. He and Amanda were yet to properly talk about how they felt, about Adam Spencer, Greg Armstrong, and how they were processing it all. Nonetheless, Daniel felt that he and Amanda finally had a good shot at rekindling the brother–sister bond that had been damaged so badly when they were teenagers.

He texted Molly back, reminding her of their drinks with Kelly and Charlie. His phone buzzed again.

Don't worry, I'm there for you, ready and willing to kick her ass if you need me to. Love you xxx

He grinned, texted *Love you* back, and dropped the phone back in his pocket.

As he left the empty task force room, he looked back. The previously chaotic base was back to being a blank canvas, ready for another team to take it over with a new case. *Or indeed me again*, Daniel thought. He knew it wouldn't be long before he had another investigation to lead. Before another killer was ready to shock the city and push Daniel to the edge.

But he was ready.

Until next time.

THE END

A NOTE FROM THE PUBLISHER

Thank you for reading this book. If you enjoyed it please do consider leaving a review on Amazon to help others find it too.

We hate typos. All of our books have been rigorously edited and proofread, but sometimes mistakes do slip through. If you have spotted a typo, please do let us know and we can get it amended within hours.

info@bloodhoundbooks.com